MERCILESS

By

Heleyne Hammersley

Praise For Heleyne Hammersley

Praise For Heleyne Hammersley

"If you like your police procedurals full of drama, gasps and OMGs then this one is for you!" **Sharon Bairden – Chapter In My Life**

* * *

"The pace of the book is spot on for the content and it works so well with the story as it ramps up towards the end as the story starts to get to its completion adding to the tension." **Donna Maguire – Donnas Book Blog**

* * *

"This is a well thought out plot and the tension builds throughout the book right up until the final reveal." **Marion – Goodreads**

* * *

"A good read that will keep you guessing until the end." **Nicki Southwell – Goodreads**

* * *

"A fast paced thriller. A road trip with a difference. Very good story and definitely an author to look out for!" **Theresa – Goodreads**

* * *

"I highly recommend this author to anyone who enjoys a gripping thriller. I sincerely hope there is at lot more to come (and soon) from Ms Hammersley." **Graeme – Amazon Reviewer**

* * *

"Gripping to the last and, again, unputdownable." **SueC – Amazon Reviewer**

Also by Heleyne Hammersley

Fracture
Forgotten
Closer To Home

For my cousin, Jan Wager

JANUARY

CHAPTER 1

The sun was just turning the skyline pink as Sam Cooper wheezed her way along the canal path. Her breath plumed around her head in clouds of steam which drifted lazily away on the faint breeze. The path's surface was gravel and unaffected by the frost which coated the bushes and trees, allowing Sam safe passage as she crunched towards the lights around the lock, her usual turning point where she could switch off her head torch and return in the dawn light. She was trying to clear her brain before work; trying to block out the memory of raised voices and regretful tears.

She hadn't wanted to fight. Abbie had come home in a foul mood and had been determined to squabble about anything and everything until the row found a well-worn groove, and Sam had almost been tempted to tune out. Why did she have to live on a fucking boat? In the summer, Abbie had loved the open hatches and the regular swell of the water as other narrowboats passed by leaving cheery waves and hellos in their wake. But this was her first winter on the canal and she was starting to loathe it. Sam knew that the confined space wasn't for everyone. That having to empty the chemical toilet on a frosty morning was a chore, and that hearing the groan of ice around the hull as the canal froze could be eerie, but she had been convinced that Abbie would love the romance and cosiness of it after the first few cold weeks.

Sam had been so wrong. Now it looked like she was going to have to make a choice. Give up the narrowboat that had been her home since her grandfather had left it to her in his will, or give up Abbie.

She jogged on, trying to focus on her breathing and the steady crunch of gravel under her trainers. She didn't use her MP3 player when she ran. She'd have enjoyed the rhythm of music chosen to suit her mood or her pace but, as a detective with South Yorkshire Police, she knew the perils of not being aware of your surroundings, especially in lonely places in poor light. She always ran with her phone in her hand – just in case.

The white-topped lock gates were up ahead and Sam slowed down, about to head home for a shower. She normally ran right up to the second gate before turning back but, this morning, she was tempted to stop short and go back. It might allow her a few more minutes to try to smooth things over with Abbie.

'Fuck it,' Sam murmured and picked up her pace, trying to outrun her frustration.

The lock was full; the bottom gate closed allowing the water to build up against it. In the half-light it was like obsidian, its smooth surface broken by an unexpected shape. Sam slowed down and walked to the edge of the lock, trying to work out if it was a trick of the light or if somebody had thrown something into the water.

It looked like a black bin bag, bobbing gently, half-submerged but, as her eyes adjusted to the gloomy darkness of the enclosed water, she could make out more detail. The surface of the object was ribbed or rippled and it appeared to have a lot of air trapped inside. There was something floating next to it. A pale shape against the dark water.

'Shit,' Sam hissed as she recognised a hand. It wasn't a bin bag, it was a down jacket. And it was still being worn.

Two seconds later, she was giving her location to the emergency services.

'So you found the body?' Detective Inspector Kate Fletcher asked her colleague. Sam nodded, trying to control the shivering that wracked her limbs.

'I saw her floating there and called it in.'

'And you just happened to be passing?' Kate heard the slight scepticism in her tone, the one she used for anybody who had just found a body; understanding with an underlying hint of suspicion. But this was one of her team. She took a breath and tried again.

'What were you doing down here, Sam? It must have been barely light.'

Sam wrapped her arms more tightly round her upper body. She looked tired and shaken. Her short blonde hair stuck up around her temples like she'd been running her hands through it, and her blue eyes skittered around as she spoke. Kate was used to her being quiet and calm and in control but the slim, hoodie-clad figure in front of her looked more like a junkie in need of a fix than a valued colleague.

'I was running. I run most mornings,' Sam said.

'Here?'

'I've got a boat in the Ings Marina. It's where I live. I like to run the towpath because it's level. Not much of a challenge.'

She gave a self-deprecating grin and, in the familiar expression, Kate recognised the DC that she knew. Her colleague wasn't under suspicion and Kate needed to stop treating her as though she was. She was cold and probably in shock.

'Get yourself over to the ambulance.' Kate pointed to the waiting vehicle, parked behind a hedge on the closest access road to the canal towpath. 'They'll have blankets. Get warm. I'll send Hollis on a coffee run while we wait for the dive team to finish. Plenty of sugar?'

Sam smiled gratefully and followed Kate's instructions.

A shout from the lock caught Kate's attention before she could follow through on her promise of hot drinks, and she looked across to the huge black-and-white gates. The divers had finished and were ready to remove the body from the water. She watched as they gently guided the covered body tray to the canal's edge where an overall-clad team was waiting to haul it up into the tent that they had erected across the path – a Viking funeral in reverse. Behind the tent, Kate could see blue-and-white tape preventing access from the south, just beyond the point where a footpath intersected with the towpath. Similar tape prevented her from accessing the lock unless she donned appropriate clothing and showed her ID. Kate estimated that nearly a quarter of a mile of towpath was cordoned off – they weren't sure yet whether this was a crime scene but she knew that the SOCOs would make certain that, if it were, they kept it as secure as possible.

DC Hollis came shuffling towards her in his SOCO suit and shoe covers. He looked frozen. His slender frame and long limbs made him look like the world's biggest toddler in a badly fitting romper suit.

'Anything?' she asked.

He shook his head. 'Body's female. Fully dressed. No obvious sign of injury. The divers are having a quick break and then they'll get back in to search the lock. Kailisa's here and he's not happy.'

Kate smiled. The pathologist was renowned for his attention to detail and his empathy with the victim, but his people skills were sometimes a bit lacking. She knew that he'd do a thorough job despite the conditions, but also that he'd resent any unnecessary interruption from her or her team.

'Do you want to get warmed up?' she asked Hollis. 'There's supposed to be a support van around somewhere with hot drinks. Sam could use one. She's at the ambulance.'

'She okay?' Hollis asked, struggling to unzip his overalls and pull his suit-clad arms free. 'Can't be much fun finding something like this before breakfast.'

'She's doing fine,' Kate said. 'Did you know she lived down here? On a boat?'

Hollis shrugged. 'I think she mentioned it. She's not one for sharing details of her life, though. I'll go and get that drink.'

Kate watched as he finally removed his overalls, deposited his shoe covers in a waiting bin for later examination and ducked under the tape. She'd wanted to be the one closest to the action, to see the body lifted from the water but she'd also wanted a chance to talk to Cooper. Unable to be in two places at once, Kate had allowed Hollis to assess the scene, to be her eyes and ears. He needed the experience and, after the events of the summer, she had learned to trust him completely. Since her return to South Yorkshire from Cumbria just over a year earlier, she'd managed to build up a reliable team around her, and Hollis was a key part of that. He was a steadying influence on the others, good in a crisis and an empathetic and skilled interviewer.

A figure jogged towards her along the canal bank.

'We've found something that you might like to see, inspector.' The crime scene tech bent over to catch his breath as he waited for Kate to suit up and follow him across to the lock. The large black-and-white gates were both closed, the long wooden beams that they were attached to jutting out almost as far as the towpath. Beside these swing beams were mooring points, chunky mushrooms of metal, also painted black and white. She'd noticed that there had been some scrutiny of the area near the top lock gate, and glanced down to see what was so significant. Plastic markers surrounded a set of scuff marks in the gravel, frozen in place by the hard frost of the previous night. There was a long scrape, right down to the hard earth surface of the path, and a patch where the gravel was piled up near the edge of the lock.

'What am I looking at?' she asked.

The man bent down and pointed a gloved finger at the longer groove.

'Looks like somebody might have been pushed. There are indications that more than one person stood here and the patterns and disturbances in the gravel may suggest a struggle.'

'May? Is that the best we've got?'

The man shrugged. 'It's enough to put a question mark above any suggestion that it was an accident. But it's not much. Doctor Kailisa's with the body if you want to speak to him.'

Kate walked along the path to the tent, safe in the knowledge that she'd been invited. Inside, Kailisa and his team were taking photographs and measurements. The woman's body was still on the buoyancy tray and still clothed. Icy water dripped from the down jacket forming a puddle on the plastic sheeting beneath her. Her hair was long and dark and obscured much of her face but Kate could just make out a smudge of bright lipstick and a carefully tended eyebrow. Her legs were clad in tight leggings and she wore one ankle-high leather boot. The other foot was encased in a soggy pink sock reminding Kate of a sausage on a cheap fry-up.

'DI Fletcher,' Kailisa said without looking up at her. 'I suppose you want to know manner and time of death.'

'I know better than that, doctor,' Kate responded with a grin that he couldn't see. She'd worked with the pathologist from the Doncaster Royal Infirmary before and knew that he wouldn't commit to anything until he'd performed a thorough examination and that he was above speculation. 'I was just wondering if there was anything that could be seen even by a lay-person.'

He shook his head.

'There may be a head injury, the back of her skull feels like it might be fractured, but until I get a proper look I know nothing. We haven't even found any identification.'

Great, Kate thought. *An unidentified body and an unknown cause of death*. 'I assume that my team will be kept informed.'

Kailisa turned to look at her, his dark brown eyes serious. 'If this is anything more than an accident you will be the first to know.'

Kate removed her protective clothing, ducked under the tape barrier and went to check on Cooper and Hollis. They were huddled together on the back step of the ambulance, hands wrapped around cardboard cups of steaming drinks.

'You okay?' Kate asked Cooper.

The DC smiled weakly and took a long pull on her coffee. Kate looked at Hollis for confirmation and he shrugged slightly.

'Would you mind getting me a coffee?' she asked him. 'It's bloody freezing on that canal bank.' His eyebrows dipped into a frown of annoyance until he clearly realised that she wanted a chance to talk to Sam on her own. He leapt up tugging a forelock and headed in the direction of the support van.

'Must've been a shock to–' she began but Cooper cut her off.

'It's not my first body, you know,' she snapped. 'Just wrong place, wrong time.'

'I know,' said Kate. 'But it's still not what you expect to find on your early morning run. So close to your home, as well. I had no idea you lived on the water. Must be peaceful.'

Sam gave her a wry smile which seemed to suggest that Kate had no idea what her life there was really like. 'Do they know who she was?' Sam asked, changing the subject before her boss could ask anything else about her personal life.

'Not yet. I might have to ask you to have a look. It could be somebody you recognise from the local area. Perhaps another boat owner. Kailisa needs to do a full PM so maybe he'll find some ID in one of her pockets.'

'Unlikely,' Sam said. 'Most women carry stuff like that in a handbag rather than in their pockets.'

'The divers are still looking in the lock. They might find something.'

Cooper shook her head. 'My guess is a mugging. That's why there's no bag. Some scroat tried to get it off her, and when she clung on, he swung her into the water.'

Kate thought about the scuffmarks at the edge of the lock. Had there been a struggle? The scenario made perfect sense. How often had she done safety training where women were told to let go of their bags and give up their belongings rather than risk their lives? But how many really listened when faced with losing their valuables?

Just as Kate was about to commend Cooper on her insight, her phone rang. She responded with a questioning hello even though her display clearly showed her that it was Raymond, her DCI, ringing. Force of habit.

'Fletcher. You still down by the canal?'

'Yep. Just about to finish up. Not sure that this is one for us, but Cooper has an interesting theory. She–'

'Get yourself back here,' he interrupted. 'I've got one that definitely *is* for us. Woman called an ambulance this morning to attend to the death of her father. Once the body was removed she confessed to his murder. She's in Interview Three and she's asking for *you*.'

CHAPTER 2

Raymond was waiting in his office when Kate got back to Doncaster Central, and he didn't look happy. His complexion, usually flushed, looked like he'd been standing too close to a fire and his huge hands flapped irritably at his side like the flippers of a particularly dangerous prehistoric creature.

'Where the hell have you been?' he asked as soon as Kate entered the room. She took an involuntary step back as if the spray of his spit might be an acid attack.

'The canal. Just outside the town centre. Sam Cooper found a body this morning.'

'I know that! I meant since I rang you. I've been waiting.'

Kate looked at her watch. She had spent another few minutes with Sam, then checked on Hollis, filling him in on her conversation with Raymond before finally grabbing one of the SOCOs and asking him to email her the photographs of the disturbed gravel. She wasn't entirely convinced by Cooper's theory but the evidence could support it. She'd asked to be informed immediately if the woman's bag turned up, or her missing boot, and she'd left Hollis at the scene in case any form of ID was found.

'I...'

Raymond pointed at a chair and sat down at the desk that dominated the small room. His bulk reduced the space even further and Kate couldn't help but wonder if he'd chosen the desk deliberately to intimidate anybody that he invited into his office.

'Look, put that on hold for now. I'm sure your team can deal with it. I need you to talk to the woman who was brought in an hour ago. She's admitted killing her father but that's all she'll say until she sees you.'

'What's her name?'

'Caroline Lambert.'

It didn't ring a bell. 'And why does she want to talk to me?' Raymond shook his head.

'She won't say. She called the doctor this morning. The duty GP turned up and couldn't certify cause of death as he wasn't the father's regular doctor so he rang the police and the duty undertaker. The undertakers got the body to the DRI morgue where the case has been referred to the coroner. Then the daughter confessed to killing him.'

'How?'

'How what?'

'How did she kill him? Why was the body removed? Surely the scene should have been sealed off and the pathologist called?'

Raymond shook his head. 'It wasn't necessarily a suspicious death. Poor bloke had been ill with liver cancer for a few months. His daughter said he'd died in the night, the doctor checked the medical records and confirmed the illness. The father had been seen by a GP in the last few days so the doctor allowed the body to be removed. Anyway, the daughter confessed once the body was en route to the DRI. I'd assume a PM will be organised in light of what the daughter has said.'

'So why confess?' Kate asked.

'My guess is that she was worried that there might be a PM and she wanted to pre-empt it in case something obvious showed up. Overdose possibly, or suffocation.'

'Has she asked for a solicitor?'

'Nope. The only person she's asked for is you.' He stared at her accusingly as though he thought she was keeping something from him.

It made no sense. Why would somebody she'd never met turn themselves in for murder and refuse to speak to anybody else?

Only one way to find out.

A uniformed officer was standing outside Interview Three as Kate approached carrying two cups of coffee and a packet of chocolate digestives which she'd managed to stuff under one arm for safe keeping. A thin file containing the arresting officer's report was under her other arm. The PC smiled at her awkward approach and opened the door to allow her to pass before following her inside.

Caroline Lambert was sitting at the table, both feet on the floor and both hands resting on the grubby table-top. Her eyes flicked up as Kate sat down opposite her but her face showed no emotion. Kate studied her, assessing her age, height and general demeanour more from habit than necessity. Caroline Lambert looked like she was in her late thirties or early forties, her blonde hair showed no sign of grey and her make-up was subtly but expertly applied – obviously a woman who cared about her appearance. The police-issue grey tracksuit contrasted with her perfectly shaped and polished nails and her straight-backed posture. Her pale blue eyes flicked from Kate's face to the coffee and back again but she still didn't speak.

'Thought you might like a drink,' Kate said, pushing one of the cups across the table. 'I brought milk and sugar.' She dug in her pockets for the sugar sachets and milk containers and placed the biscuits next to her cup. Still no response. Kate sugared her coffee and watched as Caroline slipped the lid off her own and took a sip. She grimaced slightly and put it back on the table.

'It's not really what the canteen's known for,' Kate joked. 'The Michelin star's more for the food than the beverages.'

A faint smile.

'Caroline, you do understand what's happening here?' Kate said, trying to work out if the woman opposite was fully aware of her surroundings. She looked like she could be in shock; her lack of emotion was unsettling and she didn't seem aware of her situation at all.

'I'm under arrest for the murder of my father,' Caroline said. 'I confessed and I'm willing to make a statement.'

Her accent was northern, her vowels blunt instruments bludgeoning her words but, beyond that, Kate couldn't really tell where she was from.

'Okay,' Kate said. 'Then I'll need to record our conversation.' She switched on the tape recorder, stated the time and date and the people present, and then opened the file that Raymond had given her.

'Caroline, you've said that you'll only talk to me? Do we know each other?' Kate had met a number of people who claimed to have been at school with her, or who knew her as a child, since her return to South Yorkshire, and there were quite a few that she couldn't remember at all. She usually just nodded politely and noncommittally but this woman was too young to have been in any of her classes at Thorpe Comp. Maybe a friend of her sister, Karen?

'Not exactly,' Caroline said. 'I grew up on the Crosslands Estate, round the corner from where you used to live. My dad still lives... lived... there. I vaguely remember your family. You have a sister, don't you? And your dad worked at the pit.'

Kate shifted in her seat, uncomfortable with the way the conversation was turning to her past.

'I'm sorry,' Caroline said, as if she could sense her discomfort. 'I read about you in the *South Yorkshire Times* after the case with the children. Returning hero catches child killer, something like that. I probably got the details from there, but I do remember a few things about you. My best friend from school lived next door to you for a while. Susan Gough? I used to play in her garden sometimes and she was a bit in awe of the 'big girls' next door. I just wanted to talk to somebody who I had a connection with. It made sense when I asked for you but I'm not sure it does now. I apologise if I've caused you any inconvenience.'

Her tone and vocabulary were as formal as a Victorian school teacher, making Kate wonder again if she had realised the seriousness of her situation.

'I'm sorry, I don't remember her,' Kate said. 'Do you want to tell me what happened this morning? Do you want a solicitor present?'

Caroline smiled sadly. 'I'm not sure that I need one. I just want to make an official statement.'

Kate looked down her notes. 'You said this morning that you'd killed your father. Is that true?'

Caroline lifted her head and met Kate's eyes, her expression one of defiance. Kate had been wrong; this woman knew exactly why she was here. She took a deep breath, preparing for her confession but the words, when they came, were almost disappointingly banal. 'That's true.'

'You called for the doctor, allowed your father's body to be taken away and then confessed to the attending police officer.'

Caroline glanced at the tape recorder and said, 'Yes,' clearly and loudly. Kate wondered if she'd watched a lot of police dramas – her behaviour suddenly appeared to be almost scripted.

'How did you kill your father?'

Caroline sighed, her eyes flicking backwards and forwards as though she was working out where to start. This obviously wasn't part of a script; she looked genuinely confused and conflicted.

'My father was diagnosed with stage four liver cancer a couple of months ago. It was aggressive and he was in a lot of pain. It wasn't treatable so the hospital sent him home to die in familiar surroundings. I've been looking after him, feeding him, keeping him clean, and administering his medication. Yesterday he couldn't get out of bed, the pain was too bad. He… he soiled himself and then lay in it for hours because he couldn't bear to tell me. I managed to get him cleaned up last night but it was torture for him. He asked me to sit with him for a while afterwards and we had a long talk. He told me that he didn't want to go on. That he knew he wasn't going to recover. He was in pain and he wanted it to end. He'd been struggling to take his pain medication, the tablets, so the hospital prescribed Oramorph liquid. We had two bottles in the house, to last two weeks. I kept it in a downstairs cupboard.'

Her sentences were short, clipped, stilted as she broke the events down into smaller portions, possibly so that she didn't have to confess everything in one go. She picked up her coffee with a trembling hand and took a sip.

14

'He… he also had a couple of bottles of Scotch. He'd always liked a drink and whisky was his favourite. He'd not been able to drink since his diagnosis. He asked for a glass of whisky and his morphine. I knew it would probably kill him. I'm not going to pretend otherwise. I went downstairs and opened the cupboard.'

Another sip of coffee.

'I didn't think I could do it, though. I thought about mixing the whisky with the morphine and giving him the glass but I just couldn't. I paced around for a bit and then I heard a shout from upstairs. I ran up and he'd wet himself and was crying; I don't know if it was the pain or the humiliation. That was when I decided. I cleaned him up again, got him into some dry pyjamas and went back downstairs. I took him a glass, the whisky and the Oramorph and left them on his bedside table. I knew, if he was determined enough, that he could mix it himself. Then I left him.' Her breath hitched as she tried to stifle a sob of anguish.

'What did you do?' Kate asked. 'Did you leave the house?'

'Yes. I went for a drive. I didn't want to be there if… when he did it.'

'What time was this?'

'I don't know. Probably sometime around eight. I just drove. I couldn't tell you where I went.'

'Just in Thorpe?'

'No. I remember driving past the crematorium in Doncaster. It registered with me because I suddenly realised that I had a funeral to plan.'

Caroline took a shuddering breath that turned into a sob. 'I went back home and got straight into bed. I set my alarm for six, earlier than usual and slept like a baby. I don't know if it was the relief or sheer exhaustion.'

'You didn't check on your father when you got home?' Kate asked.

'No. I think a part of me didn't want to know. I went into his room this morning and he was dead. He looked peaceful. I sat with him for a few minutes then called the ambulance. I wasn't sure what to do so I thought an ambulance would be the best idea. A police officer turned up as well and then a doctor.'

Kate looked down at the statement from the PCSO who had attended the scene. It corroborated what Caroline was saying.

'And you handed yourself in?'

'There wasn't much point in doing anything else. I left him alone with the means to take his own life. He couldn't have managed the stairs to get the drink and the drug himself. It was my fault. I killed him. It'll all come out at an inquest. If there's a post mortem it will confirm the drugs and drink in his system and my fingerprints will be on the glass.'

She sat back and placed her palms flat on the table in front of her, suggesting that she thought the conversation was over.

'Why did you wait until the body was on the way to the hospital before you confessed?' Kate asked. It didn't quite make sense. A police officer had attended the scene. Why not confess then? Why confess at all?

Caroline studied Kate for a few seconds as though weighing up exactly how to construct an answer. She didn't seem to have expected this question. 'I didn't want to turn his house into a crime scene. It was his home.'

'But, surely you know that the police will have to investigate your claim? They'll already have access to the house and they'll check that any evidence corroborates your story.'

Caroline looked startled, her eyes widened and her nostrils flared. 'They'll be in the house? Now?'

Kate nodded. She wasn't sure whether this was the case but she knew that the house would have been cordoned off until a forensic examination had been completed.

'But why?' Caroline asked. 'I've told you what happened.'

'As I said, they need to make sure that the forensic evidence backs up your story. You could be covering for somebody else, you could have killed your father in a different way, or you could simply be lying about the whole thing.'

'Why would I do that?' Caroline asked, frowning. 'Who *wants* to be charged with murder? I only handed myself in because if anybody decided that a post mortem was necessary it would look bad if I'd not spoken out. It would have been pretty obvious that he couldn't have got downstairs by himself which would have implicated me straight away.'

'You'd be surprised,' Kate said. 'People do strange things to get our attention.'

'At least he's not there. That's what I wanted. I needed him to be out of the way before I told anybody what had happened. I know it sounds a bit daft but I didn't want him to see me get arrested.'

'It's not daft,' Kate said kindly. She could see that the self-contained woman that had been sitting in front of her at the start of the interview was beginning to unravel. The story made sense and Kate wasn't getting the feeling that Caroline was hiding something despite her slightly odd demeanour. It felt like a good time to give them both a break. She stated the time for the recording, terminated the interview and went to find Raymond who, she suspected, had probably watched at least part of the conversation.

CHAPTER 3

Hollis and Cooper were back from the canal when Kate finally managed to extricate herself from Raymond's office. Her instinct had been right; he had watched part of the interview and he'd been baffled by Caroline Lambert's poise and her matter-of-fact statement. He'd even suggested that her sob, part way through, had been for effect, trying to appear more upset than she really was but Kate didn't share his cynicism. He wanted to let Lambert stew in the interview room for a while and advised Kate to take somebody with her when she went back.

'Any news on your unidentified body?' she asked Cooper, who blushed at the direct question.

'She's not my…'

'I know,' Kate said. 'Did anything else turn up after I'd left?'

'Divers found her other boot,' Hollis offered, pulling up a chair and sitting down in front of his computer. She could tell that he didn't think it was significant. 'It was at the bottom of the lock. They pulled out a few other bits of stuff that got bagged and tagged. We'll know more when Kailisa's finished with her. Still no ID, though. What about *your* mystery woman?' He swiped his ID card and his long fingers flew across the keyboard as he logged on.

Kate gave a detailed account of Caroline Lambert's story, including Raymond's thoughts about her composure and lack of emotion. She wasn't convinced that the woman was as cold as the DCI was suggesting.

'Could be shock,' Hollis suggested, supporting Kate's own theory.

'Could just be a hard-faced bitch,' said a voice from behind one of the computer monitors. O'Connor raised his head, thick beard barely disguising his grin. 'Bet the dad's rich and she's done it for the inheritance.'

'Hardly an original thought, O'Connor,' Kate fired back at the DS. 'But why not wait? He was dying anyway.'

'Tons of debt? Loan sharks threatening her? There's a lot of people owe a lot of money to some really dodgy characters.'

'I'll bear it in mind,' she said, dismissing O'Connor. He could always see a link to South Yorkshire's seedy underbelly of illegal loans, deals and trafficking even in a case like this. He was good at ingratiating himself with people lower down the pecking order in gangs and using them to get dirt on the people at the top. Raymond thought the sun shone out of O'Connor, and his collar of the leader of an illegal smuggling and distribution network the previous summer had added to his kudos. Kate wasn't convinced, though. She thought his methods and his contacts were bordering on unprofessional and she didn't especially enjoy working with him.

'A poxy ex-council house doesn't seem worth killing somebody for,' Hollis said. 'It probably wouldn't sell for much more than about eighty grand.'

'Let's go and have a look,' Kate said. 'Forensics should still be there. I wouldn't mind having a look round to see if Caroline Lambert's story adds up.'

Kate hadn't visited the Crosslands Estate since the summer. Now, in the grip of an icy winter her memories were a series of overlapping images. Events of the previous year bruised her mind with their immediacy as she scanned the old quarry site where she'd been called to view the body of a seven-year-old girl, and Kate shivered involuntarily as she caught sight of the chimney of the school's old boiler house, stark on the skyline like a thumb raised in confirmation of her survival.

Her hand went automatically to the ghost of the wound in her side, an instinctive testing that she had healed and that the scar was just a memory.

Hollis looked across at her as he changed gear. 'You okay?'

'Fine,' Kate said, taking a deep breath. 'First time back here since last summer, that's all.'

'Same for me,' Hollis said, reminding Kate that she wasn't the only one with a scar. He'd also suffered at the hands of a killer, even if his own scars weren't physical.

The privet hedges were still green in defiance of the recent frosts but the other trees on the estate were skeletal. The pavements looked dried out as if the winter cold had sapped moisture from the cement, and the roads were covered with swathes of orange-brown salt that the council scattered to prevent accidents. Kate remembered that, when she'd been a child sliding on the snow in these streets, the 'grit-lorry' had been an open-backed truck with two men with shovels on the back. They scattered salt across the roads using only muscle power and, if they saw that the kids had made a slide, they gritted that as well, despite the wails of protest. It didn't snow much anymore, though; the grit was more a precaution than a necessity.

'Left here,' she said to Hollis as they approached the short row of shops that served the estate. They'd changed almost beyond recognition, Kate noted, as Hollis turned into a wide street and parked the car outside the address that Kate had been given. The off-licence cum sweetshop of her childhood was a Chinese takeaway and the greengrocer's had been knocked through into what had been a wool and fabric shop to create a mini-supermarket. The bus shelter at the end of the row was a modern Perspex one, not the concrete structure she remembered. The graffiti looked much the same, though.

The house they were visiting looked like most of the others on the estate. Red brick with white uPVC windows and a tidy garden. Unlike the ones to either side which had lost most of their front gardens and hedges to block-paved drives to accommodate a family car, Dennis Lambert's house still retained a privet hedge and a functioning gate. Two vans and a liveried police car were parked outside neighbouring houses, and Kate was almost certain she could feel the faint breeze of curtains twitching as she pushed open the gate and climbed the short flight of steps to the front door.

She pressed the bell and stepped back. An overall-clad figure opened the door and Kate was surprised to see another member of her team blocking her way.

'Barratt? I thought you'd taken a couple of days' leave.'

He stepped outside and pulled down his hood, running his hand through his thinning fair hair. 'Swapped it. I was in the office when the call came in about this case so I legged it over here.'

Typical of the DC, Kate thought. He was keen but had a bit of a tendency to go rogue if she didn't keep him in check by giving him very specific instructions. She could imagine him dashing out of the office before any other members of the team could come in and stake a claim. She would have put money on Raymond having no idea where Barratt was or what he was up to.

'You didn't think to let me know you were on duty? That you were here?'

He hung his head like a scolded puppy. 'I rang through but you were in an interview. Left a message for the DCI but I don't know if he'll have got it.'

It sounded like an excuse but it was perfectly plausible. Kate *had* been in an interview and Raymond wasn't always the easiest person to communicate with. Kate didn't envy anybody on the switchboard trying to tell him anything that he deemed to be irrelevant or unimportant.

'What's going on in there?' she asked, nodding towards the front door.

'SOCOs have finished doing their thing. I think everybody's getting ready to leave.'

'Any sign of violence, a struggle?'

Barratt shook his head. 'Bedroom smells a bit unpleasant but that's probably to be expected, the state the old bloke was in. Otherwise nothing unusual.'

They were interrupted by the door opening. Two members of the forensics team pushed past, carrying heavy steel cases of equipment. They were followed by another member of their team laden with evidence bags.

Kate flashed her warrant card. 'Okay to go inside?'

The female colleague looked her up and down as though she were assessing Kate's suitability for an exclusive club. 'Should be. We're done. Wear shoe covers, though,' she said, gesturing towards a cardboard box next to the door.

Kate followed her instruction and stepped into the dimly lit hallway. It wasn't quite four o'clock but the days had only just started to get longer and there wasn't much light coming through the narrow windows at the top and bottom of the stairs.

'Barratt!' Kate called. 'Walk me through it.'

The DC pushed past Hollis who had remained in the doorway and, eager to show off what he knew, he started babbling. 'Kitchen's through there. Living room…'

'I know the layout of these houses,' Kate said. 'What happened where?'

Chastened, Barratt tried again. 'The father was in the main bedroom, at the front of the house. It looks like the daughter was sleeping in the back room. There were lots of her clothes and stuff scattered about.'

Kate climbed the stairs slowly, picturing the location of the upstairs rooms. She followed the landing round to the front bedroom and stood in the doorway surveying the scene. There was a musty smell cut through with the faint, acrid tang of urine. The dark wood wardrobe and chest of drawers were closed and the carpet was worn and dusty, making the whole room seem neglected. The bed was unmade, a cheap wooden frame with a sagging, stained mattress. The pillows and duvet were missing, obviously removed by the forensics team.

'What was on here?' she asked, pointing at the empty bedside table. It was the cleanest thing in the room apart from the tell-tale grey patches of fingerprint powder; the wooden surface looked recently dusted, and there were no rings or stains from cups or bottles.

'Drugs, tissues, a glass, a bottle of whisky.'

'What sort of drugs?'

'Some tablets and a bottle; tranquillisers and liquid morphine apparently. The whisky was Ardbeg.'

Kate stared at him checking whether he was being facetious but his face was serious. He was giving her as much detail as he could.

'Was the bedside table this clean?' she asked, noting the layer of dust on the dressing table and the chest of drawers.

Barratt leaned round her to get a better look. 'I suppose so. The SOCOs dusted for fingerprints but I doubt they cracked out the Pledge when they'd finished.'

Kate scanned the room again but nothing was jumping out at her. Nothing looked out of place or unusual. It made sense that the bedside table would be clean, it was the only piece of furniture in use, besides the bed. She turned and went to the back bedroom – the one matching her room in her father's old house a few streets away.

A double bed had been pushed against one wall, the duvet neatly covering the bottom sheet. The curtains were still drawn and the bedside lamp was on, fighting the deepening darkness.

'Was this light on when you got here?'

'This light was on and the one in the front bedroom. There was a suitcase full of clothes and some make-up and bits and pieces. SOCOs took the lot.'

On into the spotless bathroom. A few feminine toiletries were scattered along the windowsill above the sink, and a grapefruit-scented shower gel hung from the soap rack in the shower. The only signs of Dennis in this room were an electric shaver and a dried-out toothbrush that looked like a washed-up sea creature on the side of the sink. Kate opened the laundry hamper that lurked beneath the sink. Empty.

'SOCOs took everything. There were some clothes of hers and some soiled sheets. They took the ones from his bed as well.'

'What about in there?' Kate asked, pointing to the closed door of the 'box' room at the front of the house. She knew that it was big enough for a single bed and not much more. Her sister had occupied the same room in their childhood home. 'Anything?'

'It looks like it's being used as a junk room,' Barratt said. 'A few old bits of furniture, a couple of broken vacuum cleaners, a small desk. All covered in dust like the room hasn't been used in years.'

He led the way back downstairs to the kitchen. Again, Kate could see nothing out of the ordinary, nothing to contradict Caroline Lambert's story. The kitchen looked to be in need of modernisation but at least it was clean. The appliances looked relatively new but more functional than fashionable.

'Anything in here?' Kate asked Barratt.

'A couple of packets of paracetamol and some codeine. The codeine were on prescription in Dennis Lambert's name. Another bottle of whisky and one of gin in the top cupboard. Both open.'

Kate walked over to the window and peered out into the garden. She could just make out the shapes of a couple of grassed over flowerbeds, a shed and a greenhouse.

'Okay,' she said. 'I think I'm done. Barratt, we'll catch up tomorrow.'

She joined Hollis at the front door and slipped off her shoe covers, shaking her head at Hollis.

'Her story adds up,' she said. 'So far. Let's see what forensics and the PM turn up.'

She opened the door and had to take a step back. In front of her was a large elderly woman who looked like she was going to knock the door down with her raised fist.

'About time,' the woman spat at her. 'I was hoping they'd send *you*. We need to talk.'

CHAPTER 4

The woman introduced herself as Brenda Powley – Dennis Lambert's 'friend'. It was obvious from her intonation that *friend* was a euphemism and that their relationship had been something more at some point. She'd invited Kate and Hollis into her house – diagonally opposite Lambert's – and installed them in her cramped sitting room while she made hot drinks.

As soon as she left the room, Hollis mouthed, 'What the hell?' Kate shook her head, as baffled as her colleague.

'Right, here we go.' Brenda bustled back through the door laden with a tray, which she placed on the coffee table that nestled between a reclining chair and the faded, flower-print sofa where Kate and Hollis were sitting. Brenda passed coffee to Kate and tea to Hollis and offered chocolate digestives which they both refused. Food usually led to a more prolonged stay and Kate didn't want to spend time listening to idle gossip.

Deep wrinkles carved into Brenda Powley's face placed her in her seventies, but her grey eyes were lively and alert. As she settled into her seat, her head like an oversized egg atop a nest of chins, she looked from Kate to Hollis and then fixed her gaze back on Kate.

'I'm glad they sent *you*. I heard what you did for Anna Godwin and that other family. She said that you're from round here, that you understand what folk on this estate are like. I suppose you're wondering what this is about?'

'I assume it's something to do with the death of Dennis Lambert,' Kate said, taking a sip of her coffee. Instant and much too sweet. Brenda sighed and her face clouded with grief for a second before her eyes narrowed in anger.

'Death. Is that what you're calling it? Murder more like. I can't see any other reason why that daughter of his turned up. I only rang her to let her know he'd had a bad turn and ended up in hospital. Thought it was the decent thing to do. Got her number from Dennis's address book. I didn't expect her to come back.' Brenda's tone was defensive as though she somehow blamed herself for what Caroline had done.

Kate sat up straighter in her seat and noticed Hollis pull his notebook out of the pocket of his suit jacket.

'Murder?'

'What would you call it? Dennis was fine a couple of months ago.' She waved a hand at Kate, probably anticipating an interruption. 'Oh, I know he had cancer but he was doing well. He only ended up in the DRI because he had some pain and I had to call an ambulance. He could still get out and about, and the doctors said he might have another six months. Then *she* turned up. Five minutes later, Dennis is laid up in bed and then he's dead.'

'What exactly are you accusing his daughter of?' Hollis asked.

Brenda turned to him, an incredulous look on her face as though she couldn't believe that he didn't see events exactly the same way.

'Well, I think she did away with him. Wouldn't let me in the house, said I wasn't family and this was a family matter. Like she'd ever bothered before. Do you know, I've not seen her for more than twenty years? And then she just turns up after I rang her. Called it her *duty*. Said she was going to look after him in his final days. A bit late to start caring if you ask me. Why hadn't she bothered before?' Her chins wobbled in indignation.

Kate had hoped that this woman could add some background but it appeared that she was angry that she'd been kept away from her 'friend' in his final weeks and wanted to convince them that Caroline was a murderer. A fact that Caroline had freely admitted a few hours earlier. They were getting nowhere.

'What sort of man was Dennis Lambert?' Hollis asked, pen poised above a blank page of his notebook suggesting that her answer was of the utmost importance. Kate was reminded again why she enjoyed working with the young DC. His instincts for people were spot on and that included an almost uncanny ability to read her own moods.

'He was lovely,' Brenda said, and her pale, grey eyes drifted to a point on the wall above the cluttered mantelpiece as she remembered. 'Despite everything he'd been through he always had a smile on his face and a kind word for everybody.'

'What he'd been through?' Hollis prompted.

Brenda frowned. 'You don't know? His daughter disappeared over thirty years ago. His other daughter that is, Jeanette. Went out one night and never came back. Nobody ever saw her again. Drove his wife, Irene, half mad with grief and worry, it did. I wasn't in the least bit surprised when she did what she did.'

Kate and Hollis remained silent, forcing Brenda to continue.

'Killed herself. Took a load of sleeping pills and washed them down with gin. Mind you, she'd been drinking a lot for years. Probably addled her brain even more. It nearly broke poor Dennis. He loved that woman. Really tried to help her get over what had happened. He re-did the garden for her – she loved flowers – put in a greenhouse so she could grow chrysanths, a little pond with some goldfish, everything. But none of it made any difference to her. Then, not long after her mum died, Caroline left. He never saw hide nor hair of her until a few weeks ago.'

It was more background than Kate had anticipated but none of it was relevant to Caroline's case.

'I bet she said he killed himself,' Brenda said. 'She went out and when she got back, he'd taken an overdose. Is that it? Just like her mum?'

'We can't comment on an ongoing investigation,' Hollis said.

'Which is probably police code for "yes",' Brenda concluded. 'As I said…'

'I know, you can't say anything but I won't rest till I see her locked up for what she's done.'

Kate drained her mug and set it down on the coffee table, trying to send a clear signal that the conversation was over. It hadn't added much to their understanding of Caroline's motivation and it certainly didn't contradict the statement that she'd made earlier.

'I don't suppose you'll take an old dear like me seriously,' Brenda said, eyeing the mug. 'But, if there's anything you need to know about that family you come and ask me.'

Taking that as their cue to leave, Kate stood up. 'Thanks, Mrs Powley, You've been extremely helpful. We'll be in touch if we need any more information from you.'

She allowed Brenda to lead them to the front door.

'You'll see,' the older woman said as a parting shot. 'There's a lot more to this than you think.'

'She certainly had it in for Caroline Lambert,' Kate said, slamming the car door. 'Unfortunately it doesn't take us any further forward.'

Hollis put the car in gear and sighed.

'If anything it just backs up what she's already told us. She hasn't even denied that she intended to kill her father.'

Something was nagging at Kate. Something that Brenda had said. 'So why did she come back in the first place? It sounds like they'd been estranged for years yet Caroline said that she was doing her "duty". Why now?'

'Guilt?' Hollis suggested, leaning forward slightly as he navigated the winter-dark streets. 'Maybe she relented and wanted to make amends before he died. Terminal illness can do funny things to people's thought processes.'

Kate wasn't convinced. Why had Caroline stayed away so long? And what had happened to her sister? Curious, Kate took out her phone and texted Cooper, asking her to dig up the background to Jeanette Lambert's disappearance. Her phone rang just as she was about to slide it back into her pocket. Raymond.

'Fletcher? Got anything else on Caroline Lambert?'

'No. A bit of background from a neighbour but nothing to contradict what she's already told us.'

'Good,' he said. 'After you left she asked for a solicitor. She signed her statement and we charged her with assisting a suicide. The custody officer's going to grant her bail if we've no reason to keep her.'

'Not that I can see,' Kate said. 'Her story adds up. It looks like she left him with the means to kill himself and that's what he did. The PM might throw up something else but I'm not holding my breath. I thought you wanted me to interview her again.'

She heard Raymond sigh at the other end of the phone. It was a messy case in some ways. Kate had never dealt with assisted suicide before but it felt untidy. Usually she investigated a case, found a culprit and charged them. This was upside down. The killer had been charged but Kate still wanted to dig.

'So the coroner agrees with the GP that there's a need for a PM?' Kate prompted.

'Lambert had seen a doctor in the last couple of weeks but we have to verify the daughter's story. Do you want to attend?'

Kate didn't. She'd declined in the past when he'd suggested that she accompany him but, in those cases, she'd felt like he was posing a challenge. This offer seemed genuine. 'Do you think it's a good idea for me to be there?'

'It's an unusual case, Fletcher. I'd like your eyes on it at every stage. Feelings run high when you're dealing with so-called *mercy killing*. The press will have a field day if we mess this up.'

'I'll be there. When is it?'

'Tomorrow. Sometime in the morning. I expect your friend will be the one performing it. I'll text you the details.' He meant Kailisa. It was no secret that the pathologist wasn't a big fan of anybody who pushed him for information, and Kate had been guiltier than most of getting his back up. She remembered how stressed he'd been earlier when she'd seen him at the canal.

'Okay. I'll wear my body armour.'

After dropping the pool car at Doncaster Central and sending Hollis home, Kate didn't feel like heading up to the team office even though she knew that Cooper and Barratt would probably still be there. She texted both asking them to attend a briefing at 8.30am and then slipped into her Mini and drove home. It had been a long day and all she really wanted was junk food and mindless television. She grabbed a pizza from a local takeaway, and ten minutes later was watching the depressing weather forecast and trying to keep cheese from dripping down her top.

The programme switched to the local news, and after the usual headlines about football and the state of the roads, a familiar house appeared inserted into a backdrop that she recognised instantly.

'Shit!' Kate yelled, dropping her slice of pizza and reaching for the remote control so that she could turn up the volume. She sat, transfixed, as she listened to the presenter's dry account of the facts of the Lambert case. Raymond wasn't going to like this one bit.

NOVEMBER

(Seven Weeks Earlier)

Dear Caroline,

I don't really know what advice to give you. I know you'll do the right thing in the end. It's good that you've been to the hospital; at least you've established yourself as next of kin instead of that woman across the road. I can't help but wonder what he's like after all these years. Were you scared when you saw him? I think I would have been. Either that or I'd have given him a mouthful of abuse.

Please be careful. I know what you want to do and I completely understand why, but I'm worried that it might backfire on you in some way. Of course I want him to pay for what he did and I know that he deserves it, but what about the consequences for you? You need to plan everything so carefully otherwise you'll end up in a lot of trouble and I'm not sure he's worth it. You can't allow him to mess up your life after he's dead – that's just a waste. Please think this through. I know you're not stupid and I don't think you'll do anything rash but please, please be careful.

Love
J

CHAPTER 5

The gate opened with a rusty cough, and she waited for the yapping of a dog many years dead as she let it slam behind her. Nothing, just flakes and crumbs of paint already trying to stick to her skin, branding and binding her. She wiped her hand on the seat of her jeans with a shudder, feeling tainted. The key was worse. She dug it out from the hanging basket where it had always lurked, waiting for her return, taunting her with its dull sheen. It felt familiar, nestling into her hand as she inserted it into the lock, forcing itself and Caroline home.

She'd half expected to find Bren there, rocking in her father's favourite armchair, like Norman Bates's mother but the kitchen was empty, at least physically. The smell was the same. Not-quite-stale cooking and cigarette smoke blending with an odour of undisturbed dust and sour memories. Not much had changed, but she hadn't expected it to. Only the cooker and fridge looked like they might have been installed recently.

The carpet was different, worn and stained, not new but definitely different. The table and chairs were more modern versions of the ones that had stood there until she'd left, but not new. The curtains were lighter, airier and the windows themselves had been altered, but not recently. Each replacement had had time to settle and age, shifting its contours until it fitted perfectly then simply staying. That was always his way. Replace anything worn out with a newer but similar version that hardly looked different. Perhaps it was comforting; Caroline found it sickening, another indication of his tightfistedness, his mean spirit.

There was a note on the table, a reminder that she was the stranger.

Caroline,

Pants, vests and shirts ironed in drawers in bedroom. He'll need socks, shaving kit, soap etc.

It wasn't signed and the *etc.* could have been anything. Caroline knew nothing about men in their seventies with cancer, and didn't really want to know. She looked around for clues but the slanted bars of weak sunlight carved by the windowpanes made her feel trapped and helpless, useless. She knew she would have to go upstairs to face the rooms which were already weighing her down, threatening to collapse through the ceiling and crush her where she stood.

Delaying the inevitable, Caroline searched the kitchen for anything that could be of use. She pushed back the sliding door of a cupboard, hating the feel of the raised bumps of glass providing friction for her hand and echoing her own goose pimples. Tissues, a notepad, numerous useless objects and an electric shaver all looking like they had been in their current position for decades. She grabbed at the shaver, feeling slightly less lost and disabled. A drawer bulged with plastic carrier bags when she opened it and two spilled over, floating down to her shoes. She jerked back, disgusted by the clinging polythene, and tried to wipe them off on the carpet. More evidence of pointless hoarding. She shook out one of the bags, enjoying its efficient snap as it filled with air, and put a packet of tissues and the shaver in the bottom.

Caroline went into the hallway, ignoring the stairs that loomed over her, fixing her eyes firmly on the floor. A faded strip of carpet led to the front door – the edges didn't quite reach the skirting board, revealing irregular strips of bruised tiles. She pushed open the door to the sitting room, 'the house' as he always called it, half expecting someone or something to leap out at her from behind the door. The signs of recent occupation were more disturbing there than the desolation of the hall. One chair was pulled close to the fire, its cushions sagging, the arms worn with use, cheap sponge filling starting to spill out. On the wooden panel in the left arm stood an ashtray, empty except for the stale ash smell. A library book lay open, face down, on the floor, its plastic cover bent into a mocking smile. It was surrounded by wadded tissues and sweet wrappers. His glasses were on the top of the gas fire, sightless eyes staring at her, ownerless and accusing. Nestling next to them was a packet of butter mints which Caroline scrunched carelessly in her fist before stuffing them into the bag. She could almost smell them as she shook her hand free of the crisp plastic – sweet, sickly, cloying.

She picked up the glasses, disgusted by the oily film of his hair cream on the cheap metal arms and folded them carefully. Their case was on the sideboard next to her graduation photograph, which she couldn't resist picking up, surprised that he'd kept it. She'd only sent it as a two-fingered gesture, her way of saying, *I made it despite you*. She looked different in the photograph, younger, obviously, but also bolder, more defiant than she ever remembered feeling. She tried that self-satisfied smile now, on her older face, but it didn't quite fit. The shape was wrong, somehow, and the emotion just wasn't there anymore. Placing the photograph carefully back in its position, half hidden by cheap, postcard-sized line drawings of past holiday destinations, Caroline carelessly stuffed the glasses into their case before thrusting them into the carrier bag.

Now for the bedroom.

She made her way upstairs, the steps easing her path with the familiar cracks and creaks which had once betrayed her early morning or late night escapes, each one sounding as fraudulent as those in a fairground haunted house.

Even from the landing she could see that her bedroom had changed completely. The lemon and pale blue of her last decoration experiment remained, but that was all there was to show for the eighteen years that the room had alternated between prison and sanctuary. The bed had been moved from her preferred position under the window and occupied the back wall, covered by a faded blue candlewick bedspread which Caroline vaguely recognised. She crossed to the bed to an accompaniment of more familiar floorboard whisperings and ran her hand over the rough texture of the cover. It had roses picked out in pink and green thread, most of which Caroline had unravelled years earlier to leave a balding winter scene. As she sat on the bed, head in hands, she wondered if she really had the courage for this? Could she actually go through with it? Without allowing time for further self-indulgent reflection Caroline leapt from the bed, trying to convince herself of her own resolve and strength. A quick look in his room, grab a few things from the bathroom and out. How hard could it be?

She tried not to look at the door to the smallest bedroom. It was closed, just as it had been the last time that she'd been in this house and just as it would remain for as long as she was here. She knew that all her sister's posters and clothes had been removed a long time ago: she knew because she'd helped. There was nothing belonging to Jeanette in the house; she'd made sure of that.

Her father's bedroom smelled of someone old and ill. Not rotten exactly, more like a sweet smell of decay like cheap talcum powder mixed with body odour. The bed was unmade, the duvet thrown back, forming a triangular section like skin peeled back from a wound. He'd left in a hurry. On the bedside table a glass had been knocked over onto a pile of tissues which had dried into ridge-like wrinkles, reminding Caroline of elephant hide. She turned to the dressing table, bare except for his deodorant and watch, and caught her triple reflection in the mirror, each face a different person. The left side looked grim and determined, the right bored but the Caroline in the middle, the face-on one, was pale and frightened.

She smiled to herself and stuck out her tongue. Scared Caroline smiled in response, but she had the feeling that the reflections in her peripheral vision hadn't changed, refusing to acknowledge her show of bravado. Self-consciously, she swept the deodorant into the plastic bag that hung by her side like a faithful dog, and bent to examine the drawers. Here, at least, the smell was clean. Fresh washing bulged in the bottom drawer, shirts, jumpers, vests. She pulled out a selection at random and piled them on the dressing table, careful to ignore her reflection. The smaller top drawers contained underwear: vests, socks and old men's underpants. Grimacing, Caroline removed the top layer from each drawer and placed the items with the other clothes.

The wardrobe held new terrors. Dark and imposing, it lurked in a lightless corner of the bedroom, intimidating and threatening her. She approached slowly, another, more ghostly, reflection of herself advancing from the highly-polished, dark surface of the door like a drowned figure rising from a lake. It stretched out a hand as if to hold Caroline's own as she reached out to turn the key and then it disappeared as the door swung open.

Caroline took out a suitcase and threw it on the bed. It was soft-sided and buckled, not like the hard plastic case that had scraped her shins on the few family holidays that she allowed herself to remember. She opened the case and filled it with the items that she had collected, including the carrier bag. Finally, she reached into the wardrobe for the dressing gown, that universal symbol of the hospitalised. As she pulled it down, her fingers brushed something hanging from the clothes rail. She parted the hangers for a better view, jolted from the present by the object she had discovered. A simple plastic container no bigger than a lemon hung amid the suits, its sides woven to look like wickerwork, a ribbon in its top holding it in place on the rail. She carefully unhooked it and pulled it down for a closer inspection. It nestled in her cupped hands, pale blue and harmless; an object as familiar as the reflections she had been avoiding for the past ten minutes. Every autumn until she was nine, she had taken it from its hiding place and filled it, under careful supervision, with lavender from the huge bush in the back garden. Every autumn, before Jeanette had gone, Caroline had held it in her cupped hands, inhaling to see if any memories of the previous year's long summer lingered in the stale seeds before she poured them into the dustbin and replaced them with a new fragrance that made her nostrils twitch and her throat burn.

Caroline sat on the bed and cupped her hands around her find as if she was protecting a precious stone. Exhaling heavily, she leaned forward and inhaled, trying to discover some lingering scent of that last summer, some reminder of the family that they had once been.

Nothing. But that wasn't a surprise. After what had happened with Jeanette, there wasn't really much left of the family.

CHAPTER 6

Caroline pulled into a parking space as far away from the main entrance of the hospital as she could find and coughed out the remnants of smoke from a low-tar cigarette. Winding down the window, she threw the butt across the car park, despising herself for picking up the habit again after so many months of abstinence. It showed weakness, she knew; the first sign of trouble or stress and she was smoking. Low tar now, full strength in a few days, she knew the pattern and was prepared for the consequences of her behaviour.

It was raining gently but instead of winding up her window, Caroline held out her right hand, palm up, accepting the cooling drops as a baptism or a blessing before the ordeal ahead. She pulled her hand back into the car and studied the droplets that she had collected, some still almost perfectly round, others melting and merging into a slick sheen on her palm. Caroline shuddered as it reminded her of nervous sweat; unpleasant but strangely appropriate. She checked the clock on her dashboard; she'd planned to arrive about an hour from the end of visiting time to limit the experience to something that might just be bearable but the minutes were passing at an alarming pace. It was time.

As she left the car, Caroline checked the door carefully, twice, aware that she was still stalling rather than being genuinely security conscious. The suitcase was heavier than she remembered and she wondered uncomfortably if the extra weight was guilt or reluctance; the answer was clear from the heavy breath she let out, barely masked by the whoosh of the hospital's state-of-the art automatic door swinging away from her, beckoning her inside.

The main desk was set back at an angle from the entranceway as though the staff wanted to be as unobtrusive as possible, or as unhelpful as possible, Caroline thought wryly, scanning the walls and doors for a clue. There were at least three ways out of the foyer, discounting the most appealing which would take her back to the car. Each had a coloured sign above its double doors, different colours for each wing of the hospital. Turning from door to door, Caroline scanned the signs until she found a green one for Aspen, the ward that Dennis had been admitted to for a few days' observation.

Taking a tight grip on the handle of the case, Caroline plunged through the double door before she could even think about changing her mind and surfaced in a long corridor which drew her round a series of sharp bends and corners like the rabbit in a greyhound race; except that Caroline wasn't afraid of what was behind her but of what was still to come. The doors leading off looked like watchful eyes eager to keep her on the right path, many had cryptic signs above them warning of *X-ray* or *Medical Physics*; even the mortuary sounded more tempting than Aspen ward.

And then she was there.

This door was different as one half stood open, inviting yet sinister, waiting to close and allow her no way back if she stepped over the threshold. Forcing a smile into her eyes, Caroline stepped onto the ward expecting to see rows of beds and smiling, helpful nurses. Instead she was confronted by more doors and a small, unattended staff desk. Each doorway was just an entrance, there were no actual doors and each opening was flanked by frosted glass windows. The obvious thing to do was to walk round the central area, peering in until she was able to locate Dennis in one of these anterooms. Feeling slightly foolish and more than a little conspicuous, Caroline began her search, desperately trying to avoid the eyes that stared back at her.

He was in the second room that Caroline checked, propped up on the bed reading a *Daily Mirror* without his glasses. His close scrutiny of the newspaper allowed Caroline to study him, noting the changes, wondering which were recent, from the illness, and which had happened gradually, over the past couple of decades. He was much thinner and smaller than she remembered, ankles protruding from hospital-issue pyjamas like thin branches stripped down to the white wood. Each foot, lying on the bedcover like a dead fish floating belly up, was mapped with blue and purple veins, stark against the pallor of the flesh. The full belly and broad shoulders were gone, his rib cage looked slightly bowed and sunken, creating an almost hunchbacked effect. The hair was different, too; thinner, whiter and no longer held in place by the oil which had once darkened it to a mid-brown.

Only the eyes were the same – grey, cold and cruel. These eyes registered Caroline's presence as she moved towards him and they barely flickered with surprise.

'What're *you* doing here?' he asked without shifting position or letting go of his newspaper.

'I was about to ask you the same,' she joked, aware of how her accent had changed since they'd last spoken. She stood uncertainly at the foot of the bed before remembering the reason for her visit.

'I've brought you some things. Pyjamas, shirts, socks.'

He folded the paper and studied her closely, no doubt noting the changes in her own manner and appearance. 'How did you know I was here?'

'Bren phoned. She thought I ought to know.'

'She came in yesterday but it's a long way on the bus. She can't carry much. She didn't say she'd rung you.' He was still watching, still appraising, tempting Caroline to flirt with the idea that he felt as uncomfortable as she did; that he was no more in control of the situation than she was.

'Where do you want this?' she asked, shaking the case as if it were a naughty child.

Dennis looked around, suddenly helpless and vague, his age clear in every tic and twitch of his facial muscles. 'Empty it out and you can put the stuff in the cabinet.'

It was an instruction rather than a suggestion and Caroline did as she was told more out of habit than any sense of being helpful. She unpacked the items carefully and stacked the clothes into the shallow drawers housed inside the small bedside cupboard. The toiletries she placed in the top drawer where they would be easily accessible.

'Put that down by the chair and I'll get a nurse to put it away somewhere,' Dennis said, as she closed the suitcase. 'I can use it when I get out.'

His economy with words hadn't changed much, Caroline noted. Never bother to speak when a gesture or a look would do. Words could give too much away, they could indicate moods and feelings; a shake of the head is always much less easy to read anything into, much less easy to invest with emotions or meaning.

Emptying the case had given Caroline a focus but once the task was completed she was unsure of her next move. She checked her watch in what she hoped was a surreptitious manner.

'Don't let me keep you.' Dennis was fiddling with his newspaper. 'Thanks for bringing a few bits and bobs. You can get off now if you want.'

More ambiguity. If *you* want. He could be dying in front of her, Caroline knew, and he still wouldn't ask for her assistance. Other members of the family had said it was just his way; that he didn't like to put people out. In the past, Caroline had often felt like she was the only one who had a clear, unblinkered view; the only one who could see Dennis for what he was – manipulative, calculating and flint-hard. She was the only one who knew the truth.

'If you're staying you might as well sit down,' Dennis's instruction broke into her musings. Caught by surprise, Caroline sat and studied her hands, aware that she must look like a small child who had been told to sit still and not fidget. Feigning nonchalance, she stretched her arms, palms clasped together, fingers linked, and rolled her shoulders.

'Must have been a long drive,' Dennis commented wryly, as if noting her tiredness.

'Not bad,' she said. 'It's less than an hour. It was fairly quiet on the roads.'

Silence blanketed them again.

Caroline was surprised at how little they had to talk about after so long, but so many topics were taboo. 'So what's up with you? Bren wasn't specific. I know it's cancer.'

Dennis laughed and Caroline felt she was being mocked; so many years and that was the best she could come up with. Still, he wasn't doing any better.

'It's my liver. The doctors have said a few positive things but I haven't got long. They reckon six months at best. I had a bad turn in bed a couple of days ago. I phoned Bren and she rang for an ambulance.'

Caroline wasn't surprised at the sequence of events. Dennis never had liked to bother the medical profession if it could be avoided. 'So how long are they going to keep you in? Do you want me to find a doctor? Ask when you'll be let out?'

Dennis turned to face her and she felt suddenly impaled on the sharpness of the glance. 'No, just leave it. They'll be busy. I'm sure they'll tell me in good time.'

'Suit yourself,' Caroline said. 'Is there anything I can get you while I'm here?'

'Don't think so.' More silence.

Caroline studied the floor, avoiding taking in details of the ward around her. A telephone rang at the nurses' station reminding her of the world outside. How easy it must be to accept this as the actual, tangible world; this temperature-regulated, disinfected reality. Better than outside, safer, easier to manage. Routine meals, drugs for the pain, for the worry, drugs for the drugs. Then a comfortable death.

'Did you see Bren?' Dennis asked.

'No. She just left me a note. I didn't want to bother her,' Caroline lied. 'Is she coming to see you?'

'I thought she might.' His voice was light but his eyes betrayed his disappointment. 'She's probably busy. I expect she'll come tomorrow. You could have given her a lift.'

The accusation was clear and Caroline felt instantly on the defensive.

'Didn't think, sorry. I just packed your case and drove over here. Next time maybe. Look, I'm going to see if I can find anybody who can give me some information. *You* might not be bothered when you're getting out but *I* need to make plans.'

'Plans?'

'Somebody's got to look after you and I don't think bloody Bren's up to the job.'

Caroline walked away from his muttered protests and headed back to the nurses' station where a harassed-looking woman in a dark blue uniform was tapping a keyboard. She didn't look up, engrossed in what she was doing, so Caroline coughed gently, unwilling to seem rude but keen to get the information she needed and get out of the hospital. The woman looked up, dark eyes briefly flaring with irritation from beneath her untidy fringe as she made two final keystrokes and pushed away the keyboard.

'Can I help you?' she said, glaring at Caroline as though she were a minor royal granting an audience to an annoying fan.

Caroline smiled, trying to diffuse some of the tension that had arisen from nowhere. 'I'm just after some information about my father. I'd like to know when he's likely to be discharged.'

'Which one is he?'

'Dennis Lambert. He's been here since yesterday.'

The woman's face suddenly softened, the planes and angles flattening in sympathy. 'Ah, yes. He's…'

'He's got liver cancer. I am aware of his condition.'

'You know it's serious?'

Caroline nodded. 'I know he's not going to get better. Is there somebody that I can talk to about getting him home?'

A hacking cough came rasping from one of the rooms, desperate and deep.

'Let's go somewhere a bit quieter,' the nurse said, standing up and stepping round the desk. 'It'll be easier to talk.'

Caroline allowed herself to be led into a small room around the corner from the nurses' station which was obviously used for private consultations. It contained a pair of hard plastic chairs and a curtained hospital bed. Beneath a tiny window, a small table held a blood pressure cuff and a stethoscope, both casually arranged and unthreatening. Caroline sat down without being asked and leaned forward as the other woman did the same.

'I'm Maddie Cox. I'm a clinical nurse specialist and I have oversight of your father's condition. He's in stage four liver cancer and, as you know, his prognosis isn't good.'

Caroline struggled to contain a smile. The woman was clearly hiding behind jargon and didn't want to brutalise Caroline with plain language.

'He can be made comfortable with pain relief…'

'He's in pain?'

'He will be. At the moment he can manage it with paracetamol but, as the disease progresses we many need to prescribe morphine.'

Caroline's thoughts flitted about her brain like angry wasps, unable to settle on anything clear. Morphine. Pain. She recognised the words but couldn't quite grasp their meaning.

'He should be mobile for a while yet. He can walk and there's always the option of a wheelchair, further down the line.'

Further down the line. What did that mean? Caroline could picture a freight train bearing down on her at ever-increasing speed. 'How long?'

'Well it's…'

'How long?'

Maddie sighed. 'It's hard to say but, in my experience, cases like this usually don't drag on. Six to eight months possibly.'

Plenty of time. Too much time.

'If you'd like to speak to your father's consultant I can…'

Caroline shook her head. 'No. I'm clear about what's happening and what needs to be done.'

The nurse nodded, her mouth a flat line of sympathy and understanding.

'Well, if…' She stood, obviously expecting Caroline to do the same. Something dropped from her pocket and rolled under her chair. Caroline leaned forward to retrieve it despite Maddie's protests and saw that it was a blue plastic disc with the number 50 and the letters GA on one side. The other side was blank.

Caroline passed it back to Maddie without comment, storing away this small nugget of information about the nurse. Knowledge was power, Dennis had taught her that.

CHAPTER 7

Caroline timed her next visit to the hospital precisely – not enough time to get caught up in Dennis's misery but just enough to have a chance to talk to the nurse that she had met the previous day; if she were working the same shift. Back at her father's house, Caroline had spent the evening tapping the screen of her phone, researching her father's cancer, the stages and possible progress of the disease. It might take longer than she'd anticipated.

She negotiated the foyer with more confidence this time, the uncertainty of her previous visit banished by her faith in the seeds of her plan. This time she noticed how drab the corridors looked; scuffs and scars marred the flooring, and the walls, although bright, were battered and scraped. She breezed into Aspen ward and walked up to Dennis's bed, empty-handed this time. He was asleep. Caroline briefly considered giving him a nudge but couldn't really see much point; at least, this way, it was easier for her to re-establish contact with Maddie Cox.

The nurses' station was deserted again, the staff obviously too busy to spend time answering phones or updating records, so Caroline wandered around the ward peering into each 'room'. Most contained quartets of elderly men who looked like they were hovering somewhere between life and death surrounded by clusters of relatives who mostly looked bored. Faces turned towards her, a sudden rush of anticipation, and then settled back into their set expressions of hopelessness.

There was no sign of Maddie. One or two nurses gave her a curious stare as they ministered to patients but none wore the dark blue uniform of the clinical nurse specialist. Was she on a different shift? Was it a day off? Frustrated, Caroline paced back to Dennis's bed and considered her next move. She sat on the hard chair next to his bed and watched the steady rise and fall of his chest as he slept. He looked almost peaceful. Her resentment uncoiled inside her, a taut spring looking for release after years of strain. Finally, decisively, she pressed the call button on the handset which lay next to Dennis's arm.

Hurried footsteps approached, barely allowing Caroline time to set a concerned expression on her face and pull her chair closer to the bed.

'Can I help you?'

The nurse who arrived was slightly dishevelled-looking as though the call had dragged her from a few snatched minutes of sleep. Strands of her blonde hair hung loose from her practical bun and the dark smudges beneath her eyes made her look exhausted.

'I think his breathing's a bit funny,' Caroline lied, pointing to her father's still-sleeping form.

The nurse looked at her sceptically then leaned closer to Dennis. 'He sounds fine at the moment. He had a bit of a rough night so he's probably exhausted.'

'Rough night?' Caroline prompted.

'Unsettled. I think he wants to go home and he got a bit agitated.' She picked up the chart that hung on the bottom of the bed. 'It looks like he was given something to help him to sleep, that's all. He might be a bit groggy when he wakes up.'

'I was just worried. I spoke to Nurse Cox yesterday and she sort of prepared me for the worst. I was hoping to speak to her again. I have a few questions about bringing my father home.'

The nurse glanced over her shoulder towards the nurses' station. 'I think she's still on shift. If you give me a few minutes I'll see if she's available to speak to you.'

Caroline watched the woman walk away before turning back to her father. Sleeping pills. Another piece of information to store away for future use. Dennis's breathing was slow and steady and the effect of the heat of the ward and the rhythm of his chest was soporific. Caroline felt her eyes growing heavy as she waited.

'You're back then?' Her father's voice roused her from her stupor and she looked up to see his cold eyes watching her suspiciously. 'Thought you'd have gone back to Sheffield by now.'

'No. Still here. I told you I'm going to take you home when you're ready to leave. I had a chat with one of your nurses yesterday so I've got a bit more of an idea of what you'll need.'

Was that fear in his eyes? She couldn't be sure. And, if it was, what was he afraid of? Death? Her? 'What did she say, this nurse?'

He obviously hadn't asked. He tried to sit up and Caroline leaned forward to rearrange his pillows so he could get comfortable. There was a scum of whitish saliva in the corners of his mouth and she tried not to look at it as she spoke.

'She said it'll be a few more days. I'm going to talk to her again about what I'll need to do for you.'

This time the fear was more obvious. Visions of bedpans and sponge baths darted across Caroline's mind, the lingua franca of elderly illness. Hopefully, not this time.

'You were asking for me?' A voice behind her.

She turned to see Maddie Cox peering anxiously at her father, probably expecting him to have deteriorated rapidly; her eyes flicked back to Caroline when she was satisfied that her patient's condition hadn't changed.

'I was,' Caroline said. 'I have a few more questions about my father's care after he's discharged. I just thought you'd be the right person to ask after we spoke yesterday.'

Maddie coloured slightly and Caroline wondered if she was remembering the Gamblers Anonymous chip that Caroline had picked up for her.

'Of course,' she said, glancing expectantly from Caroline to her father.

'Not here,' Caroline said with a pointed nod towards Dennis, knowing that he would make no protest, that he'd accept whatever the professionals suggested without question.

Maddie led the way to another cramped room hidden away behind the nurses' station. It was obviously a rest room for staff as one wall was lined with cheap foam-seated chairs which looked like they'd been shoved together to make a makeshift bed. The walls were adorned with posters warning about the dangers of MRSA and other illnesses, and the window blind was closed. Opposite the row of chairs was a kitchen counter with a sink, microwave and kettle. A small fridge nestled beneath the sink. *All the basics*, Caroline thought, *with the emphasis on the 'basic'.*

'Have a seat,' the nurse said. Caroline perched on the one nearest the door, forcing Maddie to sit further inside the room; further away from anybody who might overhear.

'So what do you need to know?'

'To be frank, I didn't just want to ask about my father. It's a bit more personal than that.'

Maddie sat back in her seat, a wary expression of surprise in her eyes.

'Personal?'

'I saw your fifty-day chip from GA when you dropped it the other day. I recognised it immediately.'

She paused and waited for the implication to sink in.

'Oh, you're…'

'Yes. I'm an addict. I've been attending GA for a few months and one of my worries about staying with Dennis is that I won't be able to get to meetings should I need to. I thought I could ask you where to go.'

Maddie scowled, obviously irritated by the intrusion into her personal life. She dug her hands defensively into the pockets of her uniform top.

'You could have looked in the yellow pages. Or online.'

Caroline hung her head. 'I could have. But it's hard enough going to a new group. I thought you might let me tag along, introduce me.'

Maddie shook her head. 'I'm sorry. I don't mix work with my personal life, especially this part of my life. Use Google.' She stood up.

Caroline sighed. 'I've overstepped. Sorry. It's just that I've got such a lot going on and I know what I'm like. I'll give in eventually. I haven't had a bet in over a year but the first thing I thought about doing when I left on Tuesday was going to the bookies and then to the pub. You're right though. It's my problem. I'll find somewhere. I apologise in advance if I end up gate-crashing your meeting.'

Maddie sighed, walked over to the door and closed it quietly. 'It's not that I don't want to help. I'm just not sure it would be right. I'm looking after your dad. I don't want patients or their families in my personal life. You can understand that.'

'I do. And I feel embarrassed for putting you in this position. Hopefully he'll be out of here soon and you can forget this happened.'

Maddie held the door open for her and allowed her back through to the nurses' station. As soon as she'd turned her back on the nurse, Caroline's face cracked into a self-satisfied smile. She'd seen the look on Maddie's face as the nurse had listened to her sob story. This wasn't the end of the discussion.

Caroline closed the lid of her laptop. She'd taken Maddie's advice and searched online for GA meetings in Doncaster. There were two regular ones but neither was near the infirmary. However, two meetings gave her a 50/50 chance and she wasn't in a hurry; she'd find the right one eventually. She stretched out her arms, easing the tension in her muscles. It was good to be home. She'd decided against spending another night at her father's house. One had been enough. The memories and the grime had both been off-putting in different ways and she couldn't bear the thought of being watched by Bren every time she stepped out of the door.

She looked around the room, taking pleasure in the bright décor and the modern furnishings. She loved this house and the area, and had no regrets about moving back to South Yorkshire despite her initial misgivings. Dore was far enough away from Thorpe for the village to barely cross her mind but close enough for her to get back if she needed to. Now she needed to.

She'd tried to get as far away as possible when she'd left home for university, and Bristol had been the perfect place. Three years of freedom and a geography degree gave her the confidence to move even further south and west, and she'd spent the next twenty years in and around Plymouth working for the city council as a planner. Thorpe had always been there, though, in the back of her mind – a throbbing tell-tale heart. Thorpe and Jeanette. She'd always known that she'd have to come back – for her sister.

She slipped the laptop onto the coffee table and went through to the kitchen – her favourite room in the house. Standing at the sink to fill the kettle she gazed out at the back garden with its long stretch of lawn and carefully tended shrubs, both looking muted under a blanket of frost. She missed the garden during the winter; missed the feel of warm earth under her fingers and the satisfaction of edging the lawn and cutting back the plants. Caroline always felt connected to her mother when she spent time gardening; a deep-rooted link that was almost genetic. Her mum had loved the garden, loved her roses and chrysanthemums. Until Jeanette disappeared. Nothing had been the same after that. Her mum had barely left the house and her interest in the garden had dissipated almost overnight.

Caroline poured hot water onto her teabag, still looking at the garden. The patio at the bottom would need a clean after the winter to get rid of the algae and moss. It was the only thing that she'd had to change before she could live in the house. She'd had the greenhouse dismantled and the patio laid before she'd been able to move in any of her furniture. She could barely remember what the garden had looked like when she'd first viewed the property.

Her father had bought their council house after the first wave of sell-offs in the 1980s. It had been more expensive than if he'd bought it when he'd first had the opportunity but Caroline knew that he'd done it because of Jeanette and their mother's subsequent depression. It meant that he could make alterations, to make the place theirs, but all she'd felt at the time was trapped by the memories of her sister.

At nine years old, Caroline had been desperate to move away, to start again but she'd understood that selling the house was impossible and that, if she was going to leave, she'd have to do it by herself. So she'd worked hard at school, convinced that if she could get a good job she'd be able to live wherever she wanted. She'd considered university when she'd started her GCSEs and by the time she was seventeen, she'd known what she wanted to study and where.

She would have probably stayed in the southwest despite having no real ties there. A few failed relationships had convinced her that she wasn't likely to get married and have a family; she was too broken and too closed off and she didn't really enjoy sharing her space with anybody. But the inheritance had changed everything. She had only met her mother's brother, Ted, twice but she had been aware that he had a job that was something to do with lorries. What she hadn't understood as a child was that he'd owned a haulage company and, after he died, his solicitor told her that he'd sold it in the late nineties for a substantial sum of money. Widowed and childless, he'd left it to her. So she'd moved back but still kept her distance; she was financially independent and she could rub Dennis's nose in it by sending him details of her new address in Dore. Letting him know that she was close. Watching and waiting.

Bren's call had still come as a shock, though. Even though another part of the reason for Caroline sending her contact details was for something like this, she hadn't really expected her father to keep her phone number, much less allow Bren to use it, so the call had left her shaking with confusion and anxiety and anticipation.

CHAPTER 8

The first GA meeting that Caroline had attended had been in a room at Doncaster library. The person leading the group had been very earnest and the five other attendees had welcomed Caroline without suspicion. But no Maddie.

The Methodist church was her second option. It was on a side street just off one of the main roads heading south out of Doncaster; secluded and out of the way. From what Caroline had learned from Google, the two groups were run by the same branch of Gamblers Anonymous but they had to use different venues on different nights. She had asked about this at the library meeting, and it seemed that there was little overlap between attendees. The Tuesday library group rarely attended the Thursday church group and vice versa.

The Methodist church was an imposing red brick Victorian building with three storeys of arched windows and a double entrance door. One side of the door had been propped open invitingly, and Caroline stepped through it into a large, oak-panelled vestibule area. She instantly felt the weight of years of religious practice and hope bearing down on her. She took a deep breath, trying to keep herself focussed on the task ahead. The library meeting had been quite small and Caroline hadn't felt compelled to 'share' her story but, from the buzz of conversation coming from behind the panels, Caroline could tell that this meeting was going to be quite a bit bigger. She placed her palm on the cold brass fingerplate, imagining her handprint captured there for eternity, and pushed open the inner door, rehearsing her fabricated version of her past in her head.

A knot of people was gathered at the front of the chapel in an open area beyond the rows of elaborate wooden pews. A few heads turned as Caroline approached but most went back to their conversations, allowing her the opportunity to examine her surroundings.

The oak theme had been continued into the main chapel, and the pews and panelling glowing softly under the harsh electric lights. The seating was arranged in two stages; the first, plush with blue velvet cushions, flanked a central aisle which ran up to an elaborate wooden pulpit dominating the back wall. A small lectern stood in front of it; obviously modesty had won over ostentation in the twenty-first century.

The second level of seating was above the first, arranged high above the main body of the chapel, supported by iron pillars; closer to God and swathed in shadow. Above the pulpit was a curtained alcove in front of the huge pipes of an organ which looked like something from a sci-fi film or a steampunk comic strip.

Caroline stood in the central aisle, head raised as she turned and took in the varying tones of the wood against the plain white of the walls; it was a modernist interior designer's heaven.

'Hi,' a voice next to her said. 'Are you here for GA?'

She turned to face a young man in a dishevelled-looking grey business suit. His dark hair was cut short on top and shaved close to his head at the sides, and his blue eyes regarded her with friendly curiosity.

'I er...' Caroline hesitated, momentarily flummoxed by the direct question.

'It's okay,' the man said with a warm smile. 'We're all in the same boat. I'm Warren.'

He held out his hand and Caroline shook it, surprised by the strength of his grip.

'I'm a bit of a regular,' Warren said. 'Two years next month. It's always a rush to get here straight from work but these meetings have given me my life back. I haven't had a bet since I started coming but I don't think I could give up meetings yet.' It was a lot to admit in a few short sentences, and Caroline assumed that the tone of these meetings was generally confessional. So much so that it even bled into casual greetings.

'He only comes for the free food these days,' a woman across the aisle said. She walked towards them with two quick strides and towered over them both. Caroline looked up into deep brown eyes set in a face that was wrinkled and creased like chamois leather and framed by a tight cap of grey hair. 'We all wish he wouldn't keep coming, though. It'd be a lot simpler to do the catering.'

Warren who smiled apologetically. 'Vegan,' he said. 'Two years of bloody houmous and carrot sticks. You'd think somebody would have come up with something a bit more imaginative. Evelyn's in charge of snacks.'

The woman nodded as though accepting a compliment. 'Seriously,' she said. 'We're a friendly bunch. The meeting's about to start if you'd like to take a seat.'

She led the way to a circle of chairs which had been set up at the front of the church beneath the forbidding wooden pulpit, and gestured to Caroline to sit down. Caroline hesitated. There was no sign of Maddie, and Caroline was reluctant to stay for another round of stories and revelations if it didn't help her to achieve her goal; but what choice did she have? Reluctantly, she took a seat opposite Warren and gazed round at the other members. As she'd expected, none of them were familiar from the meeting earlier in the week and, much like on Tuesday, they represented every walk of life. They were a mix of genders, ages and, judging by the business suits and uniforms, professions.

The meeting began in the same way as the previous one with everybody introducing themselves. Caroline kept the details of her life to a minimum but one or two others were eager to share small details from their week. Each revelation or minor victory was greeted with approving smiles, and one woman received a polite round of applause for confessing to having driven ten miles out of her way to avoid passing a betting shop where she'd lost a lot of money in the past. Then it was time for one of the group to tell their story in depth. Caroline knew that she wouldn't be asked as it was her first meeting so she allowed herself to relax a little as Evelyn asked Warren to share.

He'd just started his story, a brief account of his time at university, when he was interrupted by someone walking down the aisle.

'Hi. So sorry I'm late. Warren, please carry on.'

The woman slipped into a chair a few seats away from Caroline on the same side of the circle and instantly devoted her attention to Warren's story, allowing Caroline a chance to study her. It was the first time that she'd seen Maddie without the professional disguise of her nurse's uniform and she was surprised that such a small difference could change her perception of the woman.

At the hospital Maddie had been mostly brisk and efficient but here, leaning forward slightly to listen to Warren, Caroline saw again her empathetic nature, smiling sympathetically as he admitted his addiction. She must have had time to go home and change as she was wearing a cardigan and jeans under a smart black jacket and her make-up was much more obvious than when Caroline had seen her at work. Her hair was loose instead of pulled back into a ponytail and, in profile, Caroline could see that she was strikingly attractive.

As Maddie turned to acknowledge another member of the group, her smile froze as she saw Caroline. She looked away, but Caroline could see that for the next twenty minutes she was struggling to focus as another member told their story. She was fidgety and seemed agitated.

As the rest of the group dispersed to attack the food, Caroline hung back, hoping to speak to Maddie, make her fake apology and offer to leave. Maddie beat her to it.

'What are you doing here?' she hissed, her eyes flicking from the group of people at the snacks table to Caroline and back again.

'I'm sorry,' Caroline said. 'I did warn you that I was looking for a meeting. This is the nearest one to my dad's house. It's been a stressful few days and I just needed to come.'

'There's one on Tuesdays at the library. You could have gone to that one.'

'Sorry,' Caroline said. 'I was aware of it but I was busy. This was my first opportunity. They seem like a decent bunch of people.'

Maddie's face softened a little. 'They are. I've not been coming that long but they've been really welcoming. You'll know yourself that it's not easy walking into a meeting for the first time and telling people what a mess you've made of your life.'

Caroline nodded.

'But there's no judgement here. Just support and company.'

'Look,' Caroline said. 'I really am sorry that I've gate-crashed your meeting. Can I buy you a drink? You know, to make up for it. I'm not the selfish bitch that you're probably imagining.'

Maddie shook her head and Caroline tensed. She was going to refuse the offer.

'I'm not much of a drinker,' Maddie said. 'To be honest I'm trying to save every penny I earn so I don't often get out. And I know you're not selfish. I've seen the way you keep pestering my staff about your father. I can see that you only want the best for him.'

'Look, I'm offering to pay. Just a drink. I can keep you on the straight and narrow,' Caroline joked. 'Or I'll just buy you soft drinks. I'm driving anyway so I can't indulge.'

There was some hesitation in Maddie's expression and Caroline wondered just how much her gambling addiction had cost her. Friends? Family? Was she lonely and unsupported beyond this group? Caroline really hoped so.

She walked over to the food table and picked up a sausage roll. She didn't want it but she needed to give Maddie time to think about her offer.

Warren smiled at Caroline and gestured with a carrot stick. 'Houmous is good,' he said with a grin.

'Sorry,' she said, waving back with the sausage roll. 'I'm a dedicated carnivore.'

Warren winked at her. 'Oh well. No judgement here, right?'

Caroline smiled at him, reluctant to encourage further chat. She didn't want to get embroiled in a conversation and miss her chance to talk to Maddie. Besides, his cheeky smile was more than a little flirtatious and Caroline really didn't have time for *that*.

She was relieved to feel a hand on her upper arm and she turned to see Maddie smiling at her.

'I think I'd like to take you up on that offer of a drink. If it's still on. I'm sorry if I was a bit snappy – just tired. It's been another long day in another long week.'

Caroline swallowed her last mouthful of sausage roll and followed Maddie up the aisle to the door.

The pub turned out to be another church, which Caroline vaguely remembered from her teenage drinking days. In the early 1990s it had been a club with flashing lights and loud music – a place to hide, to be somebody else for a night – and it had been turned into a tastefully renovated wine bar complete with cut-down pews along the walls and organ pipes behind the bar.

Caroline pointed to a table, close to the entrance. 'I'll get the drinks. What do you fancy?'

Maddie stared at her for a few seconds as if she were considering which would be the safest option. 'Vodka and coke, please. I'm not driving tonight.'

Caroline slipped her coat round the back of a chair and made her way to the bar. The pub was fairly quiet – two booths occupied by couples and a group of four in an alcove that looked like it had once been a changing area for the clergy. She remembered the joke that people used to make about the place when it had first opened – to some outrage amongst the Christian community – if Jesus could turn water into wine then why not turn a church into a pub?

A peek over her shoulder reassured her that Maddie was still in her seat so she didn't need to lower her voice as she ordered a double vodka and coke for the nurse and a half of shandy for herself.

'Here you go,' she said, plonking the drinks down on the table. 'You look like you're ready for this.' Maddie had removed her jacket and was looking at her mobile phone. She smiled up at Caroline, picked up her drink and took a big gulp, her throat rippling as she swallowed greedily.

'God, that's good,' she sighed, not seeming to notice the strength of the drink or the irony.

'Bad day?'

Maddie shook her head. 'Just long. I sometimes wonder why I bothered working for a promotion. It feels like I never get home from one week to the next.'

She dropped her eyes and traced the pattern of wood grain on the table-top with the pad of her middle finger.

'I know what you mean,' Caroline said, mainly to fill the silence. 'The only good thing about my dad's illness is that it gives me a break from work.'

'What do you do?' Maddie asked.

'City council. Planning,' Caroline lied. 'And, yes, it is as glamorous as it sounds.'

Maddie laughed and took another sip of her drink. 'How long have you got off?'

Caroline faked a heavy sigh. 'As long as it takes. Compassionate leave. I work hard enough so it's not like they could refuse. Not that they're paying me, though.'

'You know it could be quite a few months yet?'

'I know,' Caroline said. 'It's fine. I'm prepared for that.'

They sat in gloomy silence for a while as Caroline tried to think of an appropriate subject to lead her to the information that she wanted. In the end, she decided on a direct approach. 'So? GA? Have you been going long?'

Maddie's dark eyes flashed briefly with annoyance and Caroline wondered if she'd overstepped, misjudged, as Maddie stood up suddenly.

'Hey, I'm sorry if… I just…' Caroline stuttered.

Maddie smiled at her. 'I'm not leaving. I just think I'll need another drink if I'm going to tell that story.'

'Okay. But let me get them,' Caroline offered. 'I'm the reason you're here telling the story.'

She batted away Maddie's feeble protest with a wave of her hand and went back to the bar.

Two more double vodkas later and Maddie was deep into her story. A nasty divorce, a gambling habit which started as a way to escape a controlling husband and a mountain of debt which was being steadily tackled after a recent promotion.

'And then there's Ethan,' Maddie said.

'Ethan?'

'My boy. Although he's hardly a boy now. He's nearly eighteen and he's doing his A-levels. He's the main reason that I go to GA. I need to clear my debts so I can help him. He wants to be a doctor and it's a long course.'

Caroline mentally examined this small titbit of information and stored it away for future use. Debts and a son. Could be useful. 'How are you getting on with clearing your debts?'

Maddie studied her drink then raised defiant eyes to Caroline's. 'Three months ago, I had a lapse. I lost two thousand pounds. It set me back but I'm on track now. Another eighteen months or so and I'll have cleared the big loan. Until then, I'll shop at Lidl and not buy any new clothes. Ethan's got a job at Asda. He's a good lad. He's saving.'

'How much do you owe?' Caroline asked, imagining tens of thousands.

Maddie shook her head, reluctant to answer.

'At my worst it was nearly fifty grand,' Caroline lied.

'God. Nothing like that. Fifteen, give or take. But it's the interest that's the killer.'

Peanuts, Caroline thought. She could wipe out this debt with a few strokes of her pen. 'Interest? You've not got one of those dodgy loans?'

'I had to,' Maddie admitted. 'I could hardly go to the bank.'

Caroline pretended to think for a minute. 'Look. I haven't been entirely straight with you. I can afford to take time off work to look after Den – Dad because I've got some money. I got an inheritance a year ago. I paid off the last of my debts, bought a small house but I've still got way more than I need. Let me lend you the money. You could pay me back in instalments, interest free.'

Maddie's eyes narrowed with suspicion. 'Why would you do that?'

'Because you've been good to my dad.'

The suspicious look was still there. 'That's my job. It's not special treatment.'

'I know. It's not just that. I know how it feels to be drowning in debt. I'm in a position to help, that's all.'

Maddie shook her head. 'It's a generous offer but I couldn't, it wouldn't be right. We're not friends or anything; I'm just looking after your father for a few days.'

She wasn't biting. Caroline could have kicked herself. She'd jumped in with her offer too soon and had probably lost her chance to have Maddie in her debt. Time to cut her losses. 'Think about it,' she said, standing up and slipping one arm into a sleeve of her coat. 'You can always let me know if you change your mind. I'd better get back. There's still a lot to do before I get my father home.' She shrugged the coat onto her shoulders, zipped it up to her chin, and stepped out into the damp night, leaving Maddie to finish her drink.

JANUARY

CHAPTER 9

Kate was surprised by the lack of odour in the DRI's autopsy labs. She hadn't been expecting to be able to smell decomposing bodies but she had imagined that there would be some sort of disinfectant to cover up anything unpleasant. Instead the air in the place smelt of nothing; sterile. Logically, she understood that extractors and circulated air kept everything fresh but the less rational side of her brain was convinced that there were more sinister forces at work, masking the real purpose of the dissection rooms, so that coming face to face with death would be more shocking.

It wasn't her first post mortem. Kate had seen her share of bodies during her twenty- odd years as a police officer and had attended a number of autopsies but this was her first without being accompanied by a senior officer. It was also her first double PM. Kailisa was going to look at the body from the canal *and* Dennis Lambert in the same morning, which meant that Kate wouldn't get a break from the gore until lunchtime. Not that she expected to feel much like eating.

She pushed open the glass door which led into the observation area, and gazed down through the internal window at the body lying on the stainless steel table below her. There was something theatrical about the positioning as if she was in the audience up in 'the gods' and the autopsy suite was the stage. Sadly there would be no encores for the woman below her. Kailisa and his team had left most of her clothing intact except for the unzipping of her jacket, presumably to be certain that she was in fact dead when they pulled her out of the lock. Kate watched as a gowned and gloved Kailisa, accompanied by an assistant, entered from a door somewhere below her and walked over to the body. The theatricality of the situation was heightened as he spoke to the assistant, ignoring Kate's presence even though she'd spoken to him in his office less than half an hour earlier.

He dictated his first impressions, the formulaic opening lines of every post mortem that Kate had attended, sounding slightly metallic through the intercom system.

'The body is of a white female, approximate age mid-thirties to early forties. She appears to be well nourished and her clothing, while not expensive, is good quality and shows few signs of wear.'

Kate watched as the clothes were cut from the body and examined but there were no clues in the pockets or on any of the labels. Everything was chain-store generic; Kailisa noted that even her underwear was from a supermarket. Her clothes were bagged and labelled before Kailisa began on the physical examination of the dead woman. He drew down a large lens from the lighting apparatus above the table and angled it along the body. No sign of trauma other than the head injury which had been discovered at the scene.

'She has had a child,' Kailisa said, focussing the light onto her abdomen. 'There is an obvious scar left from a C section.'

'Recent?' Kate asked.

Kailisa shook his head. 'No. Impossible to say how old but it's well healed. I'd say a few years. A teenager possibly.'

Kate made a note. A child meant that somebody might be depending on this woman. She might have a partner, a loving family who were missing her. Her hand dropped almost instinctively to her own abdomen and the scar she had from giving birth to her son, Ben. What would *he* do if *she* was missing?

Nothing else stood out. Kailisa gestured to his assistant, a tiny, elfin woman with a blonde crew cut and an efficient manner which she had probably modelled on her mentor. She approached with an electric razor and shaved an area of the dead woman's head, exposing the wound to her scalp. Kate leaned forward in her seat, trying to get a better look at the mess of bruised skin.

Kailisa, obviously sensing the movement above him, looked up anticipating her question.

'DI Fletcher, this is the only obvious injury. At the moment I am unable to ascertain if it is the cause of death. The injury is a blunt force trauma caused by an object with an obvious angular shape.'

'Could it have been one of the iron ladder rungs in the lock?'

Kailisa turned away and, for a second, Kate thought he was just irritated by her questions but then she saw he was looking at a spread of photographs along one of the countertops which ran along three walls of the room. He slid a ruler out of a drawer and held it next to the dead woman's head, then consulted the photograph again.

'I'd say not,' he said. 'The object we're looking for is more square-shaped than elongated like the rungs. And thicker. Perhaps the edge of the concrete canal side. I'll need to check the photographs to ascertain whether the angle is possible.'

'There was some debris brought in with the body. Stuff that the divers brought up from the bottom of the lock. Anything there that she might have hit her head on?'

Kailisa shook his head. 'She didn't hit her head on the bottom of the lock. When she was found she was almost floating. The air trapped in her down jacket would have acted as a buoyancy aid. The lock is eight feet deep at its shallowest. There is no way that she could have struck the bottom with any force. She may not have even reached the bottom. If she'd been in moving water such as a river or the sea I'd have expected a variety of post-mortem injuries but there is unlikely to be anything from when she entered the water.'

'What about something in the debris that could have been used to hit her and then was thrown in with the body?'

Kailisa sighed and Kate knew that she'd used up her quota of his goodwill for the time being. She sat back down and continued to watch as the pathologist cut the body, his scalpel like a paintbrush tracing faint red lines across her chest and abdomen as he made the initial incisions. After removing and assessing the internal organs, the pathologist turned his attention back to the head. This was the bit Kate really hated. Kailisa made an incision with his scalpel, circling the scalp, then peeled back flesh and skin, exposing the bones of the skull. The woman's face crumpled like a deflated balloon as more skin was pulled forward, exposing the whole of the top of her head.

'The damage to the skull is more obvious without the flesh,' Kailisa said to his assistant as Kate leaned forward again. 'The wound is approximately four inches long with a sharp edge rather than something rounded like a baseball bat or a cosh. The blow has fractured the parietal bone on the right side and was of sufficient force to cause skull fragments to embed in the brain. The dura is ruptured and there are indications of severe bleeding in the cranial cavity. The skin around the injury is heavily bruised and split.' He picked up a saw, obviously intending to remove the top of the skull so that he could examine the brain. Kate tried to imagine the attack. It was the right side of the head and towards the back. Could somebody have approached her from behind and then hit her? Which would make the attacker right-handed – like around ninety per cent of the population.

'Would she have been unconscious when she went in the water?' Kate asked.

'Almost certainly.'

'So she drowned?'

Kailisa smiled up at Kate. 'Drowning, as you probably know, is rather difficult to ascertain. There is a little froth in her lungs indicating that she aspirated water but it may have been a reflex. The cold shock may have stopped her heart or the head injury may have been severe enough to kill her within minutes as the pressure of the hematoma built up in her brain. At the moment, I'm uncertain. I'll make slides of lung tissue, and the results of her blood tests may also help.'

'So there's nothing obvious?'

'There is the wound to her head. The severity suggests that she may not have survived even if she had not ended up in the water.

I think that is the most likely cause of death but I need to wait for the lab results.'

'Did somebody hit her with something?'

Kailisa consulted the photographs of the scene. 'I'd say that's the most likely cause. It's hard to imagine how she could have fallen and hit her own head with such force and at this angle. We'll know more when the slides come back from the lab tomorrow. I'm sorry that I haven't got anything more definite.' He paused and picked up one of the photographs, turning it upside down and then back again. A whispered conversation ensued with his assistant, who tapped on a computer keyboard and summoned up an image which she printed out.

'What is it?' Kate asked, but he ignored her and took the printout over to the body.

She watched as he measured the wound again and compared it to the photograph.

Finally he turned to her, holding up the piece of paper. 'A house brick,' he announced. The image was clear, obviously colour laser printed; a red, angular house brick like the ones that had been made in Thorpe years before she was born. Even without the image of the ruler next to it, Kate knew that it would be about four inches wide and eight long. Her father's garden had been full of them, left over from when the house was built. He'd used them to make borders for his vegetable and flowerbeds. Looking at the image she could almost feel the weight of it in her hand. Heavy enough to inflict a fatal blow.

'Weapon?'

Kailisa turned his free hand palm up in a gesture which suggested 'possibly' then went back to his dictation.

Kate took out her phone to send a quick text to Raymond. She had been instructed to call him but he'd been in such a rage about the previous night's news report of Dennis Lambert's murder that she really didn't want to risk his wrath by suggesting that they weren't much further forward with the woman from the canal. He couldn't understand how the press had got hold of the

Lambert story so quickly and was threatening to sack any 'leakers' or 'traitors'. She knew that he'd calm down eventually but the one thing guaranteed to soothe him was a result and she didn't really have much to offer so far. She knew that it wasn't Kailisa's fault. He was methodical and scrupulous and he wouldn't want to commit to a cause of death if there was any room for doubt.

Suddenly realising that there was something missing from his evaluation, she tapped on the glass to get his attention. He looked up, clearly irritated by the interruption.

'Any clues to time of death?'

Kailisa grinned. 'I was waiting for that. It took you a while. Getting rusty, DI Fletcher?'

Kate felt herself reddening. It was a mistake. She should have asked sooner.

'Her stomach contains undigested remains of something which looks like pizza. It seems likely that she died soon after eating. As the body hadn't been spotted during daylight hours, I'd say that sometime between six and nine o'clock yesterday is likely. Unless she ate a very late meal. As she was floating in the water, there are no lividity marks to give us any further indication.'

Kate thanked him and took out her notebook. Drawing a line beneath the previous day's jottings, she wrote the date and then *Canal body. Pizza. Where from and who with?* She might have been out for a meal with somebody who could help to fill in the timeline. Or somebody who might be the murderer. Of course, it was possible that she'd eaten alone at home. Kate was familiar with the lure of pizza delivery after a long day.

Kailisa finished dictating and turned to his assistant who stripped off her gloves and gown, dumped them in a medical hazard bin and left.

'I'll start on Dennis Lambert in around twenty minutes,' Kailisa said through the intercom. 'Perhaps you'd like a break.'

Half an hour later, fuelled by surprisingly good hospital coffee, Kate listened to Kailisa's opening lines again. This time, the identity of the deceased was known to both of them and the pathologist stated that cause of death had been reported as an overdose of opioid analgesics combined with alcohol. Kate sat down, much less curious about this death. The point of the post mortem was simply to corroborate Caroline Lambert's story that her father had taken an overdose.

Kailisa spent some time examining the head and face for fibres or any other indication of suffocation. He mentioned the absence of petechial haemorrhages in the eyes indicating that the man was neither smothered nor strangled. An examination of the throat failed to find any bruising and there were no external signs of trauma. Kate knew that he couldn't be certain of cause of death until the blood results came back but he would be ruling out other causes, such as suffocation, as he examined the body.

She watched as he opened the body cavity and removed the organs one by one, weighing and dictating. The stomach was empty apart from a small amount of brownish fluid from which Kailisa took a sample for analysis. Next he removed the liver, the primary site of Lambert's cancer. Years of abuse had left it enlarged and noduled with cirrhosis. He measured the cancerous lesions and dictated size and location to the ever-vigilant assistant.

Kate was about to excuse herself, having seen enough to confirm Lambert's illness, when she saw Kailisa frown. He was looking at the notes that had been provided by the hospital; the deathly progress of the cancer which had reduced Dennis Lambert to a bedridden husk of a man.

'DI Fletcher. You might want to come down for a closer look.'

Kate leapt from her seat and raced to the mortuary doors, grabbing a gown and gloves and struggling into them as she walked across to the dissection table.

'What am I looking at?' she asked as Kailisa held up the liver for her inspection.

'This man's liver is in a very poor state. Cirrhosis has caused the most obvious changes, the rough surface and the slightly pale colour.'

He turned it on his palm as if he were examining a particularly interesting rock-pool find. 'Here, where I've cut a section, you can see a tumour.'

He pointed with a gloved finger to a yellowish mass nestled within the lobes of the liver like a malignant pearl in an oyster. 'The cancer is in the left and right lobes. Most definitely terminal.'

'We knew that—' Kate said.

Kailisa held up his free hand, palm out, and she curbed her interruption. 'Dennis Lambert would have been in some pain but it should have been manageable. The liver is enlarged but not excessively so. I am surprised, looking at this, that he was already confined to his bed. His notes suggest a much more advanced stage of the disease based on his perceived pain level and his medication.'

Kate stared at the gory organ, trying to make sense of what Kailisa was telling her. Lambert's cancer wasn't as bad as it appeared? Had he been faking? But, surely, the hospital would have performed tests to check. 'Could the notes be wrong?'

Kailisa put the liver gently back down in a dissecting tray and nodded to his assistant, who opened a large envelope and removed a sheaf of papers. 'I only have the written notes. There are no original images from an ultrasound or an MRI scan. Just an account of what these tests found.'

'Is that unusual?'

Kailisa shrugged noncommittally. 'It is slightly irregular. Perhaps they are stored on a computer and were not printed out. I think you need to find those images though just to confirm the notes.'

It didn't make sense. How could Lambert have been *less* ill than anybody thought? Why would he pretend?

'I'm sure that all will become clear when you request the original records,' Kailisa said, but his eyes betrayed some doubt. 'For the moment, I can confirm the presence of liver cancer. I will check for metastases in the other organs. It's possible that there is something else which caused him to become immobile, perhaps in the lungs or the heart. The blood work will help. I can let you know the results by telephone tomorrow. At the moment, I can see nothing to contradict the assertion that he took his own life with an overdose.'

Kate smiled as she realised that he was dismissing her and didn't want her to come back for any further information. 'That would be really helpful. Can I take the name of Lambert's consultant? I need to find those original scans.'

The assistant found the relevant details, and Kate took a quick picture with her phone – much easier than pen and paper when your hands were gloved and every available surface was either bloody or potentially contaminated.

She read the name; Mr Colin Read – based at the DRI. No time like the present.

Shrugging off her gown, Kate stepped out into the labyrinth of corridors trying to get her bearings and hoping that she was heading in the right direction for oncology.

CHAPTER 10

The oncology receptionist was unimpressed with Kate's credentials and her request to speak to Mr Read. In her mid-sixties with her grey hair scraped back into a steely grey bun, the receptionist peered over the thin frames of her reading glasses with a schoolmarm look of disapproval as Kate explained the need to clarify the details of Dennis Lambert's records.

'I'm afraid Mr Read is unavailable at this time,' the woman said, dropping her eyes back to her keyboard in dismissal.

'When will he be available?' Kate asked, trying to keep her tone pleasant despite the supercilious attitude.

'He's on holiday.'

'And when will he be back?'

The woman sighed as though giving out this sort of information was beneath her pay grade. 'In two weeks. He only went yesterday.'

'Are you able to contact him?'

The woman shook her head. 'He's taking his annual family ski holiday in the Alps. I can hardly just ring him up about a hospital matter.'

'But this is a murder enquiry. Surely he'd be willing to help?'

Silence.

'Is there somebody else I can talk to?'

Another sigh. 'We value relationships with our patients at the DRI. You could speak to another oncologist but he or she would not have detailed knowledge of this patient's case.'

Kate tapped on the desk in frustration. The woman seemed to be deliberately making this difficult. 'You do understand I'm acting for the coroner and I have the right to those records?'

The woman ignored her, tapping away at the keyboard with efficient bird-like pecks. 'And my records show that the relevant documents have been supplied,' she said with a smug smile.

'But they're incomplete,' Kate said, repeating her point.

'Then you'll have to talk to Mr Read.'

Kate clenched her fists and stomped away from the reception desk. There was no reason why the woman should be obstructing the inquiry. The receptionist was only doing her job, but Kate wished that she had some cause, however small, to arrest her and wipe that self-satisfied smirk from the woman's face. Kate looked around the reception area, seeking inspiration, or at least something to calm her down. It was more like the foyer of a mid-range hotel than a hospital waiting area; the carpet was deep blue and plush and the walls were a comforting shade of violet. Instead of posters and leaflets, the walls were adorned with prints of watercolours, and the few low tables held a range of special interest magazines and some more general celebrity gossip rags. Then inspiration struck and she went back to the reception desk.

'Hi,' she said, trying her most winning smile. The receptionist looked up and glared at her, her lips pinched together like she'd just tasted something sour. 'You said that I could speak to another oncologist. Would that be possible today?'

A quick flurry of key tapping. 'I'm not sure that it will be of any use but you could meet with Mr Tsappis in twenty minutes.'

'And he is…?'

'He's another well-respected member of the oncology department. I can make an appointment as he has had a cancellation today.'

She emphasised the word *cancellation* just enough for Kate to sense her disgust that people would waste a doctor's valuable time, leaving Kate wondering if the appointment had been cancelled because the patient couldn't face the wrath of the gatekeeper.

'That'll be fine,' Kate said. 'I'll wait.' She strode over to a comfortable-looking sofa, sat down and picked up a magazine about motorbikes. Crossing her legs, she alternately turned a page and stared at the receptionist.

Less than fifteen minutes later, a door opened behind where Kate was sitting.

'Ms Fletcher?' a voice asked.

Kate stood up and turned to face a tall, dark-haired man in an expensive-looking charcoal-grey suit. He smiled at her, his dark eyes lighting up with what looked like genuine warmth as he gestured for her to follow him into his office.

'You asked to see me, Ms Fletcher,' he began as soon as they were positioned on opposite sides of a dark-wood desk. The top of the desk was empty except for a laptop and it seemed to stretch on for acres, dwarfing the one that Raymond was so proud of in his tiny office at Doncaster Central.

'Actually it's Detective Inspector Fletcher.'

'I apologise. Rosemary didn't give me your title.'

He smiled, flashing straight, white teeth which could have been displayed on a poster on a dentist's wall. He was unsettlingly handsome; black hair cut short in the back and on the sides but forming natural waves on top, deep brown eyes and skin that looked like it had been tanned on a yacht on the Mediterranean.

'I'm leading a murder enquiry involving one of Mr Read's patients and I need to access his full medical record.'

Tsappis smiled. 'I'm sure that the relevant paperwork will have been forwarded to the coroner as soon as it was requested. If not, Rosemary can–'

'No.' Kate interrupted. 'We have the notes but we don't have any of the original scans or images or whatever you call them, only descriptions of the findings.'

'And what would you like from me?' he asked with a smile.

'I'd really like those images. Or, if not, I'd like you to text your colleague and ask him to ring me at his earliest convenience.'

'I'm not authorised to release the case notes of somebody else's patient without the consent of the relevant consultant,' Tsappis said with a shake of his head. 'I can have a look at the case myself and share my thoughts with you but that will probably only support the notes that you've got. As for texting my colleague, that would be highly irregular.'

'But you could do it?'

He stared at her as though considering her worthiness for such an honour.

'I could. But I'd like something in return?'

Kate's heartbeat picked up. Was he trying to bribe her? Did he have some sort of criminal past that he needed her to wipe from the records? Or was it just a parking ticket?'

'What?'

Another flash of that smile.

'I'd like your phone number.'

'That's fine,' Kate said with relief. 'Obviously Read will need to be able to get in touch with me, I'll give you my card.'

She dug in her pocket for a second before she realised what Tsappis really wanted. She wasn't used to being asked out, especially when she was on a case, and his direct approach had thrown her. She felt herself beginning to blush.

'That's not what I mean,' Tsappis said. 'I'm sure you're busy but I'd like to take you to dinner when you're next free. *Quid pro quo.*'

Kate had a sudden vision of Anthony Hopkins's Hannibal Lecter leering at Jodie Foster through the glass of his prison cell as he asked her to share her most intimate secrets.

'I er... I suppose so,' Kate said, handing over her business card, thrown by his request. It was unusual but hardly unethical – this man had nothing to do with any of her cases; he wasn't a witness or a suspect and he was *very* good looking. Tsappis opened a drawer on the other side of his desk and passed his own card back to her.

'I would have texted Read anyway,' he said with a sheepish grin that was worlds removed from his earlier confident smile. 'I just thought I'd take a chance on you being single. Feel free to change your mind if you think I've bullied you into it. I don't normally ask out women that I've just met but I couldn't help myself.'

If it hadn't been for the grin it would have been corny, but Kate could see that he felt a bit embarrassed by his own bravado. She surprised herself by accepting his card and his invitation.

'I'll let you know when things quieten down for me,' she said. 'But it could be a long wait.'

The team office was fairly quiet when Kate got back to Doncaster Central. Cooper was hunched over her keyboard, Hollis was talking to somebody on the phone and there was no sign of Barratt or O'Connor.

'Been having fun?' Hollis asked, hanging up the phone.

'Great,' Kate responded. 'I love the smell of formaldehyde in the morning.'

'Nothing helpful with our mystery woman?'

She gave him a brief account of Kailisa's findings including his speculation about the house brick. Hollis tapped the top of his desk with a pen while he listened, his frustration obvious.

'I really thought we might be able to ID her. Thought she might have an unusual tattoo or something helpful like that. I hate this. Somebody, somewhere must be missing her especially if she's got a kid out there. She's been missing from home for two nights and nobody's come forward.'

Kate understood his frustration even though hers was tinged with a creeping feeling of unease. The missing woman could be somebody like her. Somebody who lived alone, had minimal contact with family, and had little going on in her life besides work. Was that why she'd accepted Tsappis's invitation? It was unsettling to realise that, if she went missing, there would be nobody to make the initial report, nobody to be told to wait twenty-four hours, nobody to pace up and down with worry and fear.

'Have you checked that no missing person reports have come in overnight?'

'I keep checking,' Hollis said. 'That's who I was just on the phone to. Nothing.'

'Cooper, anything?' Kate called over to her colleague.

A shake of Sam's head. 'I've got all the CCTV I can find from the area. So far I haven't found anybody who looks like her. Not that surprising though. Cameras are few and far between down there. There's one above the access gate to the marina, one on the road that runs parallel with the towpath and another at the major junction further down. Can't find her on any of them. That's assuming she was on foot. If she was driving it's hopeless because we have no idea what car we might be looking for.'

'You don't know her?' Kate asked. 'She doesn't live at the marina?'

Cooper shook her head. 'I had a look at some of the pictures from the scene. I'm fairly certain that I haven't seen her before.'

'Could you show some of your neighbours one of the least disturbing pictures? Ask around, see if anybody knows her?' Hollis suggested.

Cooper flushed and shifted in her seat. 'I... er...'

Kate leapt in, sensing the DC's unease. 'It might be best if you or Barratt does that,' she suggested to Hollis. 'These are people who Sam knows, it might not be appropriate.'

Cooper flashed her a grateful smile and went back to her keyboard. Kate didn't know much about Cooper's life outside the job but that fact itself was very revealing. She knew quite a bit about the others, even Raymond spoke about his wife and kids from time to time and his crippling mortgage on the new house, but Cooper never revealed anything about her personal life unless asked a direct question. It wasn't that she was secretive; she just never talked about herself in the way that the others did.

'What about Dennis Lambert?' Hollis asked. 'Anything weird in the PM?'

'Not really. He had cancer, he was dying. The bloods should be back tomorrow. Kailisa suggested that his cancer wasn't advanced enough to keep him bedbound and the notes were missing some scans, so I've asked one of the oncologists to get Lambert's consultant to contact me. No signs that he was suffocated or strangled. Nothing really to contradict his daughter's story that he killed himself with an overdose. I don't see any way to move forward on that until the rest of the results come in.'

'There is one thing,' Hollis said. 'Lambert was in hospital for a while before Caroline took him home. Is it worth asking on the ward? Get some impressions of their relationship, that kind of thing? At the moment, Caroline Lambert's story seems to stack up but she might have let something slip or not been entirely honest about her relationship with her father. Brenda Powley thinks that there's something not right.'

It was a good idea, and the hospital wasn't too far from the Ings Marina.

CHAPTER 11

The five-minute drive from Doncaster Central to the town's Royal Infirmary took nearly half an hour because the rain that had been threatened for the last few days had finally materialised, as snow. The traffic had slowed to a crawl and the heater in the pool car seemed to have given up even trying to demist the windscreen.

'Are we there yet?' Hollis asked, in his best petulant toddler voice.

Kate took another swipe at the windscreen with a duster and extended her reach to include Hollis. 'Shut up or you won't get an ice cream,' she said over his pretend outrage, as she finally turned into the visitors' car park. 'Thank God for that. I thought we'd never get here.'

The car park hadn't been gritted and the trek to reception had them both tiptoeing across the icier stretches like new-born foals. At one point, Kate had to cling on to Hollis for support. He gave her a knowing grin as she grabbed his arm.

'See. Every woman needs a big strong man at some point. Even you.'

Kate was about to retaliate when she lost her grip as he slipped on a pile of slush and nearly lost his balance. 'Looks like you could do with one as well,' she joked, hitting a clear patch and picking up pace as the doors to the main reception were finally within sight.

There was another delay as the young man on reception had to get his supervisor to ensure that he was able to give out the relevant information, then a seemingly endless walk, escorted by another member of staff, to the ward where Dennis Lambert had been treated.

'Finally,' Kate breathed as their escort pushed open one half of the double door barring her entry and gestured for them to go inside. A nurses' station stood a few feet beyond the door and beyond that, Kate could see doors which presumably led off to the patients.

'Can I help you?' a voice asked. 'Visiting time's over until half past seven.' A woman in uniform poked her head above the counter which ran in a semi-circle around the nurses' station. 'I'm afraid you'll have to wait until then.'

Kate quickly flashed her ID. 'We're not here to see a patient; we'd like to ask a few questions about somebody who was here in November.'

'That's a long time ago,' the woman said with a regretful smile.

'It's only six weeks,' Hollis said.

'Can you imagine how many people come through these doors in six weeks? The turnover of beds is high in this ward. Most patients are assessed here and then moved on to specialist services.' She brushed a stray strand of mousy brown hair from her face. Her tight bun was coming unravelled and was threatening to collapse if she didn't give it some serious maintenance.

'Please,' Kate said trying not to sound too desperate. 'Five minutes.'

The woman sighed and scowled up at Kate, her pale grey eyes narrowing with frustration. 'Look, we're short-staffed. If you can talk to me here while I finish this report, you can have your five minutes.'

It wasn't ideal but Kate could see that it was the best she was going to get. 'Okay.' She leaned over the counter top. 'Dennis Lambert. Admitted on November twenty-first last year with stage four liver cancer.'

The nurse was tapping on the keyboard. 'What about him?'

'Do you remember him? Anything about his case?'

'I do, actually. He was admitted while I was on shift. I remember because he'd been here two days before anybody came to visit him. I thought it was a bit sad that he had nobody. Then an elderly woman turned up and a family member came as well.'

It fit with what Kate already knew. The elderly woman must have been Brenda Powley.

'Were you involved in Mr Lambert's care?' Hollis asked.

The woman stopped typing and looked up at him, a faint smile playing on her lips. 'I'm involved in everybody's care here. We all are. It's not like we can pick and choose. And nor can the patients.'

She wasn't being difficult, Kate could see that she was willing to help, but it was probably impossible for her to have spent much time with Dennis; he'd have been one among many.

'How long was he here?' Hollis asked.

'If you give me a second, I'll find out.' She continued whatever she was doing on the computer then a few more mouse clicks. 'He was admitted on November twenty-first and discharged on the twenty-ninth. Eight days.'

'And his contact details? Is the daughter listed as his primary contact?'

Her eyes flicked down to the screen and back up again. 'Yes. Caroline Lambert. An address in Sheffield.'

This wasn't getting them very far. Kate had had visions of a stern matron who remembered everybody and who made snap and accurate judgements about her patients and their visitors. She knew that modern hospitals weren't at all like the Carry On films that she'd watched as a child but a part of her wished that it was that straightforward instead of a faceless bureaucracy where everybody was overstretched and overworked.

'Is there somebody who would have had oversight of Dennis Lambert's care?' she asked, expecting to be directed to his consultant, the absent Mr Read.

'Of course,' the nurse replied, looking slightly offended. 'There is a protocol in place for each patient depending on their needs.'

She looked back at the computer screen. 'I'm afraid that the nurse in charge of Dennis Lambert's care isn't on duty at the moment. She's not been in today. I don't know if she's off sick or if she had holiday booked. I can probably find out.'

Another dead end.

'Don't bother,' Kate said, slipping her card across the counter. 'Have her call me when she gets back, if you don't mind. And thanks for your time.'

CHAPTER 12

Dusk was settling along the canal as Kate and Hollis approached the marina. The water was turning into a black ribbon stretched between slush-sodden banks, and the air was still and icy. The marina was protected by high wire fencing and a large double gate was barring their entry; tall metal posts with folded-back spikes like lethal petals on top.

'Looks like they take security seriously,' Hollis said, clicking his seatbelt loose and opening the car door. He strode over to a keypad mounted on a wooden post just in front of the fence, next to the gate, obviously intended to allow access only to those in the know.

Kate watched as he frowned in the dim light then pressed a button. Even inside the car with the windows closed, she heard a buzzing sound as he was connected via intercom with somebody inside the marina.

'Yes?' a voice said, the tone unfriendly.

'Police,' Hollis responded. 'Routine enquiries. Can you open the gate?'

'Wait there.' A loud click as the other person rang off.

Less than a minute later, a figure appeared from the shadows surrounding what appeared to be a clubhouse. A man. Short, middle-aged, and swathed in a scarf and a down jacket which looked to be at least a size too big for him. The scarf covered the lower portion of his face and a black woollen hat was pulled down low across his eyebrows.

'I'll need ID!' he shouted as he approached.

Hollis took out his warrant card and held it out in front of him looking like he might be trying to ward off evil spirits.

The little man scrutinised it and then nodded towards the car. 'Hers as well.'

Kate heard Hollis's sigh as he stomped back to the car.

'He needs your ID.'

'I heard,' Kate said. 'Here.' She passed over her warrant card with no intention of leaving the warmth of the car until she absolutely had to. Hollis trudged back to the gate and held up Kate's ID which was met with another intense look.

'All right. When I open up, drive through. Park over there.'

He pointed towards the clubhouse.

Hollis returned, passed Kate her ID back and rubbed his hands in front of the heater to try to get warm.

'I take it you heard all that?'

Kate confirmed that she had and they waited for the gates to swing open. Following the man's instructions, she pulled up in an empty parking space beneath one of the darkened windows of the long low building which dominated much of the compound. Through the car window, she could see an open expanse of canal, bordered by gravel and concrete with black metal bollards at regular intervals, waiting for boats to tie up. It wasn't immediately obvious that there were permanent moorings there, though. Perhaps that was another security feature.

The man had pulled the scarf down from the bottom half of his face to reveal a scruffy grey beard and oddly feminine pink lips.

'Hugh Newstead.' A hand was thrust out to Kate before she'd even managed to get out of the car and stand up properly. He'd obviously had a good look at their IDs and realised that Kate was the superior officer. 'I do security and run the clubhouse.'

'DI Kate Fletcher,' Kate said, trying to shake his hand and ease him back away from the car.

'What can I do for you? Your young man didn't say.'

Hollis coughed from the other side of the car and Kate knew, from the sound, that he was covering a laugh. *Young man.*

'We're investigating an unidentified body that was found in the canal yesterday. It's possible that the woman may have been living at the marina.'

Newstead stared at her for a second as though considering whether to enlighten her and then shook his head.

'There's not many stay this time of year. Most of the boats are just kept here over the winter. One or two stay on, mind, have residential permits and pay their council tax. We're licensed for that, it's all above board. But I'd have known if it was somebody living on the water. I know every one of our residents and all our regulars.' He stood up a bit straighter and Kate could see that he was proud of his position.

'She might have been a visitor? Maybe she had friends here?'

Another shake of the head.

'Doubt it. I see most people who come and go. There's not many up and down the cut this time of year. Have you got a picture?'

Hollis dug out his mobile phone and found the image that Kailisa had sent. The woman was clearly dead due to the paleness of her skin and the blue tinge to her lips but there was no sign of the injury to her head. Newstead studied it for a few seconds.

'Nope. Never seen her before.' He looked almost disappointed. Perhaps he'd been hoping that he could solve their case with one glance.

'Is there anybody else here that we could ask? People on the boats?'

'There's not many here, like I said. There's a young lad on *Midnight*. I think it's his dad's boat. He's been here a few days. Reckons to be writing a book. There's Sam and Abbie on *Emily Jane* and I think Frank might have been down at the weekend but he's not here now. He might be back in a couple of weeks – I could get him to ring you.'

'That would be a great help,' Kate said, passing him her business card. 'If we could just have a quick chat with the people that are here as well.'

'I suppose so. Go left behind the clubhouse, that's where the moorings are. *Midnight's* four down on your left. *Emily Jane* is second on the right.'

As soon as they were out of earshot, Hollis giggled.

'Bit of a jobsworth that one, eh? "Your young man." Cheeky get.'

'He obviously read the situation perfectly,' Kate said with a grin. 'Now get on, lackey, and find me those boats.'

The narrowboats were moored in diagonal rows from two pontoons, creating a herring bone effect.

'Very tidy,' Hollis said. 'I bet Hugh makes them use a set square to park up properly.'

'Moor. They're moored not parked.'

Hollis gave her a *whatever* shrug and led the way along the first pontoon.

Midnight was an appropriate name for the boat where the young writer was staying. About fifty feet long and painted in a deep blue that was almost black, it stood out from the more traditional red-and-green boats which surrounded it. The name was inscribed across the bow in a lighter shade of blue outlined in white. The paintwork looked fresh and gave the appearance of a well-kept vessel. Smoke was trickling up from a small chimney on the roof and the lights were on in two of the windows.

Hollis looked at Kate his eyebrows raised in a quizzical expression. 'What do I do? Leap on and knock on the door?'

'Try a tap on the window, it might be less intrusive.'

Hollis stepped closer to the boat and rapped sharply on one of the lighted windows. A face appeared: young, dark hair, heavy frown. Hollis held up his ID and the face retreated to reappear twenty seconds later, looking round the door.

'You looking for me?' the young man said. He was probably in his early twenties, tall and skinny with a greasy mop of dark hair and a sullen expression.

'Not especially,' Kate said. 'We're trying to establish the identity of a body that was found in the canal yesterday.'

The slumped expression suddenly became animated. 'A body? Here?'

'About a mile away,' Kate said.

'Oh wow! That's perfect. I'm trying to write a crime novel. Talk about atmosphere.' He looked from Kate to Hollis then back again, his eyes alight with excitement. 'Glad to be of assistance,' Hollis said in a voice heavily spiced with sarcasm. 'If you'd have a look at a photograph and let us know if you know her, or if you've seen her around, that would be great.'

The man's eyes followed Hollis's hand to his pocket as he got his phone out, his eagerness visible in the slight tremor in his hand as he took the device and studied the image. 'She's dead, yeah? In this photograph?'

Hollis ignored the question. 'Do you recognise her?'

The young man continued to stare at the photograph. 'Doesn't look familiar. Hard to say, though. Her face looks a bit slack somehow.'

Kate could see that he was trying to store every detail; trying to find ways to describe the pallor and the dark, wet hair. 'Thanks anyway,' she said, pulling Hollis's arm back. She dug in her pocket and passed the man her card. 'If you do think of anything, let us know.'

He nodded vacantly, eyes lost somewhere in his imagination, and Kate wouldn't have minded betting that his novel would feature a body pulled from water.

'Right, let's see what sort of weirdos live on the *Emily Jane*,' Hollis said with a shake of his head as he led the way back along the pontoon.

Emily Jane was much more like Kate's expectations of a narrowboat with its green and red livery and garden chairs on the roof. There was a small patch of artificial grass between them and a low wooden table off to one side. Cigarette butts overflowed an ashtray that had been placed next to one of the chairs.

This time, Kate tapped on the first window she could reach.

'Shit, you're back early,' a voice said within.

'Police,' Kate said. 'I'm DI Fletcher. Could you come out so we can have a word?'

The small double doors were pushed open from inside and a mass of red hair appeared. 'Police? Is it Sam? Has something happened?'

'Sam?' Kate asked.

The woman stepped further out, her face pale against the shock of hair that some would have called Titian, others, less charitably, dark ginger. She was wearing a purple hoodie and tight jeans which hugged her slim figure. 'DC Sam Cooper. Isn't that why you're here?'

Kate was thrown. Why would she be there about Sam?

'I'm sorry,' she said, and then she remembered what Newstead had said. *Abbie and Sam on Emily Jane.* 'Ah, this is Sam's boat. Sorry, I didn't make the connection for a minute. So, you are?'

The woman looked from Kate to Hollis. 'You're Kate Fletcher. Which means that you're probably Dan Hollis. Sam always says you're a lanky bugger.' She stuck out a hand. 'I'm Abbie.'

Hollis was obviously as clueless as Kate. He accepted the handshake, eyebrows lost in his fringe as he turned to Kate with a questioning look.

The woman obviously knew who they were but Kate could have sworn that they'd never met before. 'I'm Sam's girlfriend. Abbie? She must have mentioned me.'

'Oh, course, sorry,' Hollis said in a smooth attempt to cover his confusion. 'You know how it is. Down here on official business, everything's out of context.'

Abbie wasn't fooled. 'You had no idea, did you? Typical. So why *are* you here if it's not about Sam?'

Hollis showed her the photograph and asked the usual questions but Abbie shook her head.

'Never seen her before, sorry. Is this the woman Sam found? She was a mess when she got home yesterday. Bloody job, does her head in sometimes.' Abbie looked away from the photograph and ducked back through the doorway of the boat. 'Look,' she said, turning back to Kate. 'Can you not tell Sam that you've seen me?'

'But... you live here, don't you? With Sam.' Kate was baffled.

'Not for much longer. That bloody dead body was the final straw. I have to get off this canal. You only just caught me. I've just finished packing. I don't want Sam to find out while she's at work. It wouldn't be fair.'

'So you're dumping her?' Hollis said, indignant on behalf of his colleague. 'And you want us to keep it quiet?'

Abbie shook her head, an avalanche of red curls falling down her back. 'No. I just can't live here anymore. It's not her, it's this sodding boat. It's not a proper home. It's not like we've not talked about it. It's just that—' Her open expression suddenly snapped shut as she realised who she was talking to. 'It's just that it's none of your business. Sorry. I shouldn't have said anything.' She went back down the steps into the living area of the boat, shaking her head.

Neither Kate nor Hollis spoke as they walked back to the car. Hugh Newstead was hovering round but they managed to get inside without being collared by him and were through the gate before Hollis broke the silence.

'Poor Sam. She's in for a crap evening when she gets back.'

'Abbie's right. It's none of our business,' said Kate. 'If she wants to talk she will.' Kate was about to warn Hollis to keep his mouth shut, Sam wasn't the type who would appreciate details of her life becoming office gossip, but her phone rang, interrupting her train of thought. She recognised the number as the front desk of Doncaster Central. 'DI Fletcher.'

'You need to get back to base, Fletcher,' said a voice on the other end that Kate recognised as belonging to Mark Evans, one of a small group of desk sergeants. 'I've got a young lad at the front desk who thinks the body that was pulled out of the canal yesterday might be his mam.'

Hollis had obviously heard every word as he floored the accelerator despite the freezing conditions.

NOVEMBER

Dear Caroline,

Is it really such a good idea you staying in the house? I know you said you'd been back and it wasn't so awful but I didn't really believe you. I just think that spending so much time alone with him isn't such a good idea. We both know what he's like, or at least, what he used to be like. He'll get into your head if you're not careful. He's done it before and he'll do it again if you give him the chance. Couldn't you stay in a B&B and just visit him every day? It might help to keep you sane if you could get away every night; keep you focused on what you intend to do.

I'm not trying to stop you going through with it, I just don't want you to get sucked in by his crap and his lies. You're stronger now, older.

If you do stay, at least take some time out for yourself. Go into town. Eat out. Go for a walk over by the quarry. Give yourself time to clear your head every day.

Stay sane.
Love,
J

CHAPTER 13

Dennis's mood hadn't improved much the next time Caroline visited. He was sitting up in a chair next to his bed reading a book. He hadn't shaved and the stubble on his cheeks and chin was Brillo pad-grey with an odd whiter patch just below his bottom lip. He was in pyjamas and dressing gown and had a cup of tea on the bedside cabinet next to him. He looked like a Victorian gentleman gone to seed, sitting in his fading library as his stately home crumbled around him. As she approached, he looked up then made a point of finishing his page and marking it with a sweet wrapper in place of a bookmark before he acknowledged her presence.

'You're back, then?'

'Looks like it,' she responded, trying to keep the interaction to a minimum. 'Any news on when you're getting out?'

He snorted. 'Like they'd tell me in advance. Eddie in the bed over there,' Dennis pointed to the empty bed opposite. 'He wasn't told until the morning they let him out. Had to ring round his family to get somebody to pick him up at short notice. I'll probably be out in the next ten minutes now you're here to take me home.'

So, his mood had changed from resignation to belligerence since her last visit. Caroline wondered whether something specific had set him off or whether his natural demeanour was re-establishing itself after he had overcome the initial shock of his hospital admission. Next he'd be looking for somebody to blame and Caroline knew that she'd be in the firing line. 'I'll ask. Find out. You seem a lot better.'

Dennis just grunted. 'Don't feel it. They'll mebbe be taking me out in a box.'

'Has Bren been in?' Caroline asked in a bid to change the subject.

His grey eyes sharpened like daggers. 'She came yesterday. You've been in my house again.'

She noted the use of the possessive *my*. He didn't want her in the house; didn't want her in his life, and the feeling was mutual, but Caroline had a job to do and no matter how much it cost her, she was going to see this through.

'Don't worry,' she said, forcing a smile. 'You can count every penny in the house when you get back. It's all still there.'

'Better be,' Dennis mumbled.

Caroline sighed, once again faced with the enormity of the task ahead. Could she really do this? Could she spend an indefinite amount of time trapped in that house with him? Again. 'Have they got your drugs sorted out? For the pain?'

Dennis shrugged. 'There's nowt they can do really. All they'll give me is paracetamol. I could get that from the Co-op.'

'Did they find out why you were in so much pain when they brought you in?'

'Because I've got cancer. Why do you think?'

He'd obviously not asked; just accepted what was happening to him unquestioningly. He was right, they might be keeping him there until he died and he'd never know because he wouldn't ask. She needed to do something, to get some information.

'I'll be back in a minute,' she said, heading to the nurses' station. Dennis might not need answers but she did. She needed to make plans; to prepare for what was to come.

She was surprised and pleased to see Maddie behind the desk. The nurse smiled at her but Caroline could see something wary around her eyes as though she was trying to be polite but was also prepared to run for her life if it became necessary.

'Hi,' Caroline said. 'I was hoping to talk to you about my dad.'

The relief was almost palpable. 'Of course. Give me a sec and I'll see if there's a meeting room free.'

Caroline waited as Maddie finished whatever she was typing and logged off the computer. She got up, picked up a tablet computer and beckoned for Caroline to follow her as she led the way through the ward and out to a corridor.

'In here,' she said, opening an anonymous brown door. 'I've got a few minutes.'

She flicked the notification sign on the door to *Occupied* and ushered Caroline inside. It was much more comfortable than either of the two rooms that the two women had met in before. The floor was plushly carpeted in deep green and the large oval wooden desk was highly polished with chairs pushed neatly up to it at regular intervals. Beneath the window was a smaller arrangement of furniture. Two low chairs upholstered in pale green and a coffee table. Maddie led the way to the chairs and pointed to the one furthest from the door.

'Sit down. At least it's comfortable in here and we can chat for a bit without getting interrupted. What did you want to know?'

Caroline took a deep breath. She had to pitch this exactly right. 'Firstly, do you know why he was in so much pain when he was admitted?'

Maddie consulted her tablet. 'He had a small obstruction to his bowel. His liver is slightly enlarged, mainly due to the cirrhosis rather than the cancer, but, as the tumours grow, they can cause pressure elsewhere. One of the lobes of his liver was causing some pressure on his large intestine. If it had continued, we would have considered surgery but, after a period of limiting Dennis's food intake and some gentle movement the problem seems to have resolved itself, for now.'

'So he can go home?'

'He can. But you need to know that it's only going to get worse. The cancer has started to metastasize; an MRI scan found tiny pinprick tumours in his left lung.'

'He didn't mention that he'd had an MRI.'

Maddie smiled sympathetically. 'I don't mean this to sound rude but you don't seem to communicate well with your father.'

Caroline laughed, a harsh bark, surprised by Maddie's directness. 'Believe me, it's mutual. We're not what you'd call close.'

'But you're willing to look after him? To see him through the final stage of this illness? It could take months and it won't be easy.'

For the first time since formulating her plan, Caroline was being offered a chance to walk away. She could leave him to the NHS, let them deal with him, put him in a hospice when the time came and allow him a quiet, medicated passing with as much dignity as death would allow. She could go back to her comfortable home and her quiet life, safe in the knowledge that, in time, she'd be free of the guilt and the responsibility without even having to lift a finger. But that wasn't going to happen. She wanted to see him suffer.

'Not an option,' she said. 'It's my duty to see this through. At least, when it's over I'll know I did the right thing.'

Maddie smiled. 'For what it's worth, I think you *are* doing the right thing. When the time comes, I'm sure he'd rather be in his own bed than in hospital or in a hospice. It's very kind of you.'

'So, when can I get him home?'

Maddie tapped again on the tablet computer. 'He's been stable for the past seventy-two hours. His medication is minimal. You could take him now if you wanted.'

Caroline felt her throat constrict. It was too soon. She had nothing in place at the house. She wasn't ready.

Maddie must have read her expression. 'I'm not suggesting that we discharge him immediately. We need to put a care plan in place, with your input of course, and we need to talk to Dennis, to check that this is what he wants.'

'He just wants to get out of here,' Caroline said.

'I know that. But we need to present him with his options.'

So it might not be that simple, Caroline thought. They might decide that she wasn't a fit carer, that he'd be better off in a hospice or some other sort of care facility. She couldn't decide if she was annoyed or relieved and was about to ask Maddie to explain further when the nurse's phone rang. She fumbled it out of her pocket, obviously embarrassed by the interruption and looked at the screen.

'I need to take this,' she said, standing up.

Caroline pretended to look out of the window, trying to listen to Maddie's end of the conversation.

The nurse walked as far as the door but seemed reluctant to go out into the corridor. 'I know,' she was saying. 'I'll get it but I need more time.' A pause. 'Just another couple of weeks. No. No, I can't afford that. We agreed on the rate. No. No that's not fair, it's not what we agreed.' The nurse went quiet, obviously listening. 'I have no choice, do I?' she said, slamming the phone down onto the table.

'Problem?' Caroline asked.

'No. It's personal. Let's get back to your father's case.'

She sat back down but her eyes kept drifting to the window or the door. She couldn't focus and called Dennis by the wrong name twice. Caroline let her waffle for a few minutes and then leaned forward and took Maddie's hand. 'I can see that you're upset. We could do this tomorrow if that's better.'

Maddie shook her head but she couldn't quite manage to fight back the tears that had been threatening since she'd sat back down.

'Is it money?' Caroline asked quietly.

Maddie nodded, the movement causing the tears to trickle down her face and fall onto the carpet in large silent drops.

Caroline watched as they were absorbed by the carpet, leaving slightly darker spots on the surface. 'I've told you that I can help.'

Maddie shook her head quickly, obviously not trusting herself to speak.

'I can lend you the money today. I'll just need your bank details. I could probably do it now, on my phone if that's what you wanted. You need to get out from under this, Maddie. If not for yourself than for Ethan.'

The other woman flinched at her son's name.

'It's honestly nothing to me. I won't be demanding repayments every few days, and I won't charge interest. I've been where you are, Maddie, and I was fortunate enough to be able to sort it out. Let me share some of my good fortune.'

Caroline let the silence hang between them. She'd said enough. All she could do was wait.

Eventually Maddie raised her eyes warily. 'Why?'

Caroline frowned, pretending not to understand.

'Why would you do that? Lend me money? What do you want?'

'Nothing, except to help you. I've seen people destroyed by their debts. Torn apart. I've known people who've lost kids, parents, jobs, everything. I was so nearly one of them. This is the first time I've been in a position to do something about it for somebody.'

'I'll think about it,' Maddie conceded. 'Can we get back to your dad's care? There's a few things we need to discuss.'

Fifteen minutes later, a tentative plan was in place. Caroline would take Dennis home the following afternoon – if he agreed – and she could be supported, when the time came, by a team of qualified carers who would help with Dennis's 'daily needs' which Caroline assumed would be bathing and dressing. He would be offered a range of medication for his pain and be assessed every few weeks by his GP in order to ascertain if any changes in his medication were deemed necessary. Maddie also gave Caroline a phone number for Macmillan Cancer Support 'just in case'.

As Caroline stood up to leave, Maddie grabbed her hand.

'Yes,' she said.

'You'll let me help?'

'Yes. For Erhan. I don't want him sucked down into this and the people that I owe money to know about him. The man on the phone even suggested that I ask my son for money as he's got a job. They know all about me.'

'Of course they do,' Caroline said. 'That's why this is better. How much do you need?'

Maddie dipped her head in embarrassment. 'I owe five thousand to the bank and the credit card companies and these… thugs… ten.

I can deal with the credit card debt and the overdraft if I can just get out from under this big one.'

Caroline knew that it probably wouldn't be that simple. 'What's the interest rate on the ten grand?'

'That's what he was ringing for. It's gone up. He wants a grand a month for the next year.'

'Twenty per cent. How about I loan you fifteen grand to get rid of him and pay off some other stuff? We'll settle terms once you've got it sorted out.'

Maddie's eyes drifted, obviously imagining what she could do without debt collectors breathing down her neck. She glanced at Caroline but couldn't hold her gaze – her embarrassment clear in the dip of her head and her flushed cheeks.

'Okay,' she said, finally capitulating. 'That would be amazing. If you do that I can clear the rest of it easily. I *will* pay you back as soon as I can.'

'I know you will,' Caroline said. 'I knew when I saw you at GA that you were really determined to sort out your life. You're strong. Stronger than me. Give me your bank details before I leave and I'll do the transfer today.'

Maddie appeared to be about to say something but Caroline changed the subject before they could descend into mutual admiration.

'Now, let's see if my dad wants to go home tomorrow,' she said, stepping out into the corridor.

CHAPTER 14

The house had changed since Caroline's last visit. As soon as she pushed open the door, she sensed a difference as though the atoms of the hallway had subtly rearranged themselves in her absence. The smell of the kitchen was less oppressive, cleaner somehow, with the odour of fried food covered by a lemony tang, and the tiles around the hall carpet looked less scuffed.

Caroline looked around, puzzled and then she realised – Bren. She must have been in and done some cleaning while Caroline had been at home. Which meant that Bren had a key. That was something which would have to change. Caroline didn't know the woman very well. Bren had lived across the road for as long as Caroline could remember but she'd not really been aware of her until she heard that Dennis had a 'lady friend'. She hadn't been interested. It was none of her business what he did, and her mother had been dead for years before he took up with Bren, but the older woman could be a problem if she had unrestricted access to the house.

Much as Caroline resented Bren's intrusion, she was glad that it was one less job that she would have to do. This was going to be difficult enough without having to do the dusting or clean the bathroom before she brought Dennis home.

Curious, she inspected the sitting room. The ashtray had been wiped clean and the surfaces gleamed. Bren was obviously a big fan of Pledge. Caroline trudged upstairs – carpet spotlessly clean – and into her bedroom. There the bed had been made up with sheets and blankets, just as she remembered from her childhood – Dennis's bed was the only one with a duvet. The top sheet had been turned down in a manner that was supposed to look cosy and inviting but, to Caroline, looked like a sanatorium bed – somewhere she could get lost and never be found.

Sighing loudly, Caroline dumped her suitcase on the floor and sat on the bed. It wasn't the same one that she'd slept in as a child, this one felt softer, more yielding as she rocked herself backwards and forwards. Her stomach grumbled reminding her that she hadn't eaten since a hurried breakfast of muesli and yoghurt, and she briefly considered walking down to the local pub for a bar meal. She quickly pushed the thought aside. She didn't want to turn up at the hospital smelling of booze and burgers.

The bed did its shaky wobble as she pushed herself upright and decided to see what Dennis had got in his pantry – even though she already knew what to expect. She trotted downstairs and into the kitchen, almost laughing out loud as she saw that she'd been exactly right. Row upon row of regimented tins and jars were stacked on the pantry shelves, their labels facing the front so they could be easily read. She pulled off the top of the old-fashioned metal bread bin, expecting it to either be empty or to be confronted with a mouldy green crust or two.

'Nice one, Bren, you old witch,' Caroline said aloud as she pulled out a fresh loaf, and a multipack of crisps. She opened the fridge and shook her head in disbelief. One shelf contained tinned meats; luncheon meat, ham, corned beef, and the next one down held packets of chocolate biscuits of the type she'd never been allowed when she'd lived there. Thick chocolate wafers and coated digestives were stacked up with Penguins and Kit-Kats. They'd always been too expensive, too much of an extravagance. It looked like Dennis knew how to treat himself now.

The fridge door was more as she remembered it. Milk on the bottom, fresh again thanks to Bren, cheese in the plastic-covered top section and, in the middle, blocks of butter and lard.

'If the cancer hadn't got you, a heart attack probably would have,' Caroline muttered, picking up a packet of lard and reading the nutritional information. She grabbed a tub of margarine and slammed the fridge door shut. As she did so, her eyes were drawn to the gaps between the fridge and the walls of the pantry. They were narrow but offered the perfect storage solution for another one of Dennis's vices. Cans of beer and lager were stacked almost as high as the fridge, stretching right to the back wall of the pantry. Different brands, different strengths, jumbled up, in complete contrast to the food tins on the shelves above. These weren't arranged for ease of selection, they were there for easy access; Dennis could just bend down and grab a can, and he obviously didn't care which one.

'No secret where I get my love of drink from. Thanks, *Dad*. And now I'm talking to myself. Maybe there's some sort of hereditary madness in the family as well. Icing on the bloody cake.'

She gathered her sandwich makings and dumped them on the table rather than make her lunch on top of the fridge as Dennis would have done. Plates were piled up in the same cupboard where they'd always been and the cutlery nestled in the same partitions in the same drawer – knives, forks, spoons, with teaspoons in the smaller bottom section. Caroline took a knife and smeared margarine thinly on a slice of bread. Then she opened a packet of crisps, grabbed a handful and sprinkled them on top of the margarine. The snack was completed by folding the bread over and squashing it down with the heel of her hand. The perfect crisp butty; childhood comfort food with maximum fat and minimum nutrition. Caroline briefly contemplated smothering the next one in tomato ketchup but decided that was regressing too far and ate it plain.

After eating, Caroline checked her watch for the hundredth time since she'd arrived. Still only half past one – at least another two hours to kill. She thought about going for a walk, but where to? She could head for the shops but that would only take about ten minutes and Bren had already supplied the essentials. There was a path across the fields next to the quarry that she remembered clearly from dog walks as a teenager – an excuse to sneak off for a quick cigarette before Sunday lunch – but, again, there was no real purpose and she worried that she might just wander for hours, lost in memories.

Dumping her plate in the sink, Caroline decided on the easiest option – daytime TV. She settled herself in the sitting room, choosing a seat in the middle of the sofa, careful to avoid Dennis's armchair which would have afforded her the best view of the screen.

She'd just picked up the remote control when a noise at the back door startled her. She listened, finger poised over the mute button of the remote. A faint knock. Then the distinctive sound of the handle turning and the door clicking open. Burglars? Unscrupulous local youths who had heard that Dennis was in hospital and decided to try their luck? Then realisation dawned and Caroline leapt from her seat just as the living room door was pushed open.

Bren. All five feet nothing of her stood in the doorway staring at Caroline as though *she* were an intruder.

Feeling like Goldilocks caught with her spoon in the porridge bowl, Caroline slowly sat down again. She picked up the remote control and turned off the television, wishing that she could point it at Bren and make her go away just as easily.

'Caroline.'

Bristling at the familiarity, Caroline forced herself to be polite. 'Brenda. How are you?'

The older woman walked into the room and perched on the arm of Dennis's chair, crossing her arms in a proprietary manner. She was very much as Caroline remembered her. Short, almost as wide as she was tall, with ankles that overflowed the tops of her shoes like dough in a mixing bowl waiting to be given a final kneading. Her features were sharp and her small eyes were hidden among a nest of fat and wrinkles, giving her face a weathered expression as though she'd spent a lot of time squinting into the sun.

'I'm fine,' she said. '*I'm* not the one in hospital.' It was a simple statement but one loaded with accusation. It was obvious that

Bren held Caroline at least partly responsible for Dennis's illness. Bren uncrossed her arms and placed her hands demurely in her lap where they lay like strange sea anemones, beached upon the bright pattern of her heavy cotton dress. 'What time are you picking him up?'

'The doctor should have seen him by about four, then he should be able to leave.'

'And you're staying?'

Caroline nodded.

'That's something, I suppose. There wasn't a problem getting time off work?'

'No. They've been quite good, really,' Caroline lied. 'I can take a leave of absence for as long as I need.'

'The house is clean for him. I gave it a good do the day before yesterday. It had got really filthy. I'm surprised you didn't notice when you picked his things up.'

An accusation. Caroline should have cleaned the house after her last visit. Or perhaps she was such a slovenly housekeeper herself that she hadn't even noticed the state of her father's home.

'And there's fresh bread and milk so you won't need to do much shopping. You can always nip up to the Co-op if he needs anything else.'

'Have you been to see Dennis much?' Caroline asked. 'He said he didn't expect you to. I suppose it's a bit difficult with the buses.'

'I've managed to get through most days,' Bren said with a smile that was almost smug. 'Our Ian's been taking me.'

Caroline was startled to realise that she'd forgotten Bren's son. Two years older than Jeanette, Ian had 'done well for himself' and set up his own company. Something to do with computers, Caroline thought. 'That's good of him.'

'He's always been a good lad, our Ian. Nothing's too much trouble for *him*.'

Bren was good. Every sentence was carefully chosen to seem innocuous to an outsider yet Caroline felt the sting behind her words as sharply as if Bren had slapped her. Yet she was an adult with every right to behave exactly how she wanted to. It was her father's house and she had more right to be there than this bitter woman whose smile never reached her eyes.

Caroline took a deep breath and gathered her thoughts. 'Bren, I know you don't like me and the feeling is mutual but, as you said yourself you're not Dennis's next of kin so you have no say in what happens to him. You have no right to sit there in judgement, no right to dictate my behaviour or to try to manipulate me into feeling guilty. The truth is, Brenda, I don't. And I don't want to be here any more than Dennis wants me here. I don't want to deal with this at all, but I have to. So, until Dennis tells me that he wants you here, until he tells me that I have to put up with your unpleasant comments and snooty looks, I'd really appreciate it if you'd just go away, and stay away.'

'You little cow,' Bren spluttered. 'How dare you...'

'How dare I what? Tell you how I feel? Stand up for myself?'

'After everything I've done for your dad.'

'And I'm sure *he* appreciates it – but *I* don't give a toss. So, while I have more right to be here than you do and until I'm told different, leave me alone. If Dennis wants to see you when he gets home then I'll respect his wishes.'

Bren crossed the room, looming over Caroline in a pathetic attempt to intimidate, which fell flat as soon as Caroline stood up.

'I won't show you out. I'm sure you can find the door by yourself.'

Bren confirmed this with a resounding slam echoed by the gate a few seconds later.

Caroline slumped back onto the sofa and sighed. This would be all round the estate in a few hours. She imagined a television screen split into quarters with a neighbour in each section; each one holding a telephone receiver to their ear and wearing identical shocked expressions.

'Oh, fuck it,' she whispered. She went back into the kitchen, grabbed her keys from the table and locked the door behind her. She needed to get away, to just drive around until it was time to go to the hospital.

She was early. Even after searching for a parking space for what felt like hours it was still only three thirty. She'd driven round back roads, through estates of rundown council houses, past abandoned factories and weed-covered slag heaps, remnants of an industrial history that had left behind scars on the landscape and poverty in the community.

She couldn't help but wonder what her life would have been like if she hadn't managed to escape. Caroline had a sudden image of herself in her early twenties, pushing a pram with a snotty toddler on her hip and no money in her purse, and thought, not for the first time, that it had been worth it. All those times she'd been called 'swot' or 'snob' because she was good at English, actually enjoyed something about school, had been endured for a good cause. She'd been to university, mixed with people from a wide range of backgrounds, and she'd travelled. But there she was, back again, unable to cut the invisible thread that bound her to this place and these people.

Realising that she was procrastinating, Caroline heaved herself out of the car, locking it quickly with a flick of the key fob, and made her way to the entrance of the hospital. A pale, low winter sun turned the huge glass doors into a blinding mirror, one in which Caroline had no desire to see her reflection. If she could just get through the next few hours, the next couple of days, then things would probably start to get easier.

Dennis was dressed and sitting in the chair next to the bed. He glanced up as Caroline greeted him but he didn't look pleased to see her. In fact, just the opposite. His skin seemed to have turned even greyer than the day before, and his thinning hair looked almost transparent. His chest looked even more sunken, his cardigan gaping open and the collar of his shirt loose around his unshaven neck, looking like a small boy dressed in his bigger brother's hand-me-downs. His breathing was loud and laboured and spittle was gathering in the corners of his mouth like the remains of an ice-cream treat.

'So, did the doctor say you can go home?'

Dennis looked at her from beneath unruly eyebrows. 'Aye, he did. But you've got to keep an eye on me.'

So that was the problem – he didn't want a babysitter, he just wanted to go back to his old life with his beer and television and fried food.

As she spoke, she was aware of Maddie hovering in her peripheral vision. She'd have got the money by now, Caroline thought. They needed to talk. 'Okay, I'll just have a word with the nurse and then we'll get you out of here.'

Maddie led Caroline back to the same meeting room as the one they'd used the previous day but instead of inviting her to sit down she just stood next to the table hugging her arms to her chest and smiling.

'I got the money this morning,' Maddie said. 'I can't thank you enough for–'

Caroline held a hand up to stop her talking. 'It's really no problem. Stop thanking me. Have you paid it off?'

'I have. He knocked a bit off because I was paying the whole lot. I can give it you back if you want.'

'It's your money now,' Caroline said. 'Pay off a credit card or buy something nice for your son.'

Maddie smiled her appreciation. 'So, you all set for getting your dad home?'

'I think so. Just need his drugs and any final instructions.'

'Drugs? There's not really much that he needs at the moment. Just standard painkillers.'

Caroline sighed dramatically. 'I know. But it doesn't seem like much. A couple of aspirin or whatever. He told me that he's had trouble sleeping and you gave him something. But what if the pain gets worse?'

'Just call an ambulance,' Maddie said.

'And end up back here every time? Can't you just give me a prescription for some sedatives, whatever he had before? And morphine in case he needs it?'

Maddie took a step back, staring at Caroline as though she'd never seen her before. 'You want me to prescribe extra medication?'

Caroline shrugged.

'You said yourself it could be a long while before… well… you know. I just want to be prepared. I don't want to keep coming back here for every little thing. You said a GP will be seeing him. If you give me enough to keep Dad going for a couple of weeks then I'll ask the doctor if I've used anything that needs replacing. I thought you'd want to help me.'

She wasn't sure if she'd got the intonation right but the hard set of Maddie's face assured her that her message was getting through.

'That's why you loaned me the money? So I'd give your father more medication than he needs?'

'Than he needs *at the moment*,' Caroline corrected. 'It's not like I'm going to be dosing him up with all sorts as soon as I get him home. I just don't want him to have to suffer. If he has another episode like the last, I want to be able to give him something for the pain rather than leaving him in agony for hours while we wait for a GP to get out of bed.'

Maddie tapped the screen of her tablet. 'Your father's already had a mild sedative. In fact he's asked for it two or three nights since he's been here. I suppose that would be okay. I can give you a prescription for a small bottle of Oramorph. Just in case. But that's all. Anything else you need, you'll have to ask the GP.'

'Of course,' Caroline said. 'I'm not trying to get you into trouble. I'm just being selfish. I want to be able to cope rather than having to ring for assistance anytime anything goes wrong.'

'You should ring for help if you need it,' Maddie said, her face softening as she obviously decided to believe Caroline. 'A quick phone call and somebody will be there in less than half an hour. Even if it's an ambulance.'

'I know. I wasn't trying to call in your debt. I'm sorry if I came across that way. I'm just scared shitless and want to be able to cope.'

Maddie led her out of the room to the nurses' station where she printed out a prescription. 'Just for emergencies,' she said, handing it over.

Caroline smiled gratefully and went back to where Dennis was waiting in his chair.

'Right then. Let's go,' she said, folding the prescription and stuffing it into her jeans' pocket. She picked up Dennis's suitcase. 'Shall I lead the way? It's not far and I've parked the car close to the entrance.'

Dennis grunted a response and stood up reluctantly. As they negotiated the corridors, Caroline tried not to turn around too often until they reached the main entrance. She waited until he caught up with her and then led him through the glass doors and across the car park.

They drove back to Dennis's house in silence.

CHAPTER 15

Caroline poured a large slug of Fever-Tree tonic into her third gin of the evening. Dropping in a handful of ice cubes, she waited for the bubbles to subside before taking a sip. She looked around the kitchen. Everything was tidy. The plates and pans were draining and the floor tiles were freshly mopped. This room had become her sanctuary. There was no TV and she rarely used her laptop as Dennis didn't have Wi-Fi and the signal on her mobile phone wasn't great. Instead she sipped gin and brooded.

Two weeks. Two weeks of cooking, cleaning and trying to make conversation. It had been much harder than she'd imagined – not the physical work but the mental effort and the emotional strain. She'd nearly waded her way through a bottle of gin and was trying not to attack Dennis's stash of whisky. It was expensive stuff and she didn't want to get into an argument with him.

They'd managed to be civil; Dennis had complained for the first two days but then he'd appeared to simply resign himself to his new situation and had allowed Caroline to prepare his meals and clean his house. He'd even managed to walk to the local pub and have a few pints. He wasn't supposed to be drinking, the consultant had told him that alcohol could kill him but, when Caroline reminded him of this, he just said, 'I'm dying anyway so I might as well enjoy myself.'

He hadn't touched his whisky, though, so maybe it was mostly bluster.

The real problem was Bren. She kept turning up and turning up her nose. Nothing Caroline did was good enough. Her cooking left a bad smell, her dusting wasn't thorough, and her vacuuming was infrequent. If this was going to work out how Caroline wanted, then Bren had to go.

Sighing to herself, Caroline took another mouthful of her drink and checked her watch. Nearly ten o'clock. Dennis's programme would be about to finish and she knew that he wouldn't want to watch the late news. Ten was just about bedtime. If she could get him out of the way she could start to make plans for the coming weeks.

They'd established their relationship; it hadn't been named or even spoken about but Dennis was starting to accept her role as carer and she'd done nothing to make him suspicious, nothing to give him grounds to question anything that she'd done but she could sense his resentment in every word and gesture. He wanted to be left alone to get on with dying but she couldn't allow it. He had to be made aware of everything that he'd done; of her suffering and that of her mother and sister.

He probably thought that she might go to the police. Maybe that's why he wasn't complaining or asking too many questions. It was much too late for that, though. If she'd been going to talk to the police she'd have done it much earlier; surely he must have realised that by now. When they spoke to each other, the words were tight with tension and suspicion on both sides. Caroline saw him for exactly what he was, and she could tell that he was aware of how little he knew about her; he had no idea what she might be capable of doing to him or to his reputation on the estate. All he had were his memories and assumptions about her and she was going to prove him wrong. Very wrong. She wasn't a child anymore and she wasn't frightened of him.

'I'm going up now!' he shouted from the sitting room door. She wasn't sure what response he expected, whether he wanted her to tell him to sleep tight or that she'd see him in the morning. Instead she chose silence. It wasn't easy. Her natural instinct was to be polite; to at least acknowledge that he'd spoken. But this was Dennis. Polite was pointless.

As soon as she heard the toilet flush and his bedroom door creak closed, she slipped the sedatives from her pocket. Diazepam.

She'd looked up the drug online. Two strips slid out of the packet, each containing ten tablets. Not many. Not enough, but it would have to do for now. She placed two on the counter top, took a teaspoon from the drawer below and, using all her weight, she crushed the tablet beneath the spoon and ground it down as hard as she could. The cracking sound was too loud in the stillness of the kitchen, and she found herself coughing to cover the noise. When she'd ground the tablet to powder she did the same with the other one.

Satisfied that she'd left no lumps, she used the side of her hand to coax the powder from the counter top into a cup. She gave it a sniff. Nothing. Dipping a tentative finger into the cup, she removed a tiny amount and placed it on her tongue. Was there a slight bitterness? She wasn't sure but she was prepared to take a chance.

She opened the pantry door and took a bottle of milk from the fridge. The milkman didn't normally arrive until after Dennis had had his morning cup of tea and, even if the delivery was early, frugality would force her father to finish off this bottle before starting a new one. Pouring a small amount of milk into the cup, she used the teaspoon to stir it into the powdered drugs until it formed a thin paste. She then poured the paste back into the milk and gave it a good shake up ready for Dennis's morning cuppa and cornflakes.

'Do you want me to ring the doctor?' Bren asked again, the anxiety clear in the quaver in her voice.

Dennis was slumped at the kitchen table, still unshaven and in his pyjamas. He'd keeled over soon after breakfast, his head lolling forwards over the empty bowl, and was complaining of feeling woozy and tired.

He shook his head. 'I'll be fine. Just a bit tired. I think I might go back to bed.'

Caroline hovered. She knew that her father wouldn't agree to the doctor being called but, even so, she'd held her breath while she waited for his answer to Bren's question. He didn't feel steady enough on his legs to leave the table so now, half an hour later, Caroline knew that she was going to have to help him back up to bed.

Gritting her teeth, she managed to hook a hand under one armpit, half pulling, half guiding, as he took a few wobbly steps.

'I don't think I'll manage the stairs. I'll just have a lie down on the sofa. Be right as rain in a couple of hours. I didn't get much sleep last night so I'm probably just over tired,' he mumbled, some of the words slurring together.

Bren tutted in protest but followed them along the hallway and into the sitting room. 'Shall I get you your quilt?' she offered.

'No. Stop fretting,' Dennis snapped. 'Just leave me alone for a bit. I'll be fine.' He dropped onto the sofa and stretched his legs out.

Caroline fussed with the cushions, trying to look like she was making him comfortable, but Bren stepped in.

'He'll wake up with a crick in his neck if you leave him like that. Here.' She leaned in to make adjustments but Dennis's expression stopped her.

He was scowling, unable to hide the fury and frustration in his eyes. 'I said leave me alone. *Both* of you. Get out!'

Bren reared back as if he'd struck her, her face a mess of confusion and hurt. 'I was–'

'Just go,' he hissed.

Caroline smiled at Bren and pointed to the door. 'You heard him.'

Shaking her head, Bren left the room muttering to herself.

'And you,' Dennis said to his daughter. 'Just bugger off.'

'Happy to,' Caroline said. Leaving him sprawled out and looking uncomfortable, she followed Bren into the kitchen.

'I really think you should call the doctor,' Bren said. She cleared Dennis's bowl and mug from the kitchen table, dumped them in the washing-up bowl and gave both a thorough scrub. Caroline picked up the empty milk bottle but Bren snatched it away from her. 'That'll need a wash before it goes back.'

A short dunk in the suds and a quick run under the hot tap and the evidence of Caroline's tampering had been erased without her having to lift a finger.

'You heard what he said,' Caroline said. 'And you know what he's like. If he says he doesn't want the doctor then I think we should respect that.'

'What if he passes out or goes into a coma?' Bren asked. 'What will you do then? Just wait?'

Caroline was so tempted to say yes – that she'd just put the television on and watch *Loose Women* while she waited for him to die. It was a valid question, though. What would she do?

'I'd ring for an ambulance. It's not like he'd be able to stop me.'

Bren grunted and started drying the mugs and bowls, putting everything back in the right place as though it was her house and not Caroline's. She moved around the kitchen, obviously familiar with every detail, from the cold tap that needed an extra twist to tighten it to the fridge door which needed a hard tug to open. Every movement suggested that she belonged there and that Caroline didn't.

'I think you should go now,' Caroline said. 'He said he doesn't want you here and you should respect that.'

'Yes, well,' Bren huffed, folding her arms across her ample chest. 'He said the same to you. Are you going to go as well?'

'You'd like that, wouldn't you? You'd like me to leave you to it. But what happens when he has another funny turn? Are you going to pick him up? Are you going to give him bed baths and change his shitty pyjamas when the time comes? Because it will. This is only the start and if you think any different then you're just kidding yourself. Dennis needs me more than he needs you, so I'm staying.'

To underline her determination, Caroline plonked herself down at the kitchen table and stared Bren down.

'There's no need to be like that,' the older woman said. 'I'm sure we can both help Dennis in different ways.'

Caroline shook her head. 'I don't think so. And I'd like his key back. While I'm staying here, I want to keep an eye on who's coming and going, and I don't want you just walking in as if you own the place.'

Bren's expression darkened and she thrust her hands into the pockets of her cardigan as though she wanted to cling tightly to the key and stop Caroline from taking it. 'You can't take it off me. Dennis gave it to me. I'll give it back when he asks.'

Caroline smiled. 'I've seen a solicitor, Bren. I'm in charge of Dennis's decisions if he isn't able to make them for himself.' It was a lie but clearly Bren was shocked. 'I need to be able to look after the house when he can't.'

'And his money, no doubt,' Bren spat. 'Do you think I don't know what this is about? That's the only reason you're back – out for what you can get. You're a greedy cow, with your flashy car and expensive clothes. You wait till I tell him what's been going on. You'll never see a penny of his if he knows how you've treated me.'

'Key,' Caroline said, holding out her hand. 'Otherwise I'll take out a court order and have you banned from the house. I'm sure my lawyer could draw up a petition tomorrow.'

She had no idea if such a thing were possible but nor did Bren and she was of a generation who were intimidated by legal jargon. She studied Caroline's face as if she were searching for weakness or a sign that this was a joke. She obviously saw no sign of either as she removed the key from her pocket and handed it to Caroline.

'Don't think I won't tell him about this when he's feeling better,' she warned. 'You won't get away with it.'

She took one last long look at Caroline and flounced out of the back door which Caroline locked behind her with the key that Bren had just given her.

'Step two,' she whispered to herself.

CHAPTER 16

The weather had turned milder as though it was determined to dash anyone's hopes of a white Christmas and, with the elevated temperatures, it had started to rain.

Caroline hunched in the doorway of the Methodist church, zipping up her waterproof jacket and taking a step further back into the entranceway to avoid the worst splashes of rainwater as they ricocheted from the steps. She'd waited until it was fully dark to leave Dennis's house, wary of Bren's curtain-twitching and tendency to enlist help from other neighbours if she could.

Two days earlier, a man Caroline had never seen before had turned up at Dennis's door asking to speak to him. He claimed to be a friend from the pub and that he was concerned about her father's well-being as he hadn't seen him for a few days. When Caroline suggested that his concern should have manifested itself in stopping Dennis from drinking so much, he'd slouched away – as far as Bren's front gate where he stood shaking his head at her sitting room window. She didn't bother to tell Dennis that he'd called. Not that Dennis would have cared – the sedatives seemed to be doing their job quite well; most of the time he didn't really know what day it was.

The inner door to the church opened and two people stepped out. Caroline ducked her head, hoping not to be recognised as they passed, deep in conversation. She recognised Evelyn and Warren from the meeting she had attended but neither paid any attention to her; Caroline wasn't even sure that they'd seen her as she leaned more deeply into the shadows. Two more people left, one giving her a small nod as he passed, but still no Maddie.

Just as she was about to open the door and look inside, Caroline's patience was rewarded and Maddie stepped out into the vestibule. She saw Caroline immediately and gave her a wary smile.

'The meeting's finished. Looks like you got here a bit too late,' she said, zipping up her coat and tucking her scarf tightly round her neck.

'I've been here a while,' Caroline admitted. 'Trying to muster up the courage to go in. I couldn't face it, though.'

The wary smile gave way to something more sympathetic as Maddie asked, 'Why not?'

'I've been struggling a bit and I'm not very happy with myself at the moment. I know I wouldn't be judged but I just couldn't face talking about the crap that's going on in my life.'

Maddie gave her an understanding smile. 'We've all been there. You really ought to try to get to a meeting. It *will* help, if you can face it.'

'I know. I'm just a bit out of my depth at the moment. I'll try again next week. I don't suppose you fancy a drink?'

'Not really,' Maddie said, slipping her hands into thick woollen gloves. 'I need to get back for Ethan; he's in the middle of his mock exams and he's stressing out.' She set off down the steps, obviously intending to end the conversation.

'Must be a relief to know that you'll be able to help him with uni next year,' Caroline said, trotting down after her. 'And after that. It's a long course, medicine.'

Her words had exactly the desired effect. Maddie stopped and turned round.

'Look,' she said. 'I appreciate your help but that doesn't make us friends or anything. I've told you that I'll pay you back as soon as I can. If you want you can have it in writing, we'll draw up a payment plan so I can give it back in instalments. Whatever you want.'

'What I want,' Caroline responded, 'is for you to come and have a drink with me. I just need somebody to talk to for an hour or so. I don't care about the sodding money.'

Maddie stared up at her, her expression unreadable. Caroline waited.

'Okay,' Maddie conceded. 'One drink. And I'm buying this time.'

She marched off along the pavement, leaving Caroline to hurry after her.

Maddie's choice of pub was very different from the wine bar that Caroline had chosen for their previous meeting – a chain establishment with a strangely inappropriate tartan theme running through the bar area. The carpet was green plaid, the dusty-looking curtains dark blue and black checks, and the seats were upholstered in varying shades and patterns possibly representing various Scottish clans. It looked like a Highland gathering had vomited across the whole pub.

It was fairly quiet for a Thursday night, the traditional big night out in Doncaster, probably linked to the day that factory workers used to get paid – when there were still factories in the area. There was a group of women crowded round a table in an alcove next to the roaring log fire and a couple of older men nursing pints at the bar but the rest of the tables were empty. Caroline wondered if Maddie had chosen the place specifically because she'd expected it to be quiet.

'What can I get you?' Maddie asked, draping her damp jacket across the back of a chair.

'Half a lager, please.'

Caroline watched her as she crossed the cavernous room to the bar. The set of her head and her purposeful stride suggested that she was angry with Caroline for manipulating her, but that wasn't important. They were here. It was time for the next part of the plan and Caroline had a good feeling about Maddie's willingness to comply. Especially if she'd judged the nurse correctly.

Maddie plonked the drinks on the table – coke for herself, Caroline noticed – and sighed heavily. 'So, what do you want to talk about?'

Caroline took a big gulp of her lager, relishing the cold fizz as it cooled her throat. 'My dad,' she said. 'He's in a bad way.'

'It's only to be expected,' Maddie stated, her tone devoid of sympathy. 'You knew what you were getting into when you decided to look after him. He's only going to get worse.'

'I know. It's just not what I anticipated, though.'

Maddie leaned forward, frowning as she urged Caroline to say more. 'In what way?'

'He's not sleeping and he's in constant pain. I've tried the Diazepam but it barely calms him down, and the Oramorph barely seems to touch the pain.'

Maddie looked down at the table-top as though she was deciding whether to get involved. 'Has he seen his GP? That should be your first port of call, really. Get the doctor in and he might be able to prescribe something stronger.'

Caroline shook her head. 'I've tried that,' she lied. 'Dad won't have him in the house. I got the GP round but Dad refused to speak to him or to be examined. It's like he's determined to suffer through this and there's nothing I can do.'

'To be honest, Caroline, that's his choice. If he won't see the GP there's not much you can do.'

Maddie didn't seem as sympathetic as Caroline had expected. She was clearly following rules and protocols but that was probably to be expected. She wouldn't risk her career over one patient – unless she had to.

'I need something stronger,' Caroline said. 'Something to kill the pain and get him to sleep.'

'Then ask your GP.'

'I've already asked. He won't prescribe without examining Dad first. I feel like I'm just going round in circles. I thought you might help.'

'How?' Maddie's voice was cold.

'Like you did before. Prescribe something.' Caroline was careful to emphasise *before*. Maddie had already crossed a line and a reminder might make her aware of her precarious situation – but even before she'd finished her sentence, the nurse was shaking her head.

'You know I can't do that. I've already put my job on the line once. I can't risk it.'

'I know. I understand,' Caroline said. 'But if I went to the hospital and asked for a repeat of the prescription that you gave me, would that put you at risk?'

Maddie flushed. 'You wouldn't.'

'I wouldn't want to. But I'm trying to help a dying man. It's not like I'm going to kill him – he's not got long left anyway. I just want him to be comfortable. Come and see him if you want. Put your mind at rest that I'm trying to do the right thing.'

'You know I can't,' Maddie repeated. 'I can't go to see him and I can't give you another prescription. Even if I wanted to, it would look suspicious if I went into his patient record this long after he's been discharged. Look. I'll give you all the money back that you gave me. I'll borrow it from somewhere else. I'll pay you back next week.'

Caroline smiled. 'I don't suppose it would look good if a patient's daughter had given you a lot of money and suddenly you're writing unofficial prescriptions for her?'

Maddie's shoulders sank in defeat. She couldn't explain her way out of the money if anybody questioned her behaviour towards Dennis. It would look like she'd been paid for the prescription. One word from Caroline and her career would be in tatters.

'You really are a bitch, aren't you?' Maddie said, dark eyes flashing with anger and humiliation. 'You've got me exactly where you want me and I didn't see it coming.'

Caroline risked a wry smile. This had been almost too easy; she hadn't expected Maddie to capitulate so quickly. Caroline hadn't wanted to have to threaten Maddie but she could understand why the nurse was so reluctant to help. She tried to picture herself as Maddie must see her; ruthless, manipulative and without a conscience. Dennis had done his work well. His little girl was a real credit to him when she had to be. But, even as she heard her barely veiled threats, Caroline hated what she'd allowed her father to mould her into; what he'd made her. She needed this to be over so that she could move on and finally become her own person, if she could work out who that might be. And, for it to be over, she needed to use Maddie.

'I'm sorry you feel that way,' Caroline said. 'All I'm trying to do is what's best for my father. I know how people can suffer when they're in the last stages of cancer and I don't want that for him. I know he's not helping himself but I still have to do something. Nobody needs to know about this arrangement; nobody needs to find out. All you have to do is prescribe a stronger tranquilliser and up his dose of morphine. As I said, it's not like we're killing him. If anything, I think it's the compassionate thing to do.'

Maddie stared at her as if she was listening to a foreign language. 'Compassion? I doubt you'd know the meaning of the word. What about doing the *right* thing? The *ethical* thing?'

'What's the right thing?' Caroline asked, surprised that Maddie was showing a spark of resistance. 'Is it right to let somebody die in agony? Is that ethical?'

Maddie shook her head. 'There are regulations around drugs and end-of-life care. They're there for a reason. How do I know you're not just going to give him a massive overdose because you're tired of looking after him?'

So close, Caroline thought. Maddie had nearly hit on the truth but the plan was much more complex than she could ever have guessed and Caroline's reasons were rooted much more deeply than in the events of the past few weeks. For a second, she was tempted to tell the nurse everything. The whole story. But what good would that do? She'd only end up sounding insane, and Maddie would probably go to the police just as Dennis had threatened to do all those years ago. No, this was the best way. Keep quiet and stick to the plan.

'You'll just have to trust me, I suppose,' Caroline said. 'If I wanted to kill him I could probably have managed with everything you prescribed the last time. Or I could give in when he asks for a large whisky.'

Maddie took a small sip of her coke.

'Will this be the last time?' she asked, eventually.

'It will,' Caroline assured her, even though she had no idea how much longer she would keep Dennis in his current state. 'If you give me enough to get him through the next few weeks – he can't have much longer left. Are you sure you don't want to check up on him?'

'I think the less I'm seen with you the better, don't you?' Maddie said bitterly. 'I'm hoping that I won't have to see you or your father again after this evening.'

'Then you'd better make sure I have everything that I need,' Caroline said with a smile.

Maddie glared at her. 'If I add extra prescriptions to his records, there's a chance somebody might notice. If I get caught I'll tell the authorities everything. I'll lose my job but I'll make sure that you get into a lot of trouble as well.'

'Looks like we both have something to lose then, if this goes wrong. All the more reason to not fuck it up.'

Maddie flinched at the profanity.

'So,' Caroline continued. 'Prescribe more of the same. Enough for a couple of months. Sedatives and morphine. Make the Oramorph a stronger dose as well. It wasn't working when I used the last of it and I can't give him a double dose every time.'

'How do you want me to get the prescription to you?' Maddie asked, her voice unsteady.

Caroline picked up one of the drip mats from the table, split it with a fingernail and peeled off the branding on one side to leave a blank surface. She dug in her handbag for a pen and wrote down the name and address of Dennis's local pharmacy.

'Have it sent there; I can pick it up.'

She gathered her coat and bag and stood up to leave.

'And you can forget about paying me back the fifteen grand. Keep it. At least, that way you'll not have to have anything else to do with me.'

Maddie tried to splutter some sort of protest but Caroline held up a hand to silence her.

'I know you won't believe me but I really did want to help you. It's just that I need you to help me as well.'

She put on her coat, draped her bag over her shoulder and walked away from Maddie without looking back.

It wasn't until Caroline was in her car that her actions hit her and she shook uncontrollably as she tried to fit the key into the ignition.

For the first time since she'd come up with her plan, she really believed that it might work.

And that exhilarated and terrified her in equal measure.

JANUARY

CHAPTER 17

The young man waiting in the interview room for Kate was clearly agitated. He sat hunched over, his hands clasped together on the table-top, one of his knees jiggling up and down as he tapped his foot. His dark hair was dishevelled and he looked in need of a shave. As Kate approached, his hopeful expression suddenly made him look like a child caught just on the cusp of manhood. His face was mostly angles and edges but his eyes were those of a ten-year-old promised an outing or a treat.

'Finally,' he said. 'I've been here for ages. Have you got some news about my mum?'

Kate pulled out a chair and sat down opposite him. She had the details of the autopsy report of the unknown woman in a folder which she had no intention of sharing with this young man, but which she might need to check physical details if he could tell her anything of use. She'd been told his name and that his age was eighteen but, other than that, she had no idea who he was or who his mother might be. She hoped, for his sake, that she wasn't the woman who had been pulled from the canal two days earlier.

'Right, Ethan, I need to get some details from you and then we'll look at working out what might have happened to your mother.'

'I think I already know,' he said, his eyes suddenly bright with tears. 'I think you found her body in the canal two days ago.' He was struggling to keep himself together.

'We don't know that,' Kate said, trying to reassure him. 'Can I get some details?'

Ethan nodded.

'Okay,' Kate said, carefully opening her folder to the brief notes she'd been given. 'You're Ethan Cox, aged eighteen? Is that right?'

'Yes.'

'And your mother, Maddie, hasn't been seen since she left for work two days ago?'

'I don't think so.'

'Why did you wait to report her missing, Ethan?'

He flushed at the question. 'I wasn't at home the first night. I went round to a friend's to study and have a few beers.'

'And your friend will confirm this?'

Ethan nodded eagerly. 'I was there all night. His parents and sister were there as well. I can give you their address and phone numbers.'

'Okay. I'll take those later. Can you tell me about that morning, the last time that you saw your mum? What was her mood? Did you notice anything unusual?'

Ethan took a deep breath.

'She left before me. She had an early shift; she works as a nurse at the DRI. She'd just had her breakfast when I got up, left me some coffee in the pot and two slices of bread in the toaster. There was nothing unusual.'

Kate jotted a couple of words on the top sheet of paper in her folder.

'And her mood?'

He shrugged. 'Normal. She'd been a bit down, I think. Her work is really stressful and she sometimes lets it get on top of her.'

His consideration and expression were more adult than Kate had expected. This was a young man who was clearly aware of his mother's life.

'There's nobody else at home? It's just the two of you?'

'Yes. It has been for the last ten years. My dad left us when I was eight and then he was killed in a car crash a couple of years ago. I didn't really know him.'

'And what about boyfriends? Was your mum seeing anybody?'

Ethan smiled sadly.

'No. She always said that she didn't have time for romance. That I was the only man in her life. Daft really. I'm going to university at the end of this year and I'd always hoped that she might meet somebody after I've left. You know, company for her.' He looked down at the table-top and ran his finger along a scratch in the surface.

'I think she needs something more in her life other than me and work. She's a good person, she deserves to be happy.'

Kate felt herself warming to Ethan. His compassion and understanding made him seem mature way beyond his years. She really hoped that she didn't have bad news. 'Okay,' she said with another swift look at her notes. 'You've provided a description of your mother. About five feet five, long dark hair, brown eyes. Any distinguishing marks? Tattoos? Scars, that sort of thing?'

Ethan shook his head. 'She hated tattoos. Always threatened to disown me if I got one. She had a Caesarean scar from when she had me but there's nothing else that I can think of.'

Kate smiled, trying not to allow her dismay to show in her face. The description fitted perfectly and she could see from Ethan's colouring that he could easily be related to the woman from the canal.

'Do you have a picture of your mum? Maybe on your phone.'

Ethan scrabbled in his jeans pocket for his phone. He tapped in his password and flicked at the screen, obviously trying to find the best shot of his mother.

'There's this one,' he said, passing the phone to Kate. 'It was taken at my eighteenth birthday party. My mates thought I was a bit sad for inviting her but she'd promised not to stay long.'

Kate studied the image in the screen. The woman was wearing a dark red dress that made a stunning contrast with her olive skin and dark hair. She was holding a glass of wine and smiling into the camera, looking slightly self-conscious. 'Is this recent?' Kate asked.

'Last October.'

She continued to look at the phone screen, reluctant to allow Ethan to see what might be in her eyes when she looked up.

There was no doubt. This was the woman from the canal. 'When did you expect her home?' Kate asked, delaying the inevitable.

'Late evening,' Ethan said. 'She sometimes went to a meeting after work.'

'Meeting?'

Ethan looked down at the table-top again. 'GA. Gamblers Anonymous. She'd had a bit of a problem. But she was getting on top of it. She told me last month; said I was old enough to know what she was really like. She hoped I'd learn from her mistakes. I don't think it was her GA night, though. I wondered if she'd been offered an extra shift at the hospital. She did that sometimes, slept at work for a few hours then carried on. She usually let me know, though.'

Kate nodded, trying to work out the best way to break the sad news to him.

'It's her, isn't it?' Ethan asked suddenly. 'The body in the canal; it's my mum?'

Kate slid the phone back across the table and held Ethan's defiant stare. He wanted the truth and he was trying to be strong.

'I think so, yes,' she admitted. 'The description matches and your photograph confirms it. We may need you to formally identify the body; she's been examined but they'll try to make her look just like she did when she was alive. I'm so sorry, Ethan.'

The young man had started to breathe quickly and unevenly, obviously trying to contain his emotions. Kate wanted to hug him. He reminded her of her son Ben when he was upset, trying to fight the little boy inside who just wanted to cry and run to his mum.

'What... what happened to her?' Ethan asked. 'Did she drown?'

'We don't know for certain, yet,' Kate admitted. 'We're still waiting for some test results to confirm what we suspect.'

'But she wasn't attacked? It was an accident?'

'Ethan, I'm sorry. There's not much more that I can tell you at the moment but, when we do know something, I promise I'll let you know.'

'And you'll tell me the truth? I'm not a kid, you know.'

'I'll tell you the truth. It might be hard for you to hear it but I'll make sure that you know everything that we find out.'

He stood up as if to leave.

'When can I see her?'

'Tomorrow, probably. Is there somebody that can go with you? It's not something you should have to do on your own. An uncle or aunt?'

Ethan's face clouded with resentment.

'I said I'm not a kid. I can handle it. She's my mum.' His voice broke on the last word and he collapsed back into the chair, his body wracked with sobs.

'I know this is awful, Ethan,' Kate tried to reassure him. 'But we're going to do everything possible to find out what happened to your mum. Can you help us? If I give you some paper and a pen, could you write down the names of her friends, family members, anybody else that you can think of who might be able to help? And I'll need the details of her GA meeting. Somebody there might have some information. The more we know about her life, Ethan, the more likely we are to find out the truth about her death.'

It sounded trite, rehearsed, and Kate hated the statement as soon as it was out of her mouth but it galvanised Ethan. He held his hand out for a pen.

'I'll write down everything I know about her life. Whatever I can do to help.'

Kate slid a piece of paper over to him and took a pen from her inside jacket pocket.

Ten minutes later, Kate was racing upstairs to the team office, armed with the details of Maddie Cox's life. Ethan had been thorough; the list consisted of friends from years earlier, work colleagues, and details of the day and venue of her regular GA meetings. He'd added his own details, including his mobile and home phone numbers and his contact details at school. Kate reminded him to include details of the friend he'd stayed with that first evening.

Kate's sorrow for the boy had deepened when he'd scanned through the pitifully short list, smiled up at her, and told her that he hoped it would help. He still didn't know that they were looking for a murderer somewhere on his list. And, if the killer wasn't on the list, somebody from Kate's team would question him again for more names, more details. Ethan wasn't a suspect, not in Kate's view, but he might end up feeling like one as the investigation gathered pace.

She'd texted Hollis as soon as she'd seen Ethan off the premises and he'd followed her instructions to assemble the members of her team. Barratt was swinging on his chair as he chatted to Cooper, and Hollis was at his computer searching for something on the internet. O'Connor was absent which wasn't much of a surprise to Kate. Although officially one of her team, he was often far too involved with his own investigation into local gangs to be of much use. Raymond's orders though; she had to keep him. The atmosphere was one of expectation. At last they had a lead on the body from the canal and now, with an identity, they could start to make some real progress and trace her movements and contacts. Three pairs of eyes turned to her as she slapped her notes down on her desk.

'Right, listen up,' she said. 'We have an ID for the woman in the canal. Maddie Cox, aged forty-one. Works at the DRI as a clinical nurse specialist. Cooper, find out what that means. What's her role? Who does it bring her into contact with? She was last seen at home two days ago, leaving for work after breakfast. We have a list of friends and colleagues. The son, Ethan, appears to be the only family.'

'Is he a suspect?' Hollis interrupted.

Kate paused, remembering Ethan's tears and desperation to retain control. 'Not at this time, but keep an open mind. He's got a solid alibi that we can easily follow up on.'

'We need to check that she was at work two days ago, what she did there, and if anybody noticed anything unusual about her. Barratt, get over to the DRI and talk to her colleagues. She attended GA meetings regularly. We need to find out who she spoke to, who she was close to there. According to Ethan, there's a meeting tonight. Barratt, can you get down there and ask around? See if anybody knows anything about her life. Was she in a lot of debt? That sort of thing.'

Barratt raised two fingers to his forehead in a mock salute and leapt out of his chair.

'What else?' Kate asked the remaining members of her team.

'CCTV,' Hollis said. 'Now we know who she was and where she worked, we can check cameras around the hospital and try to trace her movements on the night before she was found.'

'Good. Sam?'

'A clinical nurse specialist is somebody who's studied to Master's level,' Sam said from behind her monitor. 'She'll have had a specialism. Presumably, from what the son said, oncology.'

Kate felt the beginnings of a blush at the second mention of Nick Tsappis's field of expertise. She'd been trying not to think about her conversation with him or about his business card that hung heavily in her trouser pocket. This wasn't the time.

'Thanks, Sam,' Kate said. 'Could you…?'

'I know, I know, CCTV,' Cooper said with a grin. 'I can try the phone companies as well. We can get her records now we've got a name. Did you get a network?'

Checking Ethan's notes, Kate was impressed to discover Maddie's mobile number and the network provider. The boy had been thorough. Kate passed the details on to Cooper and checked her watch. 'Look, guys. It's getting on for seven. We can pick this up tomorrow. There's no point in trying the hospital this late and there'll be nobody at the council who can give us CCTV tonight.'

She couldn't resist a sympathetic glance at Sam Cooper as she made a note of Maddie Cox's phone details and then started the log-off process on her computer. Sam was in for a tough night when she got back to her boat.

CHAPTER 18

'God, I hate hospitals,' Hollis said as the doors slid open with a welcoming hum. 'They smell funny and everybody always has this false quietness about them. I can't believe we're back here *again*.'

'Everybody hates hospitals,' Kate said, scanning the walls for the sign that would take them to the ward where Maddie Cox had worked. 'I bet even the people that work here hate the place.'

They walked in silence down the corridor, Kate lost in childhood memories of visits to her mother when she'd been hospitalised for cancer treatment when Kate was eight. She hadn't had to face the memories last time, probably because she'd been in a hurry and was being rushed through the corridors, but this time she was inundated with images of holding Karen's hand and trying to keep her sister quiet as they padded along narrow corridors in search of her mother.

Kate hadn't really been aware of her surroundings the previous day. Everything had been such a rush. The corridor was wider and brighter than the ones in her memory and the doors off were pale wood with porthole style windows rather than the darkly painted solid ones that she recalled from previous visits. The floor was tiled with a mosaic in green and white and an orderly was busy with a mop and bucket making sure that the place was clean for visiting hours.

'This is it,' Hollis said pointing to a closed double door. 'Aspen ward.'

'Aspen?' Kate looked round at the corridor. 'This is where we were yesterday.'

She pushed one side of the door, expecting it to be locked, but it yielded to her touch and allowed them access to the semi-circular nurses' station. A familiar face looked up from a page of notes that she was reading.

'Back so soon, detectives?'

Kate stared at her, still waiting for her brain to process the coincidence.

'I assume you're here for further information.'

'Yes,' Kate said. 'Well, actually, no. We're here about another matter. Can we talk in private?'

The nurse sighed and picked up the telephone next to a keyboard. A hushed conversation ensued and then she stood up. 'I've called for somebody to cover me for twenty minutes. It's all I can spare.'

She led them to the deserted staff room behind the desk. There was an air of neglect to the mugs draining next to the sink and the battered-looking fridge. The row of dilapidated chairs along one side gave the space a waiting-room-like quality as though the nurses were no different from the patients.

There was no offer of tea or coffee as the nurse pointed to the chairs.

'Have a seat.'

She leaned against the sink as Kate and Hollis settled in chairs, allowing Kate the opportunity to study her more closely. In her mid-twenties with her hair in a ponytail instead of the previous day's bun, she looked more like a college student than a seasoned professional. Only her expression gave away her experience. Her grey eyes regarded them with annoyance and her arms were crossed, closing off her body.

'I'm sorry to bother you again,' Kate began. 'I can see that you're really busy but this is important. I didn't get your name yesterday.'

'No, you didn't,' the nurse responded. 'I'm Staff Nurse McGlynn. Gemma.'

Kate caught a movement in her peripheral vision. Hollis had taken out his notebook.

'Thanks, Gemma. And thanks for yesterday. I may have been a little abrupt with you.'

'I don't see what else I can tell you,' Gemma said. 'I gave you everything I knew about Dennis Lambert yesterday.'

'We're not here about Dennis Lambert,' Hollis interjected. 'This is a different case.'

'I think you should sit down,' Kate said. 'We have some bad news.'

The woman followed Kate's instruction almost automatically as though she understood the code. Perhaps she'd used it herself, many times, to prepare a family member for the worst.

'You worked with Madeline, Maddie Cox?'

A nod in response, wide grey eyes fixed on Kate's face.

'And you haven't seen her for a few days?'

'She's not been at work. I assumed she was off sick.'

'Why did you assume that? Did she have a lot of time off?' Hollis asked.

'No. She was hardly ever off sick.' The woman was starting to look uncomfortable, preparing herself for bad news.

'And you last saw her when?'

Gemma's eyes flicked up to the ceiling as she tried to work out the answer to the question. 'Tuesday. She was here on Tuesday. We had a bad day. Two patients died on the ward and another was sent home because there wasn't much else that we could do.'

'And how did she seem?'

Gemma pursed her lips. 'Fine. Same as ever.'

'Nothing bothering her?'

A snort. 'Only the same things that bother all of us in this job: long hours with little support, that sort of thing. I'm sure you two get it.'

Kate smiled her understanding. 'Had you noticed anything different about her in the past few weeks? Was she especially stressed, depressed?'

Gemma shook her head. 'Not really. She's very professional. Good at her job. We're not really friends so I'm not sure I'd have noticed any difference unless it affected her work.'

'Did she have any friends on staff?'

'Not that I know of,' Gemma said. 'She's quite a private person. Has something happened to her?'

'Possibly,' Kate said. 'We're just talking to people who knew her, trying to make sense of what we know so far. Her son reported her missing yesterday.'

'Missing? How? Like she ran away or she's been kidnapped or something?'

Kate remained silent, hoping that Hollis had the sense to do the same.

'She wouldn't just take off. Her son, Ethan. She thinks the sun shines out of him.' The nurse stood up and walked up and down the small space. 'She'd never leave Ethan. Oh Christ. Oh shit.' Gemma collapsed into the chair next to Hollis. 'That body in the canal. I heard about it on the radio last night. You think it's her.'

She took their continuing silence for confirmation.

'But I don't understand what this has to do with yesterday. Why the questions about Dennis Lambert? Yes, she was the nurse practitioner on his case but what's that got to do with her ending up…' She tailed off, lost in her own thoughts and speculation.

'She was on Dennis Lambert's case?' Kate asked.

'Yes. Yesterday, when I said you needed to talk to somebody else, it was Maddie. I told you she hadn't been in. You left your card. I was going to pass it on to her when she came back.' Gemma's face froze as she realized the implication of her final sentence. Maddie wasn't coming back. Hollis reached out and patted Gemma's arm but she pulled away.

'I can't believe this. She was here on Tuesday and everything was normal and now…'

Kate's brain kicked up a gear. Two murders in the last couple of days and now there was a link. Coincidence? She'd been trained not to believe in coincidence, not to trust it; to examine it from all angles, strip-search it and breathalyse it if necessary before accepting it as genuine.

'Did Maddie know Dennis's daughter? Did she speak to her when Dennis was here?'

Gemma looked bewildered. 'I suppose so. If the daughter was his primary contact then she would have done.'

'But you don't remember them having any other contact? Maddie never mentioned Caroline Lambert in any other context?'

Gemma shook her head. 'Not that I recall. It would have been unusual. We're discouraged from anything other than a professional relationship with patients and their families.' She began picking at a bit of loose foam that was bursting out of the seat cover next to her leg. 'I can't believe she's gone.'

'We need to try to piece together her last movements in order to work out what happened,' Hollis said. 'You say she was in work on Tuesday?'

Gemma stopped picking at the seat and stared at Hollis gratefully. It was instinctive in her to try to help, Kate could see that, it was part of her job, her training. Hollis had struck just the right tone.

'Yes. She worked from nine to six on Tuesday. I was on from eleven.'

'So you saw her leave?' Kate prompted.

'She left just after six.'

'Did she look like she was going home or going out somewhere?'

'She wasn't dressed up or anything, if that's what you mean. She looked like she'd just changed out of her uniform like normal.'

'Did she mention any plans for the evening?'

'No. But, like I said, she was a private person. I just assumed she was going home but she might have had plans I… uh…'

Gemma sat back in her seat suddenly, struck by a memory. Her eyes lost focus as though she was struggling to remember something important.

'She was on the phone that afternoon. In here. I came in on my break to make a cup of coffee and she was sitting there.' She pointed to where Kate was sitting. 'She was hunched over a bit like she didn't want anybody to overhear her.'

Hollis was scribbling frantically. If Cooper could work her magic with her contact at the phone company she might be able to find out who had been calling.

'What time was this?'

'It must have been around four. That's the time I take my tea break when I'm on eleven to eight.'

'And you didn't hear the conversation?'

Gemma shook her head. 'She was talking really quietly. She seemed a bit agitated. I put the kettle on and got a tea bag but she was gone by the time I turned round. I didn't see much of her after that. Like I said, it was a bit of a rough day.'

'That's really helpful,' Hollis reassured her, snapping his notebook shut and sliding it into the pocket of his suit jacket. He stood up to leave but Kate hadn't quite finished. The Dennis Lambert case was still niggling at her and she couldn't let it go.

'Did you ever see Caroline Lambert here after her father had been discharged?'

Gemma frowned, clearly thrown by the sudden change of subject. 'I don't think so.'

'And Maddie didn't mention her, or her father?'

'Not that I recall.'

It could be a coincidence, then. That hen's tooth in any investigation. Just sheer chance. The nurse appeared to be baffled by her questions. It didn't feel right, though. Kate's instincts were telling her that there was something here. A link was a link for a reason and she couldn't afford to ignore it. 'Who was Maddie's boss?'

'Good question,' Gemma said with an attempt at a smile. 'Ultimately the head of oncology but there should be a doctor with oversight of this ward. Should be. Maddie and another NP were practically running the place themselves because we're a bit short of consultants. I can give you the number for oncology.'

Kate remembered Nick Tsappis' card in her pocket. 'That won't be necessary. Thanks.'

Gemma checked her watch. 'I'm really sorry but I have to get back to work. Not that I feel much like it. I wish I could've been more helpful.'

Kate thanked Gemma for her time and led Hollis back to the corridor, trying to make sense of what they'd just been told.

'What did you make of that? Maddie was Dennis Lambert's nurse.'

Hollis grinned at her. 'Seeing ghosts and shadows? It's not that big a town and the hospital covers a wide area. Most people end up here at one time or another.'

There was something solid and reassuring about Hollis's certainty. He hadn't seen what she had. He'd seen a coincidence that he could easily explain. Nothing sinister, nothing to follow up on, nothing to get concerned about.

Kate set off back towards reception, convinced that he was right, that she was really seeing shadows. And then her phone rang.

DECEMBER

Dear Caroline,

You've been there for a few weeks now so I'm not surprised to hear that everything's getting on top of you. I'm here if you need to talk. We can meet up whenever you want. I wonder if you just need to get it over and done with. Is it really worth spending any more time in that house? You're strong enough at the moment but will you be in a few days? A few weeks? Think about it. He's not worth making yourself ill over. None of this is, really. I know that you're determined to see this through but don't you think it's gone on long enough? Please think about getting it over with soon. For your own sake.

Love
J

CHAPTER 19

S he hated him. It was such a simple emotion and such a release to finally admit it to herself. At first she thought it was fear, then loathing, then an abhorrence of his state. But she'd finally been able to name it. It was hatred. Everything she'd felt had been distilled, crystallised and refined until it was diamond hard and as clear as ice. She hated him.

At least she didn't have to hide it from him. There were whole days when she ignored his pleas for a drink or something to eat and others where she gave him everything he wanted and watched in disgust as he ate and drank. Twice he'd begged her to kill him and twice she'd refused, decreasing the morphine dose until his pain was unbearable but keeping him mildly sedated so he couldn't escape the agony.

It was only fair. He deserved to suffer. He wasn't going to get an easy, dignified death: he was going to linger. She knew that the whisky was partly responsible for his pain; that his liver was struggling to metabolise it so she kept giving him small amounts; just enough to mix with the Diazepam and keep him sluggish and bedridden. And in pain.

Sometimes he had moments of perfect clarity. He knew exactly where he was, what was wrong with him and what she was doing. That's when he cried like a child and begged for release. Sometimes he called her by her mother's name, confused and desperate. She learned to ignore his pitiful whimpering and his incoherent rambling. But she was getting tired. She wanted it to be over. She needed a plan for the end.

A light knock on the door interrupted her thoughts. Bren. Caroline had told her that she could continue to visit Dennis but only by prior arrangement. She couldn't have her interrupting one of their heart-to-heart sessions where Caroline told him what a bastard he was and yelled at him until he agreed.

Wearily, she rose from the kitchen table and opened the back door. Bren looked like she'd been out for the morning. Her hair was freshly styled and partially covered with a mauve headscarf, her make-up slightly overdone, as if she'd wanted to make an effort for somebody. Her chins wobbled with the humiliation of having to knock.

'You said one o'clock,' she said to Caroline, stepping forward without being invited in.

'I know. He's asleep.' Caroline pushed the door further back, allowing Bren to manoeuvre her bulk inside.

'You said I could see him, so I intend to,' she said belligerently. 'We had an agreement.'

Caroline laughed in her face.

'An agreement. Is that what you call it? I only allow you in here out of pity. Pity for you for wanting to help him, and pity for him because he's got nobody else but you and me.'

Bren snorted. 'If I'd had my way, he wouldn't have had you here. He was fine until you stuck your nose in.'

Caroline sat back down at the kitchen table, regarding the older woman with a mix of curiosity and suspicion. She was right. Without her intervention, Dennis would probably still be going for walks round the block or even popping into the pub. Did Bren have an inkling that Dennis's condition wasn't just the natural progress of his disease? Caroline doubted it. She'd no evidence that Bren was especially perceptive and she wouldn't allow her any time alone with Dennis, supervising her visits extremely closely.

Bren removed her coat and headscarf and draped them across the back of the other kitchen chair then stared at Caroline expectantly. 'Well. Are we going to make small talk or can I go upstairs and see him?'

'Do what you want. I told you he's asleep. Feel free to go and have a look. If he's shit himself again you can also feel free to clean him up and wash his pyjamas.'

Bren reared back as though she'd been slapped. 'How dare you talk about him like that? That man brought you up and now you talk about him as if he's a naughty child. I ought to wash your mouth out, you disgusting woman.'

Caroline stood up, toe to toe with Bren. Caroline towered over the older woman by a few inches so Bren had to step back in order to look her in the face.

'Why don't you try it,' Caroline said with a smile. 'There's soap on the sink. And when you've done you can go up and say goodbye to your precious Dennis because it'll be the last you'll see of him. I allow you in here, Bren, when I don't have to. You have no rights in this situation, and it's only through my generosity that you're still in this kitchen talking to me. So, if you want to keep coming back, a little respect might be the way forward.'

Bren glared up at her, mouth opening and closing like a landed trout.

'So? Do we have an understanding? This is my house and I'll say what I want. If you don't *fucking* like it you know where the door is!'

The older woman went to pick up her coat and headscarf but then seemed to change her mind. She took a deep breath and drew herself up to her full five feet and said, 'I'd like to see Dennis, please.'

It was a minor victory but one that Caroline relished. Bren knew exactly where she stood and was aware of the consequences of her actions. It might just keep her in line for a while, and keeping her in line was a necessity.

Caroline pushed past the older woman and trudged down the hallway.

'Come on then!' she shouted from the bottom of the stairs, aware that their raised voices may have awoken her father. 'I haven't got all day.' She was halfway up the stairs before Bren appeared at the kitchen door.

'I see he's still only on paracetamol,' she said.

'I see you're still a nosy cow,' Caroline retorted, irritated that Bren had used her few seconds alone in the kitchen to do some snooping. Just as well Caroline kept the Diazepam and Oramorph in her bedroom and disposed of the empty packets and bottles deep in litter bins around the area. She couldn't tell if Bren's spluttering was further outrage or from the effort of climbing the stairs.

Caroline stood outside Dennis's bedroom door and ushered Bren across the threshold. The older woman sniffed loudly as she stepped inside the room, obviously trying to insinuate that she had a bloodhound-like sense for anything out of the ordinary. There was nothing to find – Caroline made sure of that. Anything in the least bit incriminating was long gone by the time Bren arrived for her visits. She knew that Bren was assessing everything about the room, cataloguing and checking everything against her memory of the bedroom and of Dennis. Not that he bore much resemblance to the man she had known.

The decline had surprised Caroline with its speed. She'd expected something less perceptible – a gentle easing down into lethargy and disinterest but, since she'd started the sedatives, Dennis had gone from being reasonably mobile and alert to the snorting, snoring husk that lay in the bed. She'd tried lowering the dose, alarmed at the sudden deterioration but a lighter touch left him more argumentative and more determined to have his own way. At least the sedatives did little for the pain and she could be sparing with the morphine if he wasn't fully compliant.

'How long has he been asleep?' Bren asked.

'A couple of hours,' Caroline lied. She had no idea. She'd helped him to the bathroom, given him a cup of tea with Diazepam mixed in like sugar, and left him to get on with his morning. She'd been out to buy bread and milk, safe in the knowledge that he wasn't able to leave his room and, when she'd got back, she'd read the paper and had a couple of mugs of coffee. An hour before Bren had been due, Caroline had zipped round with the vacuum cleaner, put the soiled bedding on to wash and run a flannel across Dennis's inert face. Good enough to look like she was being a dutiful caring daughter.

'Is he eating properly? He looks thin.'

Resisting the urge to yell at her, Caroline answered Bren's questions in a carefully judged tone; a calculated mix of weariness, irritation and concern. Yes he'd had a drink. Yes he'd been to the bathroom. No he'd not needed anything in the night. Not that Caroline was aware of at least because she'd had three gin and tonics and slept like a baby despite the oppressive memory-ridden bedroom and the lumpy mattress.

'It smells a bit in here. Have you been opening the windows to let some air in?'

'It smells because he sometimes shi– soils himself and I have to clean him and the bed,' Caroline said, not trying too hard to mask her irritation. 'I haven't had the windows open because it's minus three outside overnight and I don't really want him to catch pneumonia or die of hypothermia.'

Something about her tone must have registered with Dennis because he stirred, his lips making a liquid chewing motion which looked like an attempt to speak. His eyelids fluttered open and his cold grey eyes fixed on Caroline. The effect was like something from a horror film when the monster is supposed to be dead but he suddenly finds one last burst of strength and grabs the pretty girl by the ankle just as she thinks she's escaped. Caroline froze. They'd been arguing the previous night about her mum and Jeanette, and Caroline had been quite clear that she wanted him to suffer. She'd intended for him to be asleep throughout Bren's visit but he was waking up and he appeared to be fairly lucid.

'Bren,' he slurred, his eyes closing with the effort of forming the word.

'I'm here, Dennis, love.' Bren sighed, moving closer and leaning in so that she could hear if he said anything else.

He turned towards her voice and opened his eyes again. 'Not seen you for ages,' he mumbled.

Bren cast an accusatory glare at Caroline. 'It's not been that long, love. I came a couple of days ago. I'm glad you're awake. I didn't want to go home without talking to you.'

His eyes closed again. Caroline wondered if the dose she'd given him earlier was enough to keep him docile if he really struggled against the sedative effects of the drug.

'She's supposed to be looking after me,' he said. 'Caroline. She's supposed to be looking after me but she's not.'

Caroline stiffened. Was this it? Was he going to tell Bren about the drugs; about the pain and the arguments?

'She's not here,' he continued, looking directly at her. 'Irene's been with our Jeanette, but Caroline said she'd look after me and she's gone away.'

The breath that Caroline had been holding left her lungs in such a rush that she was surprised that Bren didn't notice. Her legs felt suddenly unsteady with relief. He wasn't lucid at all, he was rambling. Bren had obviously realised the same thing. She sat on the bed and stroked a few stray strands of hair from his face.

'She's here, love. Caroline's right here. Look.' She turned and pointed. 'She's been here all the time.' But he wasn't listening. His eyes had closed and his breathing was slowing.

'Looks like the show's over,' Caroline said. 'Might be best if you go now. Come back in a couple of days, if you like. I'll give you a ring and let you know when he seems like he might be able to talk to you.'

Bren opened her mouth to argue but Caroline's frosty expression seemed to trap the words in her throat. Instead of speaking, Bren jumped up from the bed with more grace than Caroline expected from a woman of her size and age and stomped off downstairs.

A minute later, the door slammed followed by the gate.

Dennis's eyes opened again and he gave her a weak smile.

'Might win an Oscar if I keep this up, eh?'

'What…? You…?' Caroline couldn't quite form a sentence. He'd been faking. He knew exactly where he was and what was happening and he'd been acting. He tried to pull himself into a sitting position, failed on the first attempt and tried again.

Caroline stepped closer and pulled one of his pillows into a more comfortable position behind his back. The action was almost instinctive; she didn't care if he was comfortable or not but shock had made her incapable of coherent thought.

'Did you like that? I didn't lay it on too thick, did I?' He smiled again, a ghastly rictus that exposed his naked gums.

'What the hell are you doing?' she managed to ask.

'Same as you,' he said. 'Just thought you should know that we can both play games. I know what you're doing, Caroline. I know that you want me dead; you just don't have the balls to go through with it. All this arguing and tormenting me. It's not to make me suffer; it's because you're scared to do away with me. You always were a mouse.'

'Why didn't you tell Bren?' Caroline asked, hearing a tremble in her voice. Was he right? Was she afraid?

He sneered at her, one side of his face curling up into a nest of wrinkles. 'What would be the fun in that?'

'You bastard!' she screamed, grabbing the pillow that lay next to his head and pushing it down onto his face. 'You fucker!'

She pressed down, hard. His hands reached up and grasped her wrists and she stiffened, prepared for a struggle but instead, she felt him pulling her hands more tightly down onto the pillow. He wanted this.

'No!' she gasped. 'Not like this. I'm not going to make it that easy.' Images of her research flashed in front of her eyes. Petechial haemorrhages, fibres in his mouth. She'd be caught.

Chest heaving, she pulled the pillow back from his face and was met with a triumphant smile.

'I knew you didn't have the guts for this, you spineless little cunt,' Dennis spat.

She put the pillow back, holding it with one hand while she curled the other into a fist and pounded her father's face through the thick layer of foam. He struggled. She leaned across him, using her weight to keep his upper body relatively still as she smashed her fist into the pillow again and again.

'Had enough?' she yelled.

He stopped struggling and went limp beneath her. There was no smile when she removed the pillow, instead his face was contorted with pain and there was blood around his nose.

Caroline quickly stripped off the pillowcase, intending to wash the blood off as soon as she could. She staggered to the bathroom, still breathing heavily, and ran cold water on a flannel before rushing back to Dennis's bedside.

As she reached out to clean his face, his eyes opened and met hers.

'Clean up your own fucking mess!' she spat, throwing the flannel at him.

CHAPTER 20

The smell was getting worse. Caroline knew that she needed to bathe him but she hadn't been able to face dragging him to the bathroom, stripping him down and holding the showerhead on him until he was vaguely clean. It was her own fault. She'd let it get this bad and now she was having to live with the consequences.

She could smell him everywhere. In the kitchen, while she was making breakfast, she caught a whiff of his fruity aroma under the sweet, smoothness of her coffee and she had to throw the drink down the sink. In the sitting room, if she watched television for an hour's relief she knew he was in the room above her, gradually rotting his way through the ceiling. She'd taken to sitting on the sofa under the window because the other chairs were directly below his bed, and she was half convinced that he would come crashing through.

It had only been a few days. Bren had been round for Christmas, laden down with presents for Dennis but nothing for Caroline. She'd brought him a portable DAB radio, half a ton of sweets and biscuits, and some new pyjamas. The same ones he'd been wearing for three days. Caroline had lightened his medication for the visit, wary but convinced that he was too groggy to say anything incriminating to Bren. She'd been prepared to pass off anything incriminating he said as rambling but he'd been quite normal. He'd had plenty of morphine which was controlling the pain quite well, when she allowed him to have it, and he'd even managed to sit up in bed. Bren had made some comments about him looking better – as if he was going to get out of this alive – but Caroline knew that she was just trying to cheer him up.

She needed to do something. She changed his pyjama bottoms regularly and he wasn't soiling himself as often in bed, probably due to him being asleep for much of the day and asking for the toilet when he was awake. He knew that Caroline hated having to get him out of bed but she hated having to change his shitty pyjamas even more. Now, the rancid smell of sweat meant that she needed to bathe him properly. She'd briefly considered asking Bren, just for that satisfaction of watching the old bag struggle, but Caroline knew that Dennis couldn't be trusted. She'd have to do it herself.

She looked round the kitchen, hoping for inspiration, anything that might make the task ahead less daunting. She'd done a lot of cleaning since she'd been there. Bren's efforts had been much like Bren; shallow, only surface-deep. Beneath the wiped table and vacuumed carpet lay years of accumulated filth that needed a thorough deep clean to make the place liveable. Caroline had started with the kitchen, scouring the grout with a toothbrush, buying a new vacuum cleaner and then shampooing the carpet, blasting the cooker with the most toxic grease remover that she could find. At first it was satisfying, she was making a visible difference, but she realised that it was displacement. What she really wanted to strip to the core was her relationship with Dennis and with her past.

At least it was winter and she didn't have to face the garden.

She drained her coffee mug, ran it under the tap and grabbed the rubber gloves that were lying next to the sink; she couldn't bear the thought of her skin touching his. As she marched upstairs she could hear him stirring. He hadn't had breakfast and the dose of Diazepam that went with it, and she hadn't given him any morphine since the previous evening. He was awake and in pain.

'About time,' he gasped as she pushed open the door to the bedroom. His sallow face was contorted in agony and he was trying to pull himself into a sitting position. 'I don't know what you're giving me but I think I need a lot more today.'

She couldn't move him, not while he was like this, he'd make far too much noise and she couldn't risk the neighbours hearing. Instead she went back downstairs and prepared a dose of Oramorph in warm tea. She considered sedating him, but if he was lucid and not in too much pain he might be able to clean himself with minimal intervention on her part.

'Here,' she said, passing him the drink. She sat in silence, watching him spill some of it down the front of his pyjamas, making no attempt to wipe his chin. When he'd finished he put the mug down on the bedside table and let out a deep breath.

'Give me a minute till it kicks in and then you can do whatever it is you've come up here for.' He stared at her rubber gloves. 'Hope those are for cleaning; it stinks in here.' Every word came with a wince or a grimace but he was making sense and was obviously in a stubborn mood. Not the best time to persuade him to have a shower.

'It's you that stinks,' Caroline said, looking at the stains on his rumpled pyjamas. 'That's why I'm wearing the gloves. You're toxic.'

He sneered at her. 'You're a fine one to talk. Do you think what you're doing to me is right? Keeping me doped up like this? What's the big plan? I'm dying anyway and it's not like you've got the guts to kill me. I suppose you're trying to make me sorry? What do you want; an apology? Not going to happen, love. You were as much a part of it all as I was.'

Caroline took off one of the gloves with a snap. 'I was nine!' she yelled, slapping him across the face with the damp rubber. 'How was I a part of it?'

He flinched back but his expression was unrepentant. 'You're as much to blame as I am.'

'And you've just lost your next dose of morphine. Let's see how you feel when you're in agony.'

His face went paler but his expression was defiant. 'Do your worst. See if I care.'

She grabbed at his filthy pyjama top, almost pulling him out of bed.

'Up! Now! You're having a shower. It'll not get rid of the poison but at least you'll not smell like a rotting pig.'

He shrank away from her, resisting her grasping hands.

'Get up!' she hissed, pulling him harder. He slipped sideways and his upper body sank to the bedroom floor, leaving his legs still under the duvet. Frustrated, Caroline grasped at his pyjama bottoms and flung his legs onto the floor to join his torso.

'If we have to do this the hard way I can guarantee that you'll have a night of agony,' she whispered, leaning so close to his face that he shrank away as she sprayed him with spittle. 'Now, at least *try* to get up.'

He rolled over and hauled himself onto all fours, breathing heavily. Slowly, he managed to raise his upper body so that he was kneeling up. Caroline grasped him under one arm and hauled him to his feet. He'd lost body mass since she'd been staying with him and his frail frame felt like that of a child. If she'd tried she could have probably slung him over her back and carried him to the bathroom fireman-style. They stumbled across the landing like a couple of drunks leaning on each other for support, and Caroline kicked open the bathroom door.

'Right, sit there.' She placed Dennis on the closed toilet lid and started to unbutton his pyjama top.

'I can do it,' he said, slapping her hands away.

'Fine. Get on with it.'

His hands shook as he laboured over each button until the garment was hanging loose from his shoulders like a becalmed flag. Caroline stepped towards him and stripped it from his upper body, flinging it out onto the landing.

'Bottoms.'

Dennis hesitated.

'Oh, come on. It's not like I've not seen it all before. Who do you think has been bathing and changing you in bed? The fucking fairies?'

He flinched at the profanity but clung to the waistband of his pyjama bottoms with a skinny claw-like hand.

'Oh fuck this!' Caroline said. 'I can easily just tip you in the bath and pull them off you.' She reached out to push him and he hurriedly let go of his pyjama bottoms, wriggling them down his hips. He eased his buttocks upwards and slipped the trousers down his wasted legs.

'Here. Have them.' He tried to throw them at her but they fell too short.

As she picked them up, Caroline realised that they were heavy with fresh urine. 'You did that on purpose, you dirty bastard.'

He just laughed as she hauled him up again and held him as he stepped into the bath, leaning on the wall to keep himself upright.

She chopped at his arm with the side of her hand and he yelled and lost his balance. Caroline caught him just before he crashed into the bottom of the bath and eased him down until he was lying on his back. She wanted to let him fall, wanted him to shatter into tiny pieces but she couldn't risk an injury that might look like she'd been neglecting him. Or worse. Caroline turned the shower on, knowing that the water would run cold for a few seconds but past caring about Dennis's comfort. She ran it on his face, up his nose, in his hair until he was shivering and spluttering. Instead of allowing it to get warm, Caroline turned the dial into the blue zone and continued to train the water on Dennis's prone body, running it from his face to his genitals and back again.

His jaw quivered as he struggled to stop his gums from chattering and his whole torso was a mass of goose pimples.

'Stop it,' he managed to croak.

'Sorry, can't hear you. What did you say?'

'Stop,' he said, louder this time. 'Just stop. I'll wash myself. I won't be any trouble.'

His lips were turning blue and the shivering was starting to subside. He was dangerously cold.

'Fine,' Caroline said and turned the heat up full.

The first scalding drops had Dennis writhing with a new agony. 'Stop it, Caroline. Just let me get up.'

She gave him one last blast of hot water on his groin and then turned the temperature down to something that he could tolerate.

'Get up, you stinking pile of shit,' she instructed. 'And I'm staying. I'm not having you falling and breaking a hip. I've come too far to have you back in hospital.'

She wiped the toilet lid with tissues and sat down, half watching her father as he soaped and rinsed. He barely resembled the man that she remembered. His flesh was grey and his thinning hair was unkempt. This man that she'd been afraid of for most of her life was nothing.

When she decided that she'd had enough, she turned off the shower and bundled Dennis into a towel, almost dragging him back to his bedroom. She sat him on a chair in front of the ancient dressing table and told him to dry himself while she changed the bedding.

'Your mum used to sit here a lot,' he said. 'When we were first married, she liked to make herself pretty whenever we went out. And then, after, she used to just sit, looking into the mirror like she didn't recognise her reflection. That's when I knew she was bad with her nerves.'

Bad with her nerves. The code he always used for depression. Her mother had been depressed for half the time that Caroline had known her. Gone were the smiles, the teasing, the little rhymes and songs that she used to sing. In their place was a shell of a person. She looked the same on the outside but she'd been hollowed out by what he'd done.

'Put these on,' she said, holding out a clean pair of pyjamas. She refused to be drawn into a conversation about her mother.

'I want to go back to sleep,' he said, struggling into the pyjama jacket. 'I'm tired now.' His voice was slurring, the effect of the extra morphine that Caroline had administered. She knelt in front of him and managed to get him into the pyjama bottoms without pushing him off the chair then she hauled him to his feet and pushed him towards the bed, leaving him in the position that he landed in. She threw the duvet over him, gathered the dirty bedding and left him to sleep. She added the soiled pyjamas to the bundle and went back downstairs.

The washing machine beeped as she set the programme for a hot wash that still wouldn't make everything properly clean – nothing could – the house and everything, everyone, in it was tainted.

It was time to end it.

JANUARY

CHAPTER 21

'Doctor Kailisa,' Kate said, answering her phone on the second ring. 'What can I do for you?'

'I think it's more what I can do for you. Do you have time for a visit? Dennis Lambert's results are back and they have shown up some interesting anomalies.'

Kate sighed. She didn't have time for this. 'Can't you just tell me over the phone?'

'I'd rather not,' Kailisa replied. 'There is some physical evidence that I would like you to see as well as the toxicology and fingerprint results. Can you call in today?'

'I can do better than that,' Kate replied, intrigued. 'I'm in the hospital now. I'll be down in about ten minutes.'

She explained to Hollis as they walked. It wasn't like Kailisa to be obtuse so whatever he'd found must be interesting. They weren't getting very far with the Maddie Cox investigation but a visit to the pathology lab might make up for the wasted time on the ward and if Kailisa said it was interesting, Kate was expecting fireworks. He was a master of understatement, making even the most outrageous injury or abnormality seem commonplace with his world-weary demeanour and his non-existent sense of humour. This could be good.

Kailisa was gowned and gloved when Kate and Hollis crashed into his domain. He gave them both a hard stare as though they were inconveniencing him even though he'd extended the invitation.

'I didn't realise that you'd be bringing company,' he said, glaring at Hollis like he'd never seen him before. Kate knew that Kailisa was precious about his lab and his victims and didn't enjoy sharing with anybody that he deemed less than worthy.

'I've got to learn sometime,' Hollis said. 'I've not been to many PMs and if I'm going to pick up anything it might as well be from the best.'

Kailisa gave him a wry smile, the transparent attempt at flattery not fooling him at all. 'Gowns and gloves, both of you. Oh, and DC Hollis?'

The DC gave him an amiable grin.

'Observe, learn, but keep your comments to a minimum, please.'

He led the way into the dissection room where Dennis Lambert's body was lying on a stainless steel table. Kate was surprised to see the corpse; she'd been expecting charts and numbers rather than any more physical findings. The pathologist stood at the head of the table and pointed to Lambert's mouth where the lips looked dry and had a purplish hue which stood out against the waxy grey of the rest of the face.

'After you left yesterday, I did further dissection of the lungs, checking for any signs of the disease having advanced further than we'd already seen. I found two tiny tumours and there was brown fluid in the upper bronchi and in the bronchioles of both lungs. A miniscule amount. I sent a sample for analysis and the results showed it to be a mixture of alcohol, probably whisky, water and an opiate.'

'That was quick,' Kate said. 'It's what Caroline Lambert said she left for him to drink. Whisky and Oramorph.'

'And tap water. There was no evidence of there being water next to Dennis Lambert's bed. Where did he get it from?'

'Residue in the glass?' Hollis suggested.

Kailisa shook his head. 'There is too much in the mixture for it to be a few drops in the bottom of the glass. I assumed that he might have gone to the bathroom and taken water from the sink in there.'

It was a possibility.

'However,' Kailisa continued. 'The blood work showed a high concentration of benzodiazepine. Enough for him to have had difficulty walking unaided.'

'What's–?' Hollis began to ask but Kate nudged his foot with her own. Kailisa didn't tolerate interruptions.

'The benzodiazepine is most likely the Diazepam that he had on prescription. I sent off hair follicles with the blood tests and they confirmed the presence of the drug. In fact they suggested that Dennis Lambert had been using Diazepam for some weeks prior to his death. In large doses. He would have been bed-bound almost from the time his daughter took him home.'

That didn't fit with what Brenda Powley had said. She'd definitely said that he'd been active up to his time in hospital. She'd been surprised at his sudden decline, but here was a possible explanation. Had his daughter been keeping him sedated?

'So how did he get the water?' Kailisa paused like a teacher expecting the correct answer from a member of his class.

'He didn't,' Kate responded. 'Somebody got it for him. Or somebody mixed the drink for him. It looks like Caroline wasn't being completely truthful.'

The pathologist nodded.

'Now, here.' He beckoned them both closer to the table. Pulling back Dennis Lambert's lips, he prised the mouth open. 'Look.' He shone a penlight inside the toothless cavity, scanning across the gum line. 'See?'

Kate remained silent. She had no idea what the pathologist was indicating. All she could see was shrivelled gums and a grey tongue.

'There is a row of tiny haemorrhages along the lower gum.' He reached round Kate and took a magnifying glass from the counter that ran along the back of the room. 'Try this.'

Kate leant forward, magnifying glass held up in front of her face, conscious that she looked like the stereotypical image of Sherlock Holmes, minus the deerstalker.

'Like this,' Kailisa said, grasping her wrist and lowering her hand towards the dead man's mouth. 'Lean in; he won't bite you.'

Was that humour? More like irritation, Kate thought, glancing at Kailisa's serious expression before leaning in further. She still couldn't make out what Kailisa had been describing. The gums were ridged with bumps and depressions where, she assumed, the teeth would have been: small blood vessels were dark blue against the pink-grey flesh. And then she saw what Kailisa had found. Tiny asterisk shapes, nearly invisible to the naked eye.

'You see them?' he asked. 'Could be from ill-fitting dentures, I've seen that before, but the dentures were not brought in with the body so I can't assess them properly.'

'Probably gathering dust in the evidence room somewhere,' she heard Hollis mutter.

'If I got you the dentures could you check?' Kate asked.

Kailisa shrugged, indifferent. This was obviously just another part of his theory. 'What else could they be?'

He picked up a glass from the counter and placed it against Dennis Lambert's lower lip. 'If I put pressure on the gums, there would be bruising. Even when the teeth have been absent for years, the flesh is quite tender with blood vessels close to the surface. You can make your gums bleed by brushing too hard so it's easy to imagine pressure from a glass causing some damage.'

Kate studied the position of the glass against the lips and gums. 'But wouldn't the pressure be even? Wouldn't it produce a long thin bruise rather than these pinpricks?'

Kailisa smiled, genuinely appreciative of her observation. 'But, as you can see, the surface of the gums has peaks and troughs where the teeth would have sat and the bruising is on the peaks. Imagine pressing your hand against a comb. You get tiny marks rather than one long line. It's the same but in reverse.'

'So he might have been forced to drink this concoction?'

'That would explain the liquid in the lungs. He may have choked.'

'Or he might have done that anyway. It's not a decision that anybody takes lightly. Isn't it possible that he gripped the glass with his gums to make sure that he went through with it? Forcing himself to do it. If he wasn't sitting up properly he could easily have choked on the first mouthful.'

Kate could see where he was going with this but he hadn't come up with anything that a good defence lawyer couldn't explain away if Caroline was formally charged with murder. At the moment the best they had was aiding and abetting under the Suicide Act but Kailisa's findings could change that if he had something that couldn't be so readily explained.

'I would have expected to see bruising on the top and bottom gums in that case but I understand your caution. Perhaps the fingerprint evidence will convince you.'

He leaned down, pulled out a drawer, and took out two sheets of paper and a glass bottle roughly the shape and size of a standard bottle of whisky.

'Caroline Lambert's fingerprints were found on the bottle and the glass. We expected that as she claims that she left them both on her father's bedside table. Dennis Lambert's fingerprints were also present although they were slightly smudged.'

'Presumably he'd used the bottle a few times. It was half empty, he might have been taking nips out of it for months.' Despite her fascination, Kate felt compelled to play Devil's advocate until Kailisa gave her something solid.

'I agree,' he said. 'But there was only one instance of each set of fingerprints. If he had been drinking from this bottle, he wiped it clean after every use.'

'That's ridiculous,' Hollis interjected. 'Who would do that? You pour a drink and put it back in the cupboard. Unless you're seriously OCD.'

Kailisa frowned at him. 'You're correct. Caroline Lambert's prints were clear but Dennis's were slightly blurred as if the bottle might have slipped in his hand.'

He passed the empty bottle to Hollis. 'Pour a drink please, DC Hollis.'

Hollis mimed a glass in his free hand and tilted the bottle, gripping it using the tips of his fingers and thumbs. Kailisa took the bottle, half-filled it from the tap and passed it back with a beaker for Hollis to use as a glass.

'Again, please.'

This time the extra weight forced Hollis to tighten his grip.

'See, this time you have to wrap your hand around the bottle to keep it steady. Dennis Lambert was frail and ill. He would have had difficulty holding the bottle, hence the smudged prints. However, there is no palm print on the glass or on the label and the fingerprints are widely spaced as in the first example of DC Hollis's pouring.'

'Meaning?' Kate asked, her brain trying to keep up.

'It is possible that somebody mixed the drink, forced the deceased to drink it, wiped the bottle and then realised their mistake. The bottle and glass would be checked for prints. They held Mr Lambert's hand to the glass but didn't consider the weight or the pouring position. Too much pressure could have caused the smudging.'

Kate tried to picture it. Caroline forcing the glass up against her father's mouth. Wiping the bottle and then panicking as she realised her error. She could have easily placed his fingers against the glass when he became unconscious. Was it enough? And would it make a difference? Did this make it murder or was Caroline Lambert still only guilty of aiding the suicide of a terminally ill man?

'I know you won't want to answer this,' she began. Kailisa gave her a tight smile. 'But do you think Caroline Lambert murdered her father rather than just left him with the means to take his own life?'

Kailisa sighed and looked down at the corpse. 'I just can't imagine a man with so much Diazepam in his system being able to walk to the bathroom and get water simply to make his final drink more palatable. I also can't imagine him being able to pour the whisky by holding the bottle in such a delicate grip. He would have dropped it. The Oramorph bottle doesn't help us, however, as it is smaller and the label is paper which is difficult to recover fingerprints from.'

Kate looked at Hollis who seemed lost in thought. 'What do you think?' she asked him.

He turned to Kailisa. 'Wouldn't there have been whisky and drugs on his pyjama top? If he'd choked, surely some of it would have dribbled out of his mouth?'

Kailisa walked over to a workbench and turned on his laptop. He tapped a few keys and then turned the screen so that Kate and Hollis could see it. It showed an image of a pyjama top laid on a white surface. Scattered around the neck area were a series of red dots.

'The cotton tested positive for alcohol and opiates. Some areas look like droplets, perhaps from his lips or chin; others are tiny and could have been emitted as Mr Lambert coughed to clear his throat and lungs.'

'But, again, that could have happened if he'd done this himself and taken too big a swig?'

Kailisa nodded slowly. 'It is possible but the pattern of droplets suggest that he was lying with his head propped up rather than sitting. If he'd been sitting we'd have expected the drops to be further down the pyjama top as they fell towards his lap.'

'And who tries to drink when they're lying down? Hollis said, excitement evident in his voice. 'She must've tried to pour it down his throat.'

It did all point in that direction, Kate had to admit, but getting a jury to believe it was a different matter. A good defence lawyer would probably come up with five or six different scenarios to explain Kailisa's findings. More than enough to instil reasonable doubt. Was it enough to re-arrest Caroline Lambert? Kate wasn't sure. She'd seen Kailisa in court, he was quiet and methodical and explained his findings carefully and thoroughly, but he refused to be drawn into speculation and that might go against them.

She rolled off her gloves and started pulling at her gown. Time to think. That's what she needed. Time to process and to come up with a strategy to take them forward.

'Thanks, Doctor Kailisa,' she said, almost as formally polite as the pathologist himself. 'You've given me a lot to think about.'

She threw her gown into a hamper next to the door and pushed open the glass doors which led her away from death and disease.

'Well?' Hollis asked, trotting after her like an eager puppy. 'Do we arrest her again? It's not looking good for her.'

Kate was just about to explain her uncertainties to the DC when her phone rang.

'Barratt? What have you got?' Kate continued her brisk pace down the corridor.

'Maddie Cox definitely attended the GA group that I went to last night. Everybody there knew her and the woman described fits the description from the son.'

'Anything useful. Had her demeanour changed over the last few weeks? Did she seem especially stressed or worried?'

'Nobody seemed to think so. They didn't know much about her personal life. Apparently that's not something she talked about. One member of the group thought that she was single and somebody else remembered that she had a son. It doesn't look like she was especially close to any of them. She usually arrived and left on her own.'

'Usually?'

'There was one incident before Christmas. A new member arrived and Maddie appeared to know her. She spoke to her after the meeting and they left together.'

Kate's pulse accelerated. She stopped walking. Could this be it? The connection between Maddie and Caroline Lambert?

'Did you get a description of this woman?' Kate asked, uttering a silent prayer to a God that she didn't believe in. Barratt was thorough, he loved details. She really hoped that this wasn't the one time where he overlooked something.

'Of course,' he said and she could hear from his tone that he was slightly offended that she might have doubted his competence. 'Late thirties, early forties. Well dressed. Minimal make-up but good bone structure. I'm quoting here. Short, fair hair. Tallish. I got the feeling that she made quite an impression on one of the group, he gave a detailed description.'

'Did he get a name?'

'It was a couple of months ago, and she hasn't been back since but he was fairly sure it was either Carol, Caroline or Karen.

Typical bloke eh? Remembers what she looked like but not quite sure about the name.'

'Excellent work, Barratt. I need you to talk to Ethan Cox and show him a photograph of Caroline Lambert, see if she was a friend of his mum. Show the same photo to this man from GA – I assume you took his contact details.'

'You think there's a link?' Barratt sounded incredulous.

'It's either one hell of a coincidence or there's a link between the two women that might help us find out what happened to Maddie.'

She hung up and turned to Hollis who was looking as stunned as she felt.

'There's another connection?'

She quickly filled him in on her conversation with Barratt, excited to see the sceptical frown replaced by a hopeful smile.

'We need to talk to Caroline Lambert,' he said. 'See what she can tell us about Maddie. We can test Kailisa's evidence on her as well, see what she has to say.'

'You get onto it. She was bailed to her own home in Sheffield. Don't ring in advance – just turn up. I don't want her prepared. Drop me off back at base on your way; I'm going to see what Sam's been digging up.'

CHAPTER 22

Cooper was at her desk when Kate got back to Doncaster Central, scowling at something on the screen. Rather than interrupt her, Kate went up to the top-floor cafeteria and grabbed coffee for them both. She tore the plastic lids from the tops of the takeaway cups and added sugar for herself and milk for Sam before cramming the lids back on and wandering over to the window.

Kate loved this view. When she was involved in a complicated case she sometimes felt like it was the only chance she got to notice the weather and the changing of the seasons. Now, deep in winter, the trees were skeletal and she could clearly see the buildings around her, including the museum – the site of many happy family outings when she'd been younger. The sky was iron grey and flat and the streets were streaked with red-brown dashes of salt to stop black ice from forming. She hadn't noticed the temperature when she'd been out earlier but she could see that it was set to fall again later and the sky was threatening more snow.

As she trudged back down to the second floor, she pondered the connection between Caroline Lambert and Maddie Cox. What was the link? Were they just both GA members who happened to have met at the hospital? Did GA members have sponsors – was that it? But wouldn't it have been unethical for Maddie to treat Dennis Lambert if she had some sort of personal relationship with his daughter? None of it made much sense when she considered that Caroline lived in Sheffield and had only been back in Doncaster for a couple of months. How could she have struck up a friendship with the nurse in such a short time? Unless there was something more sinister behind it – which is exactly what she needed Sam to investigate.

'Thought this might help,' Kate said, plonking the coffee on Cooper's desk, next to her keyboard. 'You looked like you were engrossed when I came in earlier so I didn't want to bother you.' Kate pulled up a chair and positioned herself so that she could see Sam's computer screen.

Cooper looked up, her eyes struggling to focus as if she wasn't quite sure where she was. She looked at the coffee then back at Kate. 'Oh, er... thanks. Must've lost track of time a bit.' She removed the lid from the coffee cup and took a sip. 'I've been checking Maddie Cox's phone records. Got them sent over earlier. Got her bank stuff as well.'

Cooper's typically terse conversation style had reduced to being virtually monosyllabic, and Kate wondered how much of that was fallout from the previous night. It must have been a shock to get home and find her girlfriend gone. She opened her mouth to offer some reassurance but, as though she could read Kate's thoughts, Sam launched into a detailed account of what she'd found, preventing Kate from saying anything further about the previous afternoon.

'Not many phone calls on her account. Mostly to Ethan. Same with texts. Some work stuff probably. Two calls on the day she went missing.'

'Made or received?'

'Made,' Cooper said. 'I've run them through a search engine. One's a pizza place near the market, Fabrio's, but I can't find the other.'

Kate leaned over in her chair and grabbed a thin sheaf of papers from her own desk. She shuffled through them until she found Caroline Lambert's contact details.

'Does this match?' she said, passing Sam the piece of paper and indicating the mobile number.

Cooper peered at her screen. 'Yep. Who is it?'

'Caroline Lambert.'

'The mercy killing woman?'

'The same.'

Sam shook her head. 'That doesn't make sense. What's the connection?'

'That's what Dan's gone to find out. He's on his way to Sheffield to pick Lambert up so we can ask her a few questions. We need to get somebody over to Fabrio's and find out if Maddie was there on the night that she died. Kailisa said that her stomach contents were consistent with pizza. Maybe she met somebody there.'

Sam grimaced at the mention of stomach contents, and Kate wondered if she was hungover. She looked tired and her eyes were slightly glazed. Her hands were steady on the keyboard though and she didn't smell of stale booze. Probably just tired.

'You okay?' Kate asked. Sam nodded, keeping her eyes fixed on the screen. 'You sure? Dan and I met Abbie yesterday. It looked like she was moving out.'

Cooper's face froze and Kate could see that her concern was unwanted. The DC had always been reluctant to discuss her personal life and never brought anybody to work events.

'I'm sorry,' she continued. 'It's none of my business.'

'No. It's not,' Cooper snapped, then blushed as she realised who she was talking to. 'It has nothing to do with my ability to do my job so can we please move on? I just don't want to talk about it.'

She tapped a couple of keys and her screen changed to what looked like bank account details. 'I've not had a thorough look at Maddie's bank details but there's one thing that stands out a mile. She was in debt. Most of her salary went on credit cards and she made a withdrawal of five hundred pounds every month at the same time.'

'That ties in with her GA attendance,' Kate said. 'Might be gambling debts. Was she close to paying off her cards?'

'Looks like it. But then, in early December, there's a payment of fifteen grand.'

'In or out?'

'In. And then it's taken out the next day. Looks like she took it out in cash as there's no recipient for the amount.'

Kate leaned closer, following the columns of figures until she found the amount that Sam was referring to; fifteen thousand pounds. Next to it was a bank sort code and an account number.

'Can we find out where it came from?'

'Should be able to. Finding the bank's easy enough from the sort code but we'll have to see how co-operative they are. They should give us a name but we might need to get a magistrate involved if we want access to the account.'

'A name might be enough,' Kate said. It was a considerable amount of money to pass through an account in a week. It smacked of fraud or money laundering but that made no sense. Why would a nurse be involved in anything like that? Perhaps somebody lent her the money to pay off another gambling debt.

'Find out the bank and branch,' she said to Sam. 'I think we might have found the link between Maddie Cox and Caroline Lambert.'

She watched as Cooper typed the numbers into a search site which promised to find any bank by its sort code. There it was. An HSBC branch local to where Caroline Lambert lived.

'What's the betting that Caroline gave her the money?' Kate asked. 'But what did she want in exchange?'

She thought about the PM findings. The blood tests and the fingerprint evidence didn't quite tally with Caroline Lambert's story and the long-term use of tranquillisers wasn't consistent with Dennis Lambert's condition. If Maddie had given Caroline drugs in exchange for the money, it would have been easy to have kept Dennis sedated and ultimately for Caroline to force him to drink a deadly cocktail of alcohol and morphine. But why? Was it really a mercy killing? Kailisa's results suggested that Lambert's cancer wasn't advanced enough to cause him to be bedridden and the pain should have been manageable with over-the-counter pain relief or small doses of morphine. Caroline had already confessed to murder but she'd been charged with aiding and abetting suicide;

was it all a cover? She could have murdered her father and made it look like she helped him to die in order to escape a custodial sentence. But why? He was going to die anyway. It made no sense.

Kate's phone rang. Barratt.

'I've shown the photograph to Ethan,' he began, dispensing with conversational pleasantries. 'He doesn't recognise her. But the guy from GA, Warren, is fairly sure that Caroline Lambert is the woman who attended a meeting in November or early last month and left with Maddie Cox.'

'Excellent,' Kate said. 'Are you in Donny?'

Barratt confirmed his location.

'Right. I'm going to text you a photograph of Maddie Cox. Get down to Fabrio's near the market and see if the two women were in there together on Tuesday evening.'

He made a joke about bringing back pizza for tea and hung up.

Kate scrolled through her contacts and called O'Connor. 'Got a job for you, Steve,' she said when he answered. 'You know most of the loan sharks out there, see if you can find out who Maddie Cox might have been in debt to. Probably for over ten grand. Ask if she paid it back at the beginning of December. If she didn't, then I want whoever gave her the money brought in here. I don't think her death was about money but Raymond'll kill me if I don't cover all the bases.'

O'Connor threw a few possible names at her, probably hoping to impress, and said he'd get onto them and then ended the call. Kate smiled to herself. She'd never known a police officer who was so proud of his dodgy connections. If O'Connor hadn't followed a career in law enforcement, Kate was sure that he'd have been a small-time gangster and even more sure that his arrogance would have led to him getting caught.

Jobs allocated, she turned back to Cooper.

'I need you to brainstorm something with me,' she said.

Cooper looked apprehensive.

'I have some ideas about the link between Caroline and Maddie but I need to bounce them off you to see if they make sense.

What if they met while Dennis was in hospital, became friends and Caroline offered to help Maddie out with money? They both went to Gamblers Anonymous as well so there's another possible point of contact. Then Caroline wants something in return. Drugs for her dad. She gets what she wants and uses them to kill him. Okay so far?'

Cooper looked sceptical. 'Why would she want to kill somebody who was dying anyway unless her story's true and it was a mercy killing?'

'I don't know. But Kailisa seems to think there are a few things about her story that don't add up. She might have been keeping him sedated for a while and she might have forced him to drink the whisky and morphine.'

'Okay. But I still don't get why. If she wanted his house to sell then all she had to do was wait. Same for any money he might have had. Why go to the bother when he's only got months left? Why speed it up and confess to helping him die?'

Kate kick-wheeled her chair back to her desk and logged into the computer. She did a quick search of recent cases of so-called 'mercy killing', unfamiliar with the vagaries of the law. The CPS had issued guidelines in 2009 which set out reasons why prosecution should and should not be considered despite the maximum sentence for assisting suicide still standing at fourteen years in jail. Since the new guidelines, Kate could find only one case of a successful prosecution for assisted suicide and a handful more which were still pending.

It had taken her ten minutes searching the internet to gather the information, which was easily available to anybody with an interest. Had Caroline Lambert visited the same websites? The criteria for prosecution suggested that she might escape with a fine or even have her case dismissed. She was known to the deceased, she wasn't a medical professional helping him, she didn't appear to have been paid by him, and there was no history of Caroline abusing her father. If Kailisa's findings could be disproved, then it was likely that she would walk away from this, and she probably knew it – which made sense of her dramatic confession. There wasn't even a case for her gaining financially as Dennis was going to die anyway.

'Bloody clever,' Kate muttered, drumming her fingertips on her desk top. 'But I still don't understand why you couldn't just wait.' She spun round in her seat. 'Sam. Why do people kill other people?'

Cooper turned to face her. 'Money, power, they're fucked up in the head, revenge…'

Money didn't feel right. Caroline Lambert lived in the most affluent part of Sheffield and could afford to lend thousands to somebody that she barely knew. Revenge. Was that at the heart of this case? But revenge for what? Brenda Powley had portrayed Dennis Lambert as a saint. The perfect family man. Worked hard and tried to keep his wife and daughter happy even after the loss of the elder daughter. Why would Caroline hate him enough to want him to die in pain? Kate checked the notes from the interview with the Powley woman. What had she said about the other daughter? She'd gone missing.

'Sam, did you find anything about Caroline's sister? I sent you a text after we'd interviewed Brenda Powley, thought it might be relevant.'

'Not much,' Sam admitted. 'A few newspaper articles. I could probably get hold of the case notes if you need them. They've not been digitised but there'll be a copy somewhere in the archives.'

'Just run through the bare bones for now,' Kate said. Getting hold of case files was a tedious process involving filling in forms in triplicate and following complicated chains of ownership, and she didn't want the hassle unless it was absolutely necessary.

Sam switched from the document she was viewing to a Word file. 'Jeanette Lambert. Aged fifteen. Reported missing by her father on the seventeenth of August 1986. She'd been out with friends and never came home. The friends said that she'd seemed "fine" and she'd left them at about eleven pm to go home. That's it.

No sightings, no follow-ups, she just vanished. The papers printed her picture but there was no television appeal. I suppose fifteen was close enough to being an adult so it was just assumed that she'd done a runner.'

Kate did a quick calculation. Jeanette Lambert would be in her mid-forties now. She'd have been at Thorpe Comp at the same time as Kate, a couple of years below her but they might have passed in the corridors or shared some of the same teachers. The name meant nothing but, out of fifteen hundred kids, Kate couldn't be expected to remember them all, even the ones from the same estate, not after thirty years.

'What about the mother?' she asked Cooper. 'She committed suicide.'

'1995,' Sam said. 'Took an overdose of sleeping tablets. I couldn't find out much else but the newspaper reports don't hint at anything suspicious. Do you think Dennis killed her? Could that be what this is about?'

Kate thought about it as a possible scenario. Brenda Powley suggested that Irene Lambert had been depressed since Jeanette disappeared. That would be hard to fake. The tablets would have been on a prescription. Surely a doctor would have flagged up anything suspicious. It was a possibility, but it didn't feel right. And why did she wait nine years? What the hell had happened in that house?

'Sorry, Sam,' Kate said. 'I think we're going to need the case file for Jeanette Lambert's disappearance and anything else you can find out about the mother's death.'

As Sam dialled the number for the records office, Kate's phone beeped. A text from Barratt confirming that Caroline Lambert and Maddie Cox had shared a table at Fabrio's and had left together on the night that Maddie had died.

'Shit,' Kate sighed. Caroline Lambert had become a suspect in a second murder.

Just as Kate was about to ring Hollis and update him, her phone rang.

'Dan. I was about to ring you. Lambert was with Maddie Cox on the night she died. You need to bring her in.'

Silence on the other end.

'Hollis? Dan?'

'I can't bring her in,' Hollis said. 'She's not here. The house is locked and her car's gone. The next-door neighbours haven't seen her since this morning. I think she's done a runner.'

JANUARY

Caroline,

I'm really worried about you. This is taking too long. You were supposed to spend a couple of weeks with him and then get it over with. He's got inside your head, hasn't he? I knew he would. He's the one in the wrong, Caroline. He always was. You're doing the right thing. You had a plan and you need to stick to it. You need to focus. Don't let him get to you like he did before. You really believed that you were as bad as him, didn't you? He convinced you that you were evil but you're not. You know that now. You're not that scared little kid anymore and you're stronger than him.

If you can't do it then leave. Don't let any more of his poison into your mind. You managed to convince me that getting rid of him was the right thing to do but you're not a murderer, I know that. Killing Dennis isn't murder though, it's justice. But it's not worth your sanity; it's not worth your integrity. Don't let this taint you, change you, make you less than you are. Stay strong and remember that I'm still here for you whatever the outcome.

Love
J

CHAPTER 23

The nights were finally drawing out. Not by much, but Caroline felt that she was putting the lights on slightly later every day. She thought about checking, just for something to relieve the monotony but it was too much effort, too much to remember.

The days were crawling glacially towards the end of January and she still hadn't found the courage or the determination to do what she'd set out to achieve. She was still feeding and washing Dennis when necessary, and he was still trying to engage her in conversation when he was lucid. She'd managed to keep Bren's visits to a minimum and hadn't seen her for a few days – not since she'd popped in to wish Dennis a belated happy New Year which seemed a little pointless as he had nothing to look forward to. Caroline had accused her of being cruel but Bren was defiant in her well-wishing and even gave him a kiss. If she noticed that he was a bit fragrant she'd obviously decided not to comment.

It was Bren's interference that Caroline was most worried about. It would be like her to call social services to cause trouble and let Caroline know that she was being watched. The GP had visited last week, after a call from Caroline. She knew from her research that she needed her father to have been seen by his doctor if this was going to work. They wouldn't take her word for the speed of Dennis's deterioration.

Fortunately the doctor had given Dennis a perfunctory examination. The sedatives that Caroline had given him that morning made him compliant but he wasn't really lucid. She'd explained that this was a regular occurrence and the doctor had listened sympathetically and told her to keep him rested and clean.

He'd asked about pain management and Caroline explained that the paracetamol didn't always work. He'd written a prescription for codeine and suggested that she administer it regularly and then he'd left.

She had more than enough drugs to keep him calm and comfortable but she didn't actually want him to be either. She really had to make a decision and do something.

Looking out of the kitchen window, she could see shadows forming on the roof of the house opposite. The chimney cast a thin block of black across the red tiles like the gnomon from a sundial. She'd once been able to tell the time by this shadow but she didn't enjoy looking outside. The garden taunted her.

He'd told everybody that he was doing it for Irene; only Caroline and her father knew the truth. She could still make out the remains of the flowerbeds, grassed over but still identifiable as hummocks in the otherwise flat lawn like ancient archaeological earthworks – or abandoned graves.

After Jeanette, the garden had been a riot of colour as though the brightness of the flowers could fill the gap left by her sister. The wildflower bed attracted bees and butterflies and the roses could have won awards if her mum had had any interest in showing them. But her mum had remained resolutely indoors despite her husband's encouragement. She wouldn't tend the garden and she couldn't even look at the greenhouse.

Dennis always talked about the structure as if it was his pride and joy; some great achievement that he had completed like a Herculean labour for the woman that he loved. It had taken him three weeks from digging the foundations to putting in the last pane of glass. He'd done it mostly by himself, including laying the flagstone base and cementing round the edges; apart from the night that he'd made Caroline help him. She'd made one other contribution though, and she had always been convinced that Dennis had never noticed it. In the wet concrete, next to one of the corner struts of the table, she'd inscribed initials. It was tiny, a miniature hieroglyph that contained as big a secret as those on Tutankhamen's tomb.

She'd protested and cried when he'd made her pour concrete and flatten it down but he'd silenced her with the same threat that had kept her quiet for more than thirty years. A threat he'd used just a couple of days earlier when they spoke about the events of that summer. A threat which had finally convinced her that he was beyond redemption and without remorse.

Her phone rang, interrupting the flow of memory and she grasped at it in relief, like a drowning sailor clutching a lifeline. The name on the screen wasn't a surprise. She'd been getting these calls for a few days and ignoring them.

'Maddie, what a surprise,' Caroline answered, eschewing the usual greeting.

'We need to talk,' the nurse said. 'You've been putting me off for days and I have to see you. I'm scared shitless that there's going to be an audit and somebody will find out what I've been doing. My career could be on the line.'

She sounded frantic and out of control as if she was in fear of her life, but it was just her job. If she got fired there'd be other jobs.

Caroline struggled to keep the contempt out of her voice as she responded. 'Calm down. You've done nothing wrong. Prescribing drugs is your job.'

'Calm down?' Maddie yelled. 'How can I calm down? I can't believe I let you talk me into this. Look, I'll give you the money back. You said the first time that it would be the last then you came back for more. How many more times are you going to ask me to risk my career for a few grand? I can't believe I've been so stupid.'

Caroline held the phone away from her ear, letting the other woman rant for a minute more. When she finally started to calm down, Caroline interrupted. 'Maddie? Maddie? You need to get a grip. I told you last time that that would be it. There'll be no more prescriptions, no more demands. It's done, okay? It's over.'

Silence.

'You mean… he's dead?'

'No. He's alive. But probably not for much longer. Things got a lot worse over Christmas. He's going downhill rapidly.'

'I'm still worried.'

Caroline had to use every scrap of her willpower not to throw the phone at the wall. She needed to be able to think without interruption. 'What about?'

'I already told you. We could be audited at any time and I might not be able to hide what I've done for you.'

'In which case, blame me. Say I blackmailed you.'

'I'll still lose my job.'

'But you won't go to prison. Let me take the flak.'

'I don't know. That might not work. And, anyway, I don't trust you. I think I might have to go to the police and tell them what happened. I can't sleep and I'm not eating properly. I need this to be over and done with. We need to talk properly, not over the phone. Can you get away tonight? Is there somebody to look after your father?'

'I'll arrange something,' Caroline said. 'Don't go to the police yet. Let's talk and see if we can make sense of this. There'll be a way out for you, I'm sure.'

More silence.

'You still there, Maddie?'

A sob from the other end of the line.

'Maddie. Look. I'll meet you later. Just name the time and place. We'll sort it out.'

'Somewhere public,' Maddie said. 'Somewhere where you can't intimidate me.'

'Fine. You choose. Listen, I need to get back to my father now. Text me the details.'

She hung up without allowing Maddie the chance to say anything else. The nurse didn't know it but she'd just forced Caroline's hand. With Dennis out of the way, the police would have a difficult time proving anything beyond a mercy killing and she was prepared to confess to that. She might even avoid jail if she played it right – the grieving child who just couldn't bear to see her father suffer any longer, something like that. If not she would probably only be sentenced to a few months and then she'd be free to get on with her life.

A text pinged onto her phone. Maddie again. Fabrio's at eight. It was a cheap Italian restaurant but always popular; Maddie hadn't been kidding when she said she wanted to meet somewhere public. Caroline checked her watch. It was 4.15. Plenty of time.

An hour later, she'd cleaned Dennis up and stripped his bed. She'd checked him carefully for any bruises or incriminating marks but there was nothing. She'd been careful. Hitting him through the pillow had started an avalanche of slaps and pinches but she'd managed to rein in her temper over the past few days and there was nothing obvious to suggest that she'd been abusing him. She wasn't always sure that he could feel it anyway so it felt a bit pointless. Unlike the times she stopped his medication and only gave him whisky and water to drink. The pain was etched into every line in his face when the morphine wore off and the more he drank to try to dull the pain, the worse it got. But even the sight of him writhing in agony was growing stale. She'd expected to get some satisfaction from watching him suffer, some release but, instead, she was tired and bored.

She looked down at the bedding in her arms and thought about putting it in the washing machine but she couldn't see much point. Instead she balled everything up and threw it in the laundry basket in the bathroom. He complained throughout; not always coherently but she managed to get the gist. He didn't want her there anymore. He hated her. He was going to call the police. She tried to ignore his more outrageous threats and managed to get him back into a clean bed with as little fuss as possible, being especially careful when she handled him, allowing him to do most of the work, in case any bruises showed up later.

She couldn't seem to think past what she was about to do. There was *now* and there was *later* but later everything would be different and she could only control what happened now.

Leaving Dennis dozing in bed, she went to her bedroom and opened the cupboard where she'd been keeping the morphine. She took it downstairs to the kitchen, placed it on the table and took a spoon from the drawer under the sink, placing this next to the bottle. Standing on one of the kitchen chairs, she reached up to a high cupboard with a sliding door. This had been Dennis's 'secret' cupboard for as long as she'd lived in the house. She was never allowed access to its contents and she'd rarely caught a glimpse of what lurked inside. She knew exactly what it contained – just as she knew the exact contents of every cupboard and drawer in the whole house. She took out Dennis's bottle of Ardbeg whisky – his favourite, from Islay. She'd allowed him to drink one of the blends that he kept in the sitting room but, like her father, she'd been saving this one for a special occasion.

She placed the whisky next to the Oramorph and the spoon. 'Cocktail hour,' she muttered to herself.

She wasn't sure about the dosage. She'd been keeping the morphine light, sometimes going back to over-the-counter codeine and paracetamol which seemed to work reasonably well, but she wanted to keep this final dose clean and simple. He was already sedated but the Diazepam tended to start to wear off around teatime and she'd been used to giving him more with his meal. Not today though.

She took a clean glass from the draining board – a tumbler, plenty of room for a huge dose – then she sat down at the kitchen table suddenly overwhelmed by the enormity of what she was about to do. It wasn't like she hadn't planned it, fantasised about it even, but the reality wasn't quite as she'd expected. She checked her watch. Somehow she'd lost nearly an hour. She could have sworn she'd sat at the table at 5.15 but her watch said that it was nearly six pm. She needed to move, to be decisive.

The whisky opened with a hollow pop as she eased out the cork. The bottle was over half full and she was tempted to take a gulp before she poured it into the glass. Steeling herself, she resisted the urge and held the neck of the bottle over the tumbler. As the two made contact, the glass surfaces chattered together. Her hands were shaking. She poured a generous amount into the glass, swilled it around speculatively then poured more, doubling the original measure. The tumbler was nearly a third full.

Caroline slid the cork back into the bottle and picked up the Oramorph. It was new and the top crunched as she broke the seal. She added half of the contents to the whisky. Would it be enough? She had no way of knowing. She'd looked up lethal dosages of morphine but she couldn't remember anything that she'd read. She added more, just a small amount; it would have to do. She stood up and walked over to the sink. Turning on the cold tap, she topped up the glass until the liquid was only half an inch from the top.

It didn't look unpleasant. The whisky and morphine had combined to create an amber liquid that looked a lot like cold tea. She hoped that the water might make it more palatable – not that she intended to allow Dennis any option.

There was nothing else to do; nothing else to prepare. She was ready.

The hallway was in darkness but she decided to leave the lights off as she climbed up to Dennis's bedroom. She didn't want the sudden illumination to alert him to her approach and she knew from experience how to avoid the noisiest parts of the staircase. Jeanette had taught her well.

'Dennis?' she whispered, pushing the door open.

The figure in the bed stirred.

'I've brought you a drink.'

She placed the glass on the bedside table and switched on the lamp.

'But, before you drink it, I want to talk to you about Jeanette.'

Dennis struggled to sit up, his eyes wide and unfocussed. Caroline thought he must have been deeply asleep before she had disturbed him. Oh well. Plenty of time for sleep later.

'Do you remember Jeanette?' she asked. 'My sister? I really loved her. She taught me swear words. She told me about boys and sex. Not that I believed her at the time. She was incredible. She was bright and funny and talented. I've missed her all my life. Do you miss her, Dennis?'

His rubbery lips moved as he tried to form words but nothing came out.

'No, I don't suppose you do. I used to talk to her you know, after she'd gone. Nearly every night when I went to bed. I used to tell her things that had happened at school. Funny stuff, mostly, but sometimes the difficult things. The bullying and the tormenting. I even talked to her when Mum died and I was old enough to know better. Funny, really.'

Dennis was shaking his head as if he couldn't quite make sense of what she was saying. Finally he appeared to get his thoughts together enough to speak. 'You were always my favourite, Caroline. And your mum's. Jeanette was a bit wayward. I'm glad you weren't like her.'

'Wayward!' Caroline spat. 'She was a teenager. She was normal.'

He flinched away from her outburst, his eyes glued to her face as though anticipating a slap.

'Anyway, that's ancient history,' Caroline said, holding up the glass. 'I've brought you something special. A cocktail. I think you'll like it.'

She held it out to him and he sniffed it suspiciously.

'Not thirsty,' he mumbled.

'Tough shit. You're going to drink it.'

Caroline sat on the edge of the bed and held the back of his head. Wrapping her fingers through what little hair he had left, she tilted his face upwards and put the glass to his lips.

'Drink it!'

He clamped his lips shut and shook his head like a toddler refusing to eat his greens. Caroline responded by letting go of his hair and pinching his nostrils closed. He tried to pull away from her but she was much stronger.

Finally he opened his mouth to breathe and Caroline poured a small amount of her concoction towards the back of his throat. He sputtered and coughed but most of it seemed to go down. Twice more she forced him to open his mouth while she pressed the glass against his toothless gums and poured.

After the third attempt, his jaw went slack and she was able to give him more. He swallowed without complaint until the glass was empty.

'Satisfied?' he rasped, his eyes already glazing over.

Was she? She didn't know how she felt. Not elated or jubilant as she'd expected. More relieved like she'd been carrying something heavy in a sack across her shoulders and she'd finally been allowed to put it down. She stood up without speaking to him, placed the glass carefully on the bedside table, and went back downstairs.

Time to think. She needed to make it look like she'd been trying to do the decent thing; to stop Dennis's suffering and to allow him to die without pain. Her fingerprints would be all over the bottles and the glass. Would it look like she'd made the drink and then made him drink it? Would the police be able to tell how she'd held it to his mouth from the position of her fingers? She had no way to know.

She reached under the sink for a duster and wiped both bottles carefully before taking them upstairs. Dennis was breathing but each inhalation was deep and ragged. He looked like he was asleep but he could just as easily have been unconscious. Caroline checked her watch. She'd have to wait it out for a little while until it was time to meet Maddie.

She used the duster to wipe the glass and then a thought struck her. If Dennis was supposed to have mixed the drink for himself how come his prints weren't on the glass or the bottles? She picked up the Ardbeg, picked up Dennis's right hand with the duster and tried to clamp his fingers around the bottle. Then she repeated the process for the empty glass and the Oramorph. Would that be convincing? But how did he get the bottles and glass into the bedroom? She'd intended to say that she'd brought them. But she'd wiped off her prints. If she picked up the glass, would her prints be on top of his? Would the police be able to tell? Her mind spun out of control as she tried to think her way through every possible scenario.

In the end, she picked up each item again, leaving her fingerprints, and placed them neatly back on the bedside table.

Then she retrieved the Diazepam from her bedroom – no need to hide them now – and put them next to the bottles.

Dennis's breathing had slowed further and was hitching in his chest. His right hand suddenly lifted up from the duvet and twitched in the air as though he was conducting an invisible orchestra then it settled again. Caroline sat down on the edge of the bed, removed the hand from the top of the duvet and tucked it underneath, shuddering involuntarily as she touched Dennis's clammy skin. Pulling the covers up to his chin, she got up again and looked around the room. There was nothing else that she could do. It might take hours to find out if the cocktail had been lethal; hours that she didn't have.

A glance at her watch told her that she had less than an hour to get into Doncaster and meet Maddie.

Leaving Dennis struggling for breath, Caroline went into her bedroom to get changed.

CHAPTER 24

Fabrio's was a Doncaster institution. Caroline couldn't remember a time when it hadn't occupied its corner spot near the marketplace. It was where teenagers celebrated sixteenth and eighteenth birthdays, sometimes with friends, sometimes enduring the mortification of a night out with their parents. Family-orientated with a quick turnover of tables, it wasn't the place for a romantic liaison or a clandestine meeting but Maddie had obviously chosen it because she felt safer talking to Caroline somewhere public and crowded.

The smell of garlic and herbs greeted Caroline like an old friend as she pushed open the door, and the warmth was almost overwhelming after the chill of the streets. She'd deliberately arrived late so that she wouldn't have to sit on her own while she waited for Maddie to join her, and she quickly scanned the busy tables looking for the nurse amongst the crowd. Many of the tables were occupied by celebrating families. Balloons floated up from one, trailing curled paper and silver confetti. Another was strewn with wrapping paper; a teenage girl sat among the debris, surrounded by a fortress of boxed presents. The L plates and fancy dress of a hen party dominated the furthest corner; obscenities, in lowered voices out of respect for the clientele, punctuated with peals of loud laughter.

Maddie was sitting in one of the booths opposite the door. Enclosed on three sides by the wall and high wooden partitions, they were the closest that Fabrio's offered to privacy. She looked up from the menu as Caroline approached but didn't smile. 'Thought you might not come.'

'I said I'd be here. I agree with you. I think we need to talk.'

Maddie looked surprised. She'd obviously been expecting some resistance or reluctance so Caroline's compliance seemed to puzzle her. 'You do? I got exactly the opposite impression when we spoke earlier. In fact I've had the impression that you've been ignoring my calls.'

Caroline slid onto the bench seat opposite Maddie and picked up a menu. 'I was. I've been busy. I'm sure you understand the challenges of caring for somebody with terminal cancer.'

Maddie scowled at her. 'Of course. But I don't use it as an excuse not to communicate when it's important.'

'It's not an excuse, it's an explanation,' Caroline said. 'I don't need an excuse. Is the plan to eat here or just have a drink and a chat? I haven't eaten all day and their pizzas are fantastic.'

'Have what you want,' Maddie said, shaking her head in bewilderment. 'It makes no difference to me.'

They both studied their menus. Caroline realised that she had been telling the truth when she'd said she was hungry; suddenly everything on the menu looked appealing and she was torn between pizza and pasta. Her appetite hadn't been very good since she'd been looking after Dennis and she was aware that she'd lost weight; she'd had to put another notch in her belt and some of her jumpers hung off her like sails from rigging on a calm day. She'd need to do some shopping as soon as she found time.

A waitress appeared and asked if they wanted drinks. Caroline ordered a glass of red but Maddie's order was interrupted by a scream from the hen party table. The waitress sighed and rolled her eyes, obviously having a difficult evening.

'Thought things would be quiet after New Year,' Caroline said.

'You'd think,' the waitress said, turning to her, the light sparking on the diamond stud in her nose. 'It's *never* quiet, though.'

She took Caroline's drink order, jotted down a half of lager for Maddie and was about to leave when Caroline said, 'Hang on. I know what I want to eat. Can we order now?'

Maddie looked surprised but Caroline didn't feel like waiting. She ordered dough balls and a pizza, waited until Maddie had ordered, and then added mixed olives and a salad.

'Looks like all this caring has made me hungry,' she joked but Maddie's expression didn't change.

They sat in silence until the waitress brought their drinks. Caroline scanned the room, aware that Maddie was studying her closely. Caroline was reluctant to engage in conversation until she had thought about what she intended to do about the nurse's suggestion that they go to the police. Eventually Caroline grew irritated by the other woman's staring. 'What? Have I grown another head or something?'

A smile flickered around Maddie's lips but then faded. 'No. I'm just trying to work out what sort of person you are. I don't know if I can appeal to your better nature, if you have one, because everything that I've seen so far suggests that you're a calculating, scheming bitch.'

'Whoa,' Caroline said, genuinely shocked. She hadn't expected Maddie to be like this; she'd only seen her as submissive and resigned to her position. This was new.

'What else am I supposed to think?' the nurse continued. 'You encouraged me to accept money from you and didn't tell me it came with conditions. Then you got me to risk my career and I'm not sure why. I haven't a clue what's really going on but I want it to end. That's why I wanted to talk to you.'

Before Caroline could respond the starters arrived. 'Food's good here,' Caroline commented, trying to shift the conversation until she could formulate a strategy. She knew that Maddie was right; she had seriously jeopardised her career, but that wasn't Caroline's problem. She didn't want the nurse to go to the police, especially as she was planning to contact them herself if Dennis hadn't survived the night, but Caroline wasn't sure how to stop her. She could offer more money but she suspected that Maddie had too much integrity to accept.

Starter plates cleared, the pizzas arrived and they looked just as good as Caroline remembered. Ignoring her side salad, she used her hands to tuck in, relishing the gooey cheese and rich tomato sauce. Part of her wondered how she could enjoy food so much after what she'd done but another part realised that her appetite was probably a reaction to the stress of the past few weeks. She'd done the hardest part and she was left feeling light, free.

'How is he?' Maddie asked around a slice of pizza. 'Your dad. Is he coping? I'm guessing from the morphine that he's in a lot of pain. He must have deteriorated fairly quickly after he was discharged.'

Caroline spotted the weakness immediately. Maddie's training had conditioned her to care, whatever the circumstances. No matter that she'd presented a hard exterior, her sympathy was her flaw. Caroline knew that she could wiggle her way into the crack, exploit it, set a charge and detonate it if necessary.

'He's not great,' she said, trying not to smile at the enormity of the understatement. 'He's been in a lot of pain and he asks for the morphine quite regularly.'

'You're careful, though. You don't give him more than the recommended dose?'

Caroline thought about the morphine that she'd mixed with the whisky. 'No. I've read the documentation in the box and even done some research online.'

'And is he still aware of what's going on?'

Caroline took another bite of pizza, chewing slowly, considering her response. 'Mostly,' she said. 'He has some periods when he's not sure who I am but he's usually fairly lucid. He mistook me for my mother once. Forgot that she died.'

'And the sedatives? Does he need those?'

'They help him to sleep. I only use them at night if he's had an especially bad day,' Caroline lied. 'I don't want him to be doped up all the time.'

Maddie shook her head in confusion. 'When you talk about your dad you seem so reasonable, but that time you persuaded me to give you the second prescription you were like a different person. That's why I wanted to meet here. I don't know which version of you is real.'

They continued eating, Caroline pondering what Maddie had just said. She was right to be confused. Caroline was confused. This was supposed to have been so simple. When she had heard that Dennis was dying, she swooped back into his life, intent on making the process as painful as possible. But she'd blackmailed a nurse and tortured her father for weeks only to discover that the end had given her no satisfaction and now she couldn't go back to her old life.

If Dennis were dead when she got home then she'd phone an ambulance and hand herself into the police. She'd done her research, courts were usually lenient in 'mercy killing' cases, as long as nobody could prove definitively that her account was a lie, that she'd actively murdered her father rather than just giving him the means. She might even get away with a suspended sentence.

Maddie could be an obstacle, though. If she insisted that they go to the police then questions would be asked about the amount of drugs Caroline had acquired and what she'd been using them for since Dennis had been released from hospital.

'I suppose they're both real,' Caroline said, responding to Maddie's question. 'I've done my duty in caring for my father but I've not been very ethical in the way I've gone about it.' She wiped her lips with a napkin. 'And I'm not going to go to the police. Not yet. I have to bury him first, then I can face the consequences.'

Maddie's expression tightened as she took in the enormity of Caroline's statement. 'Bury him? He's dead, then? I thought you said…'

'I'm not sure. His breathing was getting slower and shallower when I left.'

'You should have rung me, cancelled. I'd have understood.'

Would you? Caroline thought. *Would anybody really have understood?*

'Look,' Maddie said, wiping her mouth and standing up. 'I want to be angry but I know that now's not the time. We'll go to the police when this is over. I can accept whatever's coming to me if you can.'

Caroline nodded, trying to think her way out of the situation. If she went to the police and confessed to blackmail to save Maddie she'd almost definitely be jailed. Acquiring the drugs by coercion would indicate premeditation. Murder carried a much longer sentence than assisted suicide. Why should she confess? The nurse was nothing to her. She hadn't been part of the plan at first; she was just collateral damage.

'Let me give you a lift home,' she offered, trying to buy herself more time. 'We can talk about it in the car.'

Maddie tried to protest but Caroline had already left fifty pounds on the table and was shrugging on her coat.

'Come on. Five minutes. I think I've got a better plan which will keep both of us out of trouble.'

Maddie had still been reluctant to get in the car despite the wind that was knifing through the streets. The pavements were already glazing with frost and the sky was blue-black and clear. Caroline managed to get Maddie to agree to a lift home after she'd slid twice on the icy cobbles of the marketplace. She gave Caroline her address and got into the passenger seat of the BMW, sitting as far away from Caroline as possible.

They'd just set off to the west of the town when Maddie asked, 'So what's this great plan?'

'Just wait,' Caroline said, negotiating a tricky junction and turning onto the narrow lane that ran beside the canal. She checked her mirrors and then pulled into a parking place that allowed access to the bank side.

'What're we doing here?' Maddie asked. Caroline wasn't sure. She'd been driving on instinct; trying to make some sense of the situation but she couldn't see a way out for herself that didn't involve getting arrested and jailed.

'Get out!' Caroline spat. 'Get out of my car! You can walk home. Go to the police if you want but it won't do you any good. I'll just deny everything.'

'It's pitch black,' Maddie said. 'You were going to take me home. I can't walk from here, it's not safe.'

'I don't care,' Caroline said. 'I just want you out of my car and out of my life.'

Barely thinking, Caroline released her own seatbelt, grabbed Maddie's bag and leapt out of the door, slamming it behind her.

'Hey!' Maddie yelled. 'What the hell, Caroline? What're you doing?' There was a satisfying tremble in her voice.

'Come and get it, then,' Caroline taunted, pushing through a gap in the hedges and setting off at a jog along the towpath. The moon was three quarters full and the path was almost floodlit by its brightness. She took a few more steps and then slowed as she saw the lights around the lock up ahead. She had no idea what she was doing. Somewhere in her mind she thought that if she could really frighten Maddie, threaten her, whatever, she might be able to convince her not to go to the police. Luring her to somewhere dark and remote would be a good start but she wasn't sure what she could do to ensure Maddie's silence. A crunch of gravel behind her. The other woman was following.

Caroline stooped and rummaged around in the hedges searching for a weapon. Anything would do, a rock, a broken bottle. A house brick! She couldn't believe her luck as she clasped her hand round the sweaty-smooth surface.

Maddie was catching up.

Caroline sprinted off towards the lock, hoping that her memory of the area was accurate. She'd been there a few times as a kid, with her parents and Jeanette because her mum liked to watch the boats; she liked the colours and the buckets of flowers on the roofs.

As soon as Caroline reached the first black and white gate, she stopped. She could just make out Maddie's dark shape lumbering towards her, her breath rasping in the frigid air. Caroline knew what she needed to do. No time to think about it. No time to change her mind. This was the only way. If she got rid of the nurse then there was nobody to question her treatment of Dennis. The extra prescriptions would probably never be spotted. Why would anybody look once Dennis was dead? She stuffed Maddie's bag under her jacket assuming that it contained the nurse's phone and keys and she hoped that all her ID was inside. If Maddie fell in the canal and drowned it might take days for the police to identify her, weeks even. It might even be written off as an accident. And, by then, they wouldn't be interested in her connection with Caroline's case – if they even made one. She had no choice.

'Caroline. Give me my bag back. This is stupid.'

Caroline laughed. 'I've thrown it in the lock. You can fish it out if you want.'

She walked away, further down the towpath so that Maddie wouldn't feel threatened as she peered into the water.

'What the fuck did you do that for? My whole life's in that bag!'

She edged towards the lock, stopping a foot away so that she could peer down. Caroline slowly walked towards her; quietly, rocking on her feet heel to toe, heel to toe, until she was practically next to her.

Maddie looked round, her eyes widening in shock.

Caroline raised her hand and swung the brick but Maddie had taken a step to the side and she simply staggered backwards, maintaining her balance.

'What the hell?'

Caroline lunged again but Maddie was prepared and grabbed her, twisting her round and pushing her away.

'Caroline. Stop!'

Infuriated, Caroline paused, bent over, as she tried to suck the icy air into her lungs. This wasn't going to work. Maddie could see what she was trying to do.

Caroline raised her head, her breathing much calmer. 'I'm sorry. I don't know what came over me. I'm so tired and stressed.'

She lowered her voice and tried to make it tremble as if she was trying to hold back tears. 'I can't cope anymore. I don't know what to do for my dad and I don't know how to keep us both out of trouble.'

Maddie glared at her sceptically. 'So you thought you'd attack me? What the hell is wrong with you, Caroline? Put the brick down and take me home. I don't think you know what you're doing.'

It was working. Caroline detected a tiny hint of sympathy in Maddie's curt tone. 'Let's get your bag back,' Caroline said pretending to look over the side of the canal.

'You look. I'm not coming anywhere near you.'

'I think it's under there,' Caroline said, pointing into the dark water near Maddie's feet. Maddie leaned forward for a clearer view and Caroline seized her chance. She raised her hand and smashed the brick into the back of Maddie's head as hard as she could, pushing her towards the edge of the lock with the other hand. A satisfying splash and then silence. She peered down into the gloom watching as the ripples from Maddie's body swelled out towards the lock's concrete sides where they broke and died.

Caroline smiled to herself as she walked slowly back to her car.

Another loose end tied up.

CHAPTER 25

'Nice place,' Kate said as they pulled up outside Caroline Lambert's Sheffield home and climbed out of the car. It was set back slightly from the narrow lane which linked two busier roads through Dore and it looked like it was probably quite old. The surrounding houses looked like more recent additions to the land but this house had authority; it looked like it belonged there. A large, detached house, it nestled among a swathe of laurels and beech hedges, partly hidden from the lane. The double front looked like a disapproving face as the windows of the upper storeys glared down at them, and the mouth of the door was a vertical slash of disapproval.

'Not bad,' Hollis agreed. 'More than either of us could afford.'

'Better keep playing the lottery, then,' Kate said. 'Or apply for a Chief Super's job.'

Hollis laughed. 'Can't decide which is the most likely to happen. The lottery probably. Can't really see myself as a pen pusher and media whore.'

'I dunno,' Kate said, looking up at him. 'Pretty boy like you. The cameras would love you.'

She was tense. Forcing entry into a house was always fraught with difficulties, and she'd never enjoyed the feeling of being an intruder. Bantering with Hollis was helping with some of the strain but she knew that they were only putting off the inevitable.

It felt like it had taken an age to convince Raymond that they needed access and then another century or so before he could persuade a friendly magistrate to issue a warrant but, checking her watch, she was surprised to see that it was only early afternoon. Cooper was back at base trawling the CCTV from the area, hoping to work out where Caroline had gone. She'd handed in her passport to the local police station so, unless she'd bought a fake, she was still in the country. Barratt was on his way from Thorpe after checking Dennis Lambert's house – no sign of Caroline there, but the DC had been accosted by Brenda Powley and forced to drink tea and eat biscuits.

Kate was beginning to feel like her team were coming together as a unit. Each had their strengths: Hollis was shaping up to be a sensitive interviewer, Sam was great with data, and Barratt was methodical and thorough. She was still stuck with O'Connor though, who was a law unto himself. At least she'd tasked him with something that he was good at, dealing with low-level criminals and unscrupulous loan sharks. She hadn't had anything back from him yet but, if there was information to be had about Maddie Cox's gambling debts, O'Connor would find it.

'Come on, let's get this done,' she said to Hollis, striding up the path to the front door. She knocked sharply three times and waited, not expecting there to be any answer but following protocol and allowing any residents time to respond. When there was no reply, she knocked again, waited for a count of thirty seconds then raised a hand to the uniformed officers waiting in a van across the street and gestured to the back of the house.

She led Hollis round the side of the building into the back garden, studying possible entrance and exit points. Although she was convinced that Caroline Lambert had fled, Kate needed to be sure that she didn't come bursting out of a back door as the uniforms forced entry into the front. There was only one back door which looked as tightly locked as the front but, just to be sure, she donned nitrile gloves and tried the handle.

'Locked,' she said to Hollis who raised his eyebrows in mock surprise.

'There's a shocker.'

Kate smiled and stepped closer to the nearest window to peer inside. Beyond the glass the kitchen was empty and immaculate suggesting that Caroline Lambert hadn't left in a hurry – she'd had time to leave the place clean and tidy. A shout from the front of the house indicated that the front door had been opened with the 'big key', and she and Hollis rushed back round to start their search.

The hallway was packed with what estate agents loved to call 'period features'; a dark wood parquet floor, flanked by deep skirting boards and, about three-quarters of the way up the pale green walls, a disused but carefully painted picture rail. Stairs ran up to the left, turning on a half landing lit by a stained glass window in shades of cool blues and greys. The light filtered through the balustrades and carved the hall wall into segments of light and shade.

'Okay. Drugs, computers anything connected to Maddie Cox,' she reminded Hollis of the parameters of the warrant. 'And anything that will give us a clue as to her whereabouts.'

'Like an open atlas with a big arrow on one page?'

Kate scowled at Hollis. Usually she appreciated his humour but she needed him to focus on getting the search done properly. He saw her frown and looked sheepish.

'Sorry,' he mumbled.

The kitchen was spotless. The stainless steel sink gleamed in the weak sunlight and the dark marble work surfaces were free of clutter. Kate reached up and opened one of the cupboards. Tins of soup and tomatoes, an unopened packet of pasta, and another of basmati rice. Other cupboards contained crockery and jars of tea bags and coffee. Behind her she heard Hollis pull out the drawers, stir the contents and then slid them shut again. There was nothing here, but she hadn't really expected to find much in the kitchen – especially one that looked as little used as this one.

She left Hollis inspecting the fridge and washing machine and walked along the hall to the living room where, again, there was nothing out of place. The grey chenille sofa looked like it had just been delivered, there were no tell-tale dips or dents in the cushions and the nap was smooth and undisturbed. A large television dominated one corner and a compact stereo sat on a shelf above it, both dust-free. Kate stood on the deep blue hearth rug and turned full circle trying to read what the room was telling her about the owner of the house. Compulsive? Possibly. What was missing? Why did it feel like a show house?

Kate tilted her head to one side, realisation dawning. There were no pictures on the walls, no photographs, no cheap copies of well-known watercolours, nothing to add a personal touch. If it hadn't been for the confirmation from the neighbours, Kate would have doubted whether anybody had actually been living in the house. It was obvious, from the condition of her home, that Caroline Lambert wasn't likely to be careless enough to leave anything incriminating lying around and she clearly hadn't left in a hurry; the house was spotless and that would have taken time and work.

Kate trudged upstairs.

Four doors led off the main landing, all closed. Kate pushed open the one at the top of the stairs, expecting it to be the bathroom. She was surprised to see a small room furnished as a study. The walls were lined with bookshelves and the desk had been positioned so that it looked out over the garden. Kate almost yelled in frustration when she saw that the desk was empty. No sign of a PC or a laptop even though there was a router on the shelf next to the window. Wherever Caroline had gone she'd made sure that she covered her tracks thoroughly.

Kate studied the bookshelves, hoping for some sort of inspiration to strike but none of the titles jumped out at her. There was a shelf of romance novels, two or three of crime fiction and a lot of travel and reference books. Among them, Kate spotted a familiar spine; a book that sat on her own bookshelf in her flat in Doncaster. *A History of Thorpe* nestled between a book about castles of the north of England and a guide to the churches of South Yorkshire. Kneeling down, Kate pulled out the book and flicked through the pages. There was a chapter about the quarry and the brickworks, several on the pit, and one about the church. Towards the back there was a chapter which covered the building of the Crosslands Estate in the 1950s, complete with the original plans, divided into the familiar streets. Kate scanned across, looking for the house where she'd grown up, when her eye was drawn to Dennis Lambert's street. A cross had been placed in the back garden of what would become the Lamberts' home, obviously marking where Caroline had lived for the first eighteen years of her life. Using her phone, Kate took a quick photograph of the page and then slid the book back into place on the shelf before heading across the landing to the next room.

Caroline's bedroom was as neat and orderly as the rest of the house. A huge sleigh bed dominated the space which was decorated in shades of green. The duvet on the bed was neatly folded down and the pillows looked like somebody had recently fluffed them up. A large dark-wood wardrobe dominated the wall opposite the window and Kate pulled it open, expecting to see clothes organised by colour and type. Instead, she was shocked to find that the rail held only a few items, long dresses and expensive-looking woollen trousers; a dozen or so pairs of shoes were lined up in the bottom, each neatly next to its mate like sets of chromosomes, all formal and mostly high-heeled. There were no casual shoes or trainers.

Kate peered up at the top of the wardrobe. In her own bedroom it was where she stored her two suitcases, waiting for a time when she might actually get round to having a holiday. The top of Caroline Lambert's wardrobe was empty. Intrigued, Kate slipped off her shoes and stood on the bed, allowing herself a clear view.

'Not so clean and tidy up here, are you?' she mused as she saw a thin layer of dust coating two-thirds of the wood. The final third was clean. Something had been removed from the top of the wardrobe recently.

Hopping down from the bed, Kate formed an idea of what had happened to Caroline. She'd come home at some point, cleaned the house and done some packing, obviously intending to leave. She must have taken some casual clothes and shoes with her and possibly a laptop. Was this part of a bigger plan? If so, Kate was struggling to make sense of it.

If Caroline had murdered her father then handed herself in, there was no guarantee that she'd be released so quickly. Unless she'd done some research into 'mercy killing' cases. Most people were released fairly quickly after being questioned as they were deemed to be of no risk to the rest of society. Did Caroline Lambert know that? Probably, Kate thought. A woman as organised and controlled as the occupant of this house must be would have certainly done her research. But how did Maddie Cox fit in? What did she know that had led to her murder?

Kate glanced around the room again. There would be no clues there. Caroline was too careful, too methodical. Disheartened, Kate decided to give the other upstairs rooms a cursory look and leave the team to complete a more thorough search.

The third door off the landing led into a spartan guest room. The bed wasn't made up and the pine wardrobe and bookshelf were empty. The room looked like a stage set – all surface with nothing beneath to give it character. A dark blue carpet still showed the marks of the vacuum cleaner and the bedside table held a lamp and a coaster for a mug or glass. The curtains hung symmetrically and the windows looked recently cleaned. Nothing unusual. Nothing incriminating.

The bathroom was as spotless as Kate had expected. On the windowsill was an assortment of toiletries but no toothpaste. An electric toothbrush sat on its holder on top of a small medicine cabinet, the cable hanging down the side. Caroline had obviously not wanted to leave it plugged in and risk a fire. The laundry basket under the sink contained a blouse, a bra and two pairs of knickers. A grey towel was folded neatly on the towel rail and the bath mat hung over the side of the bath. Kate peered round the shower curtain and saw shower gel hanging from the soap holder, which was empty and clean.

The door to the final bedroom was slightly ajar, not fully closed as the others had been. Kate reached out her hand and gave it a slight push. It swung open easily, not obstructed by thick carpet or wayward furniture. As the light fell on the walls of the tiny room, Kate gasped. This wasn't what she'd been expecting to find in such an orderly house.

CHAPTER 26

'Hollis! Get up here, now!' Kate yelled. She heard the stomp of his size tens on the stairs and then he was behind her, staring over her shoulder.

'What the…?'

'I know. Not quite what I was expecting, either.'

She took a step into the room, desperately trying to make sense of what she was seeing but it was so unexpected that her brain couldn't quite process the information; it looked like the bedroom of a typical teenage girl, with flowery wallpaper and posters adorning the walls.

'I thought she didn't have kids,' Hollis said.

'I don't think this is a kid's bedroom,' Kate responded, taking in the detail on the posters and the garish colour scheme. 'I think it's a shrine. Look at the posters.'

A film poster for *Pretty in Pink* showed Molly Ringwald glaring down at the room from the head of the bed. Madonna and George Michael competed for pride of place on the wall opposite and David Bowie guarded the wardrobe door. The single bed was made up with sheets, blankets and a faded, pink candlewick bedspread, folded back invitingly to reveal a pillow that held the indentation of a head.

'Do you think she slept in here?' Hollis asked, his voice reduced to a whisper as though he were in church. Kate pulled open the wardrobe, ignoring Bowie's invitation to dance, and scanned the shelves and rail. Empty. She crossed the room to the rickety-looking chest of drawers and pulled out the top one. Nothing.

'Hard to tell,' she said to Hollis. 'If not, then why has she decorated it like this? It looks like my room from the eighties.'

Hollis sniggered. 'Really? I would have had you down as more the Bauhaus and Toyah type.'

Kate smiled at him. 'Nope. Wham and Spandau all the way.'

She stood in the middle of the carpet and looked around, trying to feel the full effect of the décor. It looked authentic, exactly as if she'd stepped back in time to her own teenage years. She even recognised the Bananarama poster as one that she'd cut out of *Jackie* magazine and put on her own wall, and a poster for *The Breakfast Club* was identical to one that had belonged to one of her sixth-form friends.

'This is really weird,' she said to Hollis, who was taking pictures. 'Even the wallpaper looks like it's from the eighties.'

'Maybe the previous owners decorated thirty years ago and left it when they moved out. Caroline could have kept it as a joke and then added the other stuff. It probably reminds her of when she was younger.'

'I doubt it,' Kate said. '*The Breakfast Club* came out after we'd moved to Nottingham so it must have been eighty-five or eighty-six. Same for *Pretty in Pink*, I think. Caroline would have only been eight or nine. She must have had sophisticated tastes if this is a replica of her bedroom.'

'Her sister went missing in eighty-six,' Hollis said, still staring at the posters.

Suddenly her use of the word 'shrine' made more sense. This wasn't Caroline's bedroom; it was Jeanette's. Everything in it screamed fifteen-year-old girl. She took a closer look at the Bananarama poster, taking in the detail of the corners and the barely discernible fold through the middle. Brown lines indicated where the staples from the magazine had held the poster in the middle pages. The corners were dog-eared and one was slightly torn as though it had been ripped down in a hurry and not handled with any great care.

The film posters were glossy but the edges had lost their shine and, again, the corners bulged slightly. Perhaps they'd once been hung with huge pieces of Blu Tack rather than the drawing pins that held them in their current positions.

'These are genuine; look at how the edges are browning.'

Hollis took a step inside the room and peered at David Bowie. 'These are over thirty years old? They're in bloody good condition considering they're not much younger than me.'

'They've been treasured,' Kate said. 'Caroline must have been looking after these for years. I think they were her sister's. In fact, I think this was her sister's bedroom. Not in this house, obviously, but in Dennis's house. I bet she kept this stuff safe until she had a chance to recreate Jeanette's room.'

'Creepy,' Hollis muttered.

'Maybe,' Kate agreed. 'Maybe she never really got over the loss of her sister; wanted to keep her alive in some way.'

'Alive? She was never found. We don't know that she's dead. She could have just run away and grown up in a different part of the country.'

'She's dead, Dan,' Kate said with certainty. 'I can't believe that she'd stay away from her family for so long. Maybe not her parents, but her little sister? Surely she'd have come forward by now.'

The room was giving her the creeps. It was so much like her own bedroom in Thorpe that she half expected to hear her dad shout her down for her tea or her sister, Karen to come barging in to tell her the latest in one of her many friendship sagas.

'You okay,' Hollis asked, frowning with concern. 'You look miles away.'

'This room brings back a lot of memories, that's all. Wouldn't want to be that age again.' She took a last look around and then went back to the room that Caroline appeared to have been using as a study, with Hollis following close behind. He really did seem to be unsettled by the strange bedroom.

She took her phone out of her pocket and rang Cooper's line at Doncaster Central.

'Cooper. Did you get the file on Jeanette's disappearance?' Kate asked, aware that she had used none of the usual pleasantries associated with a phone call. Cooper answered in the affirmative.

'Good. I want you to sort through it and give me the details: times, witnesses, statements and details of the police search. If you can also have a look at the newspaper reports that would be really helpful – I want to know what theories there were about this girl's disappearance.'

Kate was just sliding her phone into her pocket when it rang. Cooper.

'That was quick,' Kate joked.

'No I…' Cooper started then stopped, clearly realising that Kate wasn't serious. 'We've just had a call from East Yorkshire, went straight through to Raymond who told me to ring you back.'

'Get on with it,' Kate urged through gritted teeth. Cooper was great with computers but she could take an age to explain something.

'They've found Caroline Lambert's car.'

'Where?' Kate asked, feeling her pulse rate increase. Finally they seemed to have got a break. She just prayed that it wasn't in an airport car park or at the ferry terminal near Newcastle.

'Flamborough,' Cooper said, her tone almost apologetic. 'It was parked in the car park next to the cliffs at Flamborough Head. It's locked.'

'Right. Get onto whoever called it in and make sure that nobody touches that car until I get there.'

Cooper hung up.

'Not good news,' Kate said to Hollis. 'Caroline's car's been found near Flamborough Head.'

'Where's that?' Hollis asked.

'East coast. Near Bridlington,' Kate explained. 'It's popular with bird watchers and suicides.'

CHAPTER 27

I t was getting dark when Hollis pulled the car onto Lighthouse Road in Flamborough. They'd continued to speculate about Jeanette Lambert's whereabouts on the drive but neither had come up with a plausible theory. Hollis remained convinced that the girl had either run away or been abducted and killed and that whoever had done it had found a really good hiding place for the body.

'Do you think, between us, we could write a compelling drama for the BBC?' Hollis joked. 'We've got some amazing ideas for a plot.' He flicked on the windscreen wipers as a light drizzle obscured his view.

'I think I've lived through enough drama, thanks,' Kate responded, thinking about the previous summer. 'This weather's grim. Are we nearly there?'

Hollis checked the screen on the satnav. The red line showed that they were less than half a mile from their destination.

'Five minutes and we should see the lighthouse. Hang on.' He peered out of the side window, looking across Kate. 'The lighthouse is in the wrong place.'

Kate followed his gaze and saw a tall, pale tower which looked like it had been plonked in the middle of the green of a golf course. She remembered asking her dad, on a family outing to this part of the coast when she was about six, why the lighthouse had been placed on a golf course. He'd laughingly explained that in the 1600s, when the lighthouse had been built, the coast had looked different and that it would have been even further inland than it was now. But the golf course wouldn't have been there.

'That's not it,' she said. 'That's the old one. The new one's further along on the cliffs. Keep going.'

Hollis followed her instructions and they pulled into a car park next to the newer lighthouse where Caroline Lambert's car was cordoned off with cones and police tape. Two uniformed officers were huddled next to the whitewashed wall which ran round the lighthouse, obviously trying to keep out of the biting wind.

As Kate got out of the car, the door of a dark saloon car two parking spaces away opened and a tall figure stepped out.

'DI Fletcher?' he asked, extending a hand hidden in a leather glove.

Kate confirmed her identity and shook hands, faintly repulsed by the cold surface of the glove.

'DS Morrison,' the man said. 'East Yorkshire police. I've been waiting for you.'

He was wearing a long, dark, wool coat and his chin nestled in an expensive-looking grey scarf. His dark hair and eyes and sharp nose contributed to the impression that he could be a mafia boss. Kate noted that he hadn't allowed the two other policemen to shelter in his car and wondered if he was one of those detectives who didn't like to mix with the 'lower ranks'.

She introduced Hollis, and Morrison escorted them both to Caroline Lambert's car. It was a dark blue BMW 5 series with a two-year-old registration plate.

'Expensive,' Hollis mused. 'Wouldn't want to leave it unattended in the back of beyond for long.'

Kate saw Morrison's back stiffen slightly at the 'back of beyond' comment but he obviously chose to ignore it.

'One of the uniformed officers noticed the car during a routine sweep of the car park,' he said. 'It's parked in one of the spaces reserved for the lighthouse staff and he didn't recognise it. We tend to know who's who in the *back of beyond* and this car doesn't belong to any of the regular staff – our man would have recognised it otherwise. When he did a PNC check the number came back as of interest so he rang it in and one of my colleagues called Doncaster. We were told to leave it alone until somebody from South Yorkshire got here. Now you're here, can you tell me what it's all about?'

'The owner of the car is of interest in two murder cases,' Hollis said in a tone that sounded a bit self-important to Kate's ears. She hoped that the two men weren't going to get into some sort of territorial pissing contest before they'd even had a look at the car.

'She's connected with two recent suspicious deaths and appears to have done a runner,' Kate said, trying to placate Morrison with information. 'My current concern is that she's driven here to kill herself.'

'It's a possibility,' Morrison conceded. 'We do get a fair bit of that off the cliffs. I've lost count of the number of times I've been called to attend reports of a jumper.'

He glanced at Hollis as he said the last word as though it was a challenge to Hollis's credentials as a detective.

Kate sighed inwardly. She hated it when colleagues judged themselves and each other on the number and condition of deaths they had attended, and she prayed that Hollis wouldn't rise to the bait.

'Never seen one,' Hollis said amiably. 'I'm sure it's not pleasant.'

Morrison sniggered. 'Not pleasant? Can you imagine what falling nearly four hundred feet onto rocks does to a body? It's better when they choose a high tide and get washed out to sea. At least that way we don't have to scrape them up into a bag.'

'Fascinating as this is,' Kate said, hoping her tone conveyed exactly the opposite sentiment, 'I'd like to get a look at the car before we lose the light completely. I notice there's not a SOCO team on site yet.'

'They're on their way,' Morrison said. 'I gave it a couple of hours so that they'd be here around the same time as you. Not sure what the point is, though. All you'll get are the driver's prints and trace from her house. It's not like somebody kidnapped her and pushed her off the cliffs.'

Kate was struggling to hide her annoyance at Morrison's smug attitude and sloppy police work. He was probably right but, if there was an outside chance that there was evidence in the car linking Caroline to Maddie Cox, or anything that would shed light on the relationship with her father, then they needed to know. She stepped closer to the car and tried to peer into the driver's side window but the last rays of the setting sun were making it difficult to make out the interior. She walked round to the other side where the light was actually helpful and was surprised to see an envelope on the passenger seat.

'Not uncommon,' Morrison said when Kate pointed it out to him. 'A lot of jumpers like to leave a final farewell.'

She was prevented from berating Morrison for his lack of empathy by headlights on the lane leading to the car park.

A few seconds later, a van pulled in next to Kate's car and three figures got out.

'Right. Looks like you've got your SOCO team,' Morrison said, stuffing his hands into his pockets. 'It's past time I knocked off for the day, and I don't think you'll need me for this bit.'

'What about a dive team?' Kate asked, determined not to allow him to simply slope off home, or to the pub or wherever he might want to go. 'Surely you've contacted the coastguard?'

Morrison sighed and stared at her as if she were an infant who was having difficulty grasping a simple concept.

'If she went off at high tide, a dive team won't find her. There's nothing on the rocks – Laurel and Hardy over there have already had a walk along the coast to have a look.' He inclined his head towards the uniformed officers. 'She might wash up in a few days, she might not. Depends what time she went in the sea.'

He turned away and started walking back to his car.

'CCTV,' Kate called after him. 'I'll need CCTV for the car park. There's a camera at the entrance. It'll confirm what time she arrived. Could you sort that out for me, please? You'll know who to contact, I'm sure.'

She turned back to the suited figures surrounding Caroline Lambert's car and heard Hollis snigger.

'Nice one,' he whispered.

'Can't stand arrogant, lazy coppers,' Kate said. 'And well done for not getting into a pissing contest with him.'

'Not worth it,' Hollis said. 'He outranks me.'

'For now. You might want to think about doing something about that. Get your sergeant's exams done?'

'Maybe,' Hollis muttered, walking away from her so that he could watch the forensics team from a better angle.

Kate was surprised. He was a good DC, keen but measured in his approach, and he was good with people. He'd make an excellent sergeant but he'd never shown much interest in promotion. A summons from the car interrupted her train of thought.

'We're in,' one of the white-suited figures said. Kate strode over and peered at the interior of the BMW. Like Caroline's house, it was spotless. Kate prayed that it hadn't had a quick valet since Maddie Cox's murder.

'I need to see what's in that letter,' she said to the woman holding the door open.

The woman smiled sympathetically, her blue eyes crinkling with regret as she told Kate that she'd have to wait until it had been dusted for fingerprints. Kate took a step back and watched as the boot was opened to reveal a suitcase. After taking photographs, one of the team lifted it up to examine the rest of the boot but, apart from an unused spare wheel, it was empty.

'Can I have a look in the suitcase?' Kate asked.

The forensics officer frowned before handing her a pair of nitrile gloves.

'Give me a second,' he said before raising the camera and firing off a series of shots of the suitcase in situ, the camera clicking in rapid motion like a professional photo shoot.

Kate waited until he'd finished and then leaned into the boot.

The suitcase was red and soft-sided with a zip fastening that ran around three sides. There were attachments on the slider for a padlock but Caroline didn't appear to have been especially worried about the security of her belongings as she hadn't bothered to lock the case. Kate undid the zip and pushed back the lid, leaving the suitcase gaping like an open mouth in the boot of the car.

She called Hollis over to witness her examination of the contents and he peered over her shoulder as she carefully peeled back layers of jumpers, trousers and blouses, each one recorded by a series of camera flashes. A pair of black leather shoes and a pair of brilliant white, obviously new, trainers lay at the bottom.

'No laptop,' Hollis observed.

Kate undid the strings of a toiletries bag: deodorant, soap, miniature shampoo and conditioner, lipstick, toothbrush and toothpaste. Everything looked like it had been bought recently for a holiday or a trip.

'Why would she bother to pack a bag if she was intending to drive up here and kill herself?' Hollis mused.

It was a valid question and one to which Kate had no answer.

'Maybe she wasn't sure,' Hollis continued. 'She might have just decided to run away, to disappear. Or she might have been worried that she couldn't go through with it.'

Kate wasn't convinced. She'd not dealt with many suicides during her career but she'd never heard of anybody having a contingency plan in case they bottled out. Suicide was so final; such a clear end to the difficulties that a person might be facing.

'Dan, how did you know that she hadn't just gone out for a couple of hours this morning?'

Hollis's brow furrowed in concentration as if trying to remember the sequence of events which had alerted him to Caroline Lambert's absence.

'The neighbour,' he said. 'One of her neighbours from further down the road had seen her putting a suitcase in the car as he walked past with his dog. He said that she seemed to be struggling with it and he'd asked if she needed a hand. That would have been early this morning.'

Kate tried to picture the scene. The drive of the house was enclosed by chest-high gates and the garden was surrounded by shrubs. It would have been easy for Caroline to have loaded up her car without being seen. Unless she'd *wanted* the neighbour to see the suitcase, and seeing her struggling with it would have made the contact all the more memorable.

'I think this is a set-up,' Kate said to Hollis. 'She wanted us to know that she'd done a runner and she wanted us to find her car. I bet she's on CCTV somewhere from the A1 to here – she'll have picked a route where there's likely to be a camera.'

'So you don't think she killed herself?' Hollis asked, glancing towards the clifftop.

'Honestly? I have no idea. We need to see what's in the envelope that she left.'

'I think the SOCOs have finished with it,' Hollis said, glancing round the side of the car. Kate strode back to the passenger door and tapped one of the overall-clad figures on the shoulder. The woman turned around and her eyes briefly blazed with irritation.

'Envelope,' Kate said. 'I need to see what's inside.'

Wordlessly, the woman leaned down and picked up the white rectangle. She passed it to Kate and reached down to remove a scalpel from the foam padding of her crime scene case. 'Use this,' the woman said, holding it out handle first.

Kate inserted the tip of the blade in the gap where the flap was folded over. A flash made her blink as the SOCO took a photograph. She eased the scalpel along the top of the envelope. A single piece of paper lay folded inside.

Watched closely by Hollis and the forensics officer, she slid the paper out and unfolded it.

Two words were written across the middle in black block capitals.

'What the hell?' Hollis whispered.

CHAPTER 28

'Thanks for coming in so early,' Kate addressed her team as they gathered in the meeting room at Doncaster Central, all nursing mugs of hot drinks that she'd provided from the canteen. 'As you know, Caroline Lambert is officially missing. We have no idea whether she has taken her own life or whether she abandoned her car at Flamborough Head and has absconded. A local lifeboat crew will search the area around and below the cliffs today but they're not hopeful as, according to the car park CCTV, Caroline arrived a few minutes before a high winter tide.'

'Convenient,' mumbled O'Connor, taking a swig of his cappuccino and wiping milk foam from his moustache with the back of his hand.

For once, Kate was inclined to agree with him. 'Sam, can you show us the footage?'

Cooper turned on the projector and tapped a series of keys on her laptop. The screen was filled with a black-and-white, still image of the car park at Flamborough Head with the lighthouse and the path to the cliffs barely visible in the top right-hand corner.

'Lambert pulls in at just after one pm,' Sam said, hitting 'play'. 'The dark saloon car is her BMW.' She continued to narrate as the others watched the car pass through the public parking area and pull up into one of the 'reserved' spaces close to the lighthouse. The clock in the corner of the image continued to count the seconds but there was no movement from the car for nearly three minutes. Finally, the driver's side door opened and a figure stepped out.

Even though she'd already viewed the footage, Kate was still surprised by how clearly recognisable Caroline Lambert was as she stood next to the car looking up at the lighthouse.

At 1.09, Caroline checked her watch, held out her hand towards the car, presumably using the key to activate the central locking, and set off towards the cliff path.

'That's all we've got,' Cooper said. 'I've already been through the footage from earlier to check the number plates of any other cars parked in the vicinity. There were only three – East Yorks should be checking out the owners as we speak to see if they saw Caroline Lambert near the cliff edge.'

'Hope they've not sent Morrison,' Hollis whispered to Kate with a grin. 'Might be a quite a wait if they did.'

Kate smiled back at him. They'd had a long drive back from Flamborough the previous evening. Snow had hit parts of the A1 and slowed traffic to a crawl. It had given them time to mull over the meaning of the note left in the car but they had more possibilities than answers, which was why Kate wanted to share it with her team and get them brainstorming.

'Thanks for that, Sam,' Kate said, nudging Cooper out of the way and navigating to a different programme on the laptop. 'It's possible that this was staged.'

'How do you mean?' Barratt asked, looking annoyed. He'd spent the previous afternoon involved in the fruitless search of Caroline Lambert's house which appeared to have left him in an unusually belligerent mood. 'Surely this winds everything up. If she's dead then we can't arrest her for the murders of Maddie Cox or her dad. She probably knew she'd go to jail for a long time and couldn't face it. It's not like there's anybody waiting for her to get out.'

'It just seems incredibly convenient. A neighbour saw her leaving with a suitcase so we knew that she hadn't just popped to the shops. She arrived at Flamborough at high tide and it was one of the highest of the season. She's extremely visible in the CCTV, almost as if she chose that parking space so that she could be seen in the footage.'

O'Connor was nodding. 'So she disappears. No charges to face because she's supposedly dead while she sets herself up with another identity, another life. It's possible if she had enough money. Or influential friends.'

'She's got plenty of money,' Kate said. 'We need to get onto her bank and try to find out if she was paying into other accounts in other names. She might have stashed away thousands somewhere.'

'Fake ID, change of appearance, and she's good to go,' O'Connor continued. 'Easy enough if you know the right people. Speaking of which, I found out that Maddie Cox did owe money to one of the usual scumbags. Terry Dawlish reckons she borrowed ten K from him to pay off some gambling debts. Paid it all back with interest in one lump sum last month. Looks like she *did* have a bit of help from Caroline Lambert.'

Kate had forgotten that she'd asked O'Connor to dig around in Maddie's finances. It hardly felt important considering the other links between the two women but it was useful to have further confirmation of the relationship. O'Connor had done a good job and Kate had another one for him.

'Steve, you seem to have a good idea what it would take to change your identity and disappear. Get out there and see if anybody might have supplied Caroline with fake ID. If she acquired it in South Yorkshire, somebody will know somebody who knows who supplied it.'

O'Connor gave her a mock salute and turned to leave.

'Not yet. I need you all to see this.'

Kate projected an image of the note that she'd removed from the car onto the whiteboard. The two words had been etched onto the inside of her eyelids as she'd settled down to sleep and they'd still been there when she'd woken a few hours later.

FIND JEANETTE

'What does that mean?' Barratt asked. Kate didn't answer, waiting for a response from another member of the team.

'Jeanette was her sister,' Cooper said. 'She went missing in 1986. She'd been out with friends one evening in August and never came home. Parents reported her missing; there was an investigation, a newspaper appeal but no sign of her. I reviewed some of the case notes yesterday but there's nothing there. The investigating team didn't manage to come up with a viable line of enquiry and there was no sign of abduction or that the girl had been murdered. She was last seen at just after midnight on the seventeenth of August 1986 by a girl called Julie Atkins, a school friend. I'm trying to track her down to see if she can add anything to her original statement but, as it's over thirty years ago, I'm not hopeful.'

Barratt still wasn't satisfied.

'But what does she mean by "Find Jeanette". Does she expect us to reopen the investigation? How does she expect us to find her now if the police failed in the eighties? It's not like any new information has come to light.'

Kate looked round the room. Each member of her team seemed lost in thought, trying to make sense of the message. They were an intuitive bunch and had good instincts but she could see that they were all struggling with this one. 'What's changed?' she prompted. 'Why now?'

'Her dad's dead?' O'Connor suggested. 'And her mum. They were both alive when the girl went missing.'

'What difference does that make?' Cooper asked.

'It must be linked with Dennis Lambert's death. That's the catalyst,' Hollis said, just as he'd argued on the way back from Flamborough the previous night. 'That's changed something for Caroline. Somehow it's made her think that we might be able to find her sister.'

Kate turned to Cooper. 'Was there any suggestion in the original file that Lambert was a suspect in his daughter's disappearance?'

'No. Nothing. Both parents were interviewed extensively, together and separately. There was nothing to raise suspicion as far as I can tell. They put posters up around the estate for a couple of years afterwards, probably hoping that somebody, somewhere might have information.'

'And Caroline?'

'She was nine. A female officer spoke to her and made notes but the child was upset and didn't really add anything to what they already knew.'

'Was the house searched?'

'As far as I can tell they checked the house and the garden – including the shed. There's no suggestion that there was anything to contradict the family's story. There were a few reported sightings of Jeanette in the months after her disappearance but none of them could be confirmed and, to be honest, we expect that. The public have seen an appeal for a missing kid and suddenly he or she's in every shopping centre and on every train for a few weeks.'

'Easy enough to hide a body, though,' O'Connor observed. 'Especially a kid. Loft space, under floorboards, under a flowerbed, behind a bath panel. If it's only for a few days you could probably get away with it if you wrap it up well enough.'

The others nodded thoughtfully.

'And Lambert re-landscaped the garden soon after. New flowerbeds and a greenhouse according to Brenda Powley,' Hollis added.

It was possible, Kate had to concede. If Jeanette had died or been killed in the house, her body could have been hidden until the main thrust of the investigation died down and then a more permanent resting place could have been found. But they had no cause to suspect Lambert or his wife and, according to Brenda Powley, Lambert should have been a candidate for beatification after he died.

'We need to look at Lambert,' Kate decided. 'If Caroline did kill him she must have had a reason beyond putting him out of his misery. Kailisa says he was kept drugged and probably in pain for the last couple of weeks of his life. That smacks of torture to me and you don't do that to somebody unless you want something. Either information or revenge.'

'You think she might have been torturing her father to find out what he did to her sister?' Barratt asked.

Kate shrugged. 'I have no idea what went on in that house but I'm convinced that it's much more complicated than a mercy killing. I also think Maddie Cox was collateral damage. I suspect that Caroline manipulated her by offering her money to pay off her debts and then something happened between the two women that led Caroline to lash out and kill Maddie. She may have been protecting herself – the nurse might have been supplying drugs illegally and could have threatened to go to the police. She might have put her career on the line in some way and wanted to come clean. I doubt we'll ever know.'

Silence as the team considered Kate's words.

'Right. We need to get to work,' she continued. 'O'Connor – fake ID. Barratt, I want you to go back to the Crosslands Estate and ask about Dennis Lambert. What was he like? Was he a violent man? Did he love his kids? Get an impression that doesn't involve anything that Brenda Powley has to say.'

O'Connor and Barratt scooted off on their separate jobs.

'Sam. Find Julie Atkins. I want to talk to her. If anybody knew what sort of relationship Jeanette Lambert had with her family it would have been her closest friend.'

Cooper closed the lid of the laptop, slipped it under her arm, and left the room, heading for her own desk and her own PC where she could mine for information uninterrupted.

'Dan. You and me on the phones. Get onto East Yorkshire, see if they've had any luck with the owners of the cars that were parked up at Flamborough yesterday. If not, get the numbers and ring yourself. I'm going to do some digging into Caroline Lambert's background, starting with her previous job in Plymouth. We have no clue what this woman was really like but there might be somebody down there who can help us.'

Two frustrating hours later and Kate hung up the phone with a loud sigh. She'd spoken to Caroline's boss and three of her colleagues, two at length, and nobody had a bad word to say about their former workmate. She was punctual, polite, well-motivated according to the boss, and the others described her as considerate, quiet and extremely competent. They knew very little about her background. Two knew that she was from 'up north somewhere' and one thought she might have been from Yorkshire. The only piece of information that was of any interest was that Caroline had told two of her colleagues that she was an orphan and an only child but another remembered her mentioning a sister.

'Got anything, Dan?' Kate said to Hollis who had just hung up his own phone in a similar manner. He shook his head.

'East Yorks hadn't got round to it so they gave me the phone numbers. Dog walkers and bird watchers. Nobody noticed Caroline park up and nobody remembers seeing her on the cliff path.'

'Any luck with Julie Atkins?' Kate asked Cooper who was still immersed in her virtual world. She looked up, eyes not quite focussed and nodded.

'I've managed to find her on Facebook. She's married but still uses her maiden name as part of her Facebook name. She's Julie Wilkinson now. I've just done an electoral roll search and she lives in Rotherham, near the General Hospital.' Cooper scrawled the details onto a Post-it and passed them to Kate.

'Got her phone number as well. Only the home one, though. Her mobile would take a lot longer.'

Kate smiled. It was as close as Cooper ever came to an admission of defeat. She always believed that the information she wanted was available if she had enough time to find it.

'I think we'd be better heading round there,' Kate said. 'If I ring first it might give her time to filter her memories. I want to see her reaction when I ask her about Jeanette and her father.' Kate checked her watch. The chances of Julie being home mid-morning were remote but it was worth a try.

'Dan,' she called. 'Grab your coat, you've pulled.'

He grinned over at her.

'You wish.'

CHAPTER 29

Julie Wilkinson lived in a red-brick semi on a street of red-brick semis opposite Rotherham's largest hospital. They looked similar to the one where Kate grew up in Thorpe except that the street wasn't as wide and the houses were a little closer together. Kate assumed that they were built in the sixties or seventies when land around towns had been at a premium and the councils had been under pressure to make the most of all the available space. The road was shielded from a dual carriageway by a large beech hedge that ran the length of the street but, as Kate got out of the car, she could hear that it did little to dull the constant drone of vehicles and the wail of an ambulance approaching A&E at the hospital.

A flat-roofed garage was attached to the house and, in front of the chipped white metal door, a light blue Vauxhall Golf sat on the drive.

'We might be in luck,' she said to Hollis, pointing at the car. She stepped back and allowed him to approach the door of the house first. If Julie was home, this was going to be an interview which required a delicate touch and Kate trusted Hollis to get the most out of this situation.

Through the frosted glass in the top half of the door, Kate saw a figure approaching seconds after Hollis rattled the letterbox flap. Somebody *was* home. The door opened and Hollis introduced them both while Kate assessed the woman on the doorstep. She knew that Julie Wilkinson must be in her late forties but, if she'd met her in a pub, she'd have assumed that she was much younger. Her dark hair was carefully styled and her make-up was understated and certainly not used to hide bags and wrinkles.

Her forehead creased with confusion as Hollis explained who they were, leaving Kate slightly disappointed that there was no sign of recent Botox to explain the woman's youthful appearance.

'Is it Rob?' she asked, her voice rising as panic gripped her. 'Has something happened to him?'

Hollis shook his head reassuringly.

'We're here about Jeanette Lambert,' he said, and the lines across Julie's forehead deepened.

'Jeanette? Why? You've not found her after all this time?'

'No. That's not why we're here. We want to ask you some questions about her.'

Julie smiled, the relief obvious. Kate wasn't sure who Rob might be but she guessed a husband or a boyfriend. She was used to this reaction whenever she turned up unannounced at somebody's door. People always assumed the worst, and at least half the time, they were right.

'Can we come in?' Kate asked.

Julie nodded and led the way down a bright, cream-coloured hallway to the living room. As they followed her, Kate noticed that it wasn't just Julie Wilkinson's face that appeared to be defying time. She wore tight skinny jeans and a hoodie that was probably a size too small, both of which showed off gravity-defying hips and boobs. Whatever her secret was, Kate thought, she'd like to buy a couple of bottles.

The living room was also decorated in shades of cool cream and off-white. The sofa and chairs were beige and the laminate flooring imitated pale wood. A glass coffee table stood proudly in the middle of the room, its surface free from dust and finger marks – obviously not a house with children, or grandchildren. Kate wondered if *that* was Julie's secret. Kate knew from experience how ageing having kids could be. Not that she resented Ben, but she could count the wrinkles and scars he'd left on her body and face as though he'd written his name across her skin with a knife.

Julie offered drinks but Kate refused and Hollis followed her lead. She didn't want to give the impression that this was a cosy chat about her old friend, she wanted Julie to believe that any information she could provide would be crucial to an ongoing investigation. She wanted honesty.

'So, what did you want to ask me?' Julie settled herself in the armchair next to the window where Kate and Hollis could get a good view of her face. 'You can't have found another lead?' Her face suddenly froze as she thought of another possible reason for the visit. 'Oh. You've not found...'

'We've nothing new,' Hollis reassured her, obviously understanding that she might think that they'd found a body. 'We just want some background. Certain recent events have rekindled our interest in Jeanette's disappearance and we'd like the perspective of somebody who knew her well.'

Julie leaned forward in her chair, forearms on her knees, her expression intent. 'What recent events?'

'Her sister has disappeared,' Kate interjected before Hollis could mention Dennis Lambert's death.

'Caroline? You mean she's been abducted or something?'

Hollis picked up Kate's thread. 'We're not really sure. Her car was found in a spot well known for suicides and there's no sign of her. We don't know if she's harmed herself, been abducted or simply disappeared but we think this is somehow connected with what happened to her sister.'

Julie smiled as if she understood, even though nothing about Caroline Lambert's disappearance made any sense to Kate or her colleagues.

'What was Jeanette like?' Hollis asked, trying to steer the interview away from Caroline.

'She was great,' Julie said with a huge grin. She sat back in her chair, relaxing into her memories. 'She was my best friend from our first day at Thorpe Comp. Got me into all sorts of trouble but I didn't mind. She thought she was a rebel but there wasn't really that much for us to rebel against. She was into music, clothes, make-up. She was one of those people who made you feel special if they paid any attention to you, like a light shining on you. Everything was better when Jeanette was around.'

'Better in what way?' Hollis prompted.

Julie thought for a few seconds. 'She always had the best ideas about what to do, where to go. We used to go to Donny on Saturdays and hang about in the Arndale Centre. Most of the lasses would be in and out of the shops but Jeanette liked to go up on the balcony and watch people. She said they were like ants, busy living their pointless little lives. After school, we used to go and sit in the middle of the playing field and smoke and talk about what our lives would be like in the future. I always said that I wanted to marry a rich bloke and have a dozen kids but not Jeanette. She wanted to leave Thorpe and go to London or Manchester. She wanted to sing in a band or be discovered by a casting agency and get on the telly. Kids' stuff really, but she believed that she could do it.'

Kate could see that the woman was lost in the past, her eyes unfocussed as she remembered her friend. Nothing Julie said helped the enquiry but it was interesting to find out what sort of person Jeanette had been. Could she have been lured away by somebody promising her bright lights and fame? She asked the question and Julie laughed.

'No chance. Jeanette was really savvy. She knew that talent scouts didn't hang about in Thorpe or the Arndale Centre in Doncaster. She knew she'd have to move away at some point. She wanted to do her A Levels first, though. She was going to go to college in Donny and study for a couple of years. She could probably have gone to university, she was bright enough. All our teachers said so.'

'So you don't think she ran away?' Hollis asked.

Julie shook her head firmly. 'Not a chance. She'd have told me if she was planning anything like that. She told me everything.'

'Did she talk about her family?'

Julie tilted her head to one side and regarded Hollis quizzically. 'Why do you ask?'

'As I said. Just trying to get an impression. We've looked at your original statement and there's nothing there to indicate that there were family issues but, with Caroline disappearing, we wondered if there might be a link.'

'What? You think Caroline was involved? She was only nine when Jeanette went missing.'

'What about her parents?' Kate prompted. 'Did Jeannette ever talk about how well she got on with her mum and dad?'

'I've thought about that a lot over the years,' Julie said, nodding slowly. 'She always talked like she could wrap her mum round her little finger and she said her dad would do anything to please her mum.'

'But you're not convinced?' Hollis asked.

'At the time, I just took everything she said at face value but there were a few little things that have made me wonder ever since. She sometimes had odd bruises, mostly on her legs. I saw them in PE a few times. She always said that she'd had a fall or she'd been fighting with Caroline and I believed her. She was off school for a week as well with a broken arm. Said she'd tripped up the steps and fallen on it. Nowadays her mum and dad would probably have social services breathing down their necks but she might have been telling the truth. Apart from one thing.'

She paused and Kate could see that she was working out how to phrase whatever it was that she had to say.

Julie leaned forward again as though sharing a secret or some especially juicy gossip. 'She was at my house one night; I think it was in the Easter holidays. We'd been sitting out the back listening to the Top 40 and hadn't really been paying attention to the time. My mum came out and said that Jeanette's dad was at the door asking for her. When Jeanette got up to go and see him she was really pale and I noticed that her hand was shaking as she turned the doorknob. I didn't hear what her dad said to her but she didn't come back to say goodbye, she just left with him. I didn't see her for a while after that and when I did she said the family had been away for a couple of days to stay with her auntie in York. Thing is, I could have sworn I saw their Caroline in the Co-op two days before the day that she said they came back. I forgot all about it at the time. Just put it down to a misunderstanding but, with hindsight, I wonder if her dad had given her a good hiding for not getting home on time.'

'You didn't mention this to the police? It sounds a lot like the night she went missing. Out with friends. Home late.' Kate tried to keep the accusation out of her voice. If a friend of Jeanette's had spoken against Lambert then the investigation might have taken a different, more productive line.

'I was just a kid,' Julie explained. 'I was terrified of the police. And, like I said, a lot of this didn't really occur to me until much later.'

'You could have come forward at any time,' Kate told her. 'We get new information about old cases on a fairly regular basis.'

'I suppose so,' Julie sighed. 'But it was supposition. What if it was all in my head and I'd made things even worse for the family?'

'Did you meet Dennis Lambert?' Hollis tried to change the subject. Julie was getting defensive and that wasn't going to help them get any more information. Kate leaned back in her seat, giving him a chance to correct her mistake.

Julie shook her head. 'Not properly. He was always at work on the rare occasions when we went to her house. If he was due back we went out. There was that time he came looking for her but I only saw him briefly at the door.'

'You were friends for four years and you never met her dad?' Hollis was clearly surprised. 'Did you get the impression that she didn't want you to meet him?'

'To be honest, I never thought about it. I'm not sure she would have seen much of *my* dad. It was a different time. Both our mums stayed at home and our dads worked. When my dad came home everything changed. There was tea to get ready while he got a wash and then he'd eat and watch telly. We weren't supposed to bother him, and having friends over was bother, I suppose. If I did have anybody round we always sat in my bedroom, or the garden if it was summer.'

It made sense based on Kate's own experience. Her mum didn't like her having her friends round if her dad was at home because he worked hard and she didn't want him to be pestered. After her mum died Kate and Karen tried to look after him, but they were too young to run the house so he'd ended up doing a lot of the housework and cooking. She knew that he wouldn't want other kids getting under his feet; his own two were enough.

They were interrupted by a thud from upstairs.

'Somebody else here?' Kate asked.

Julie smiled and shook her head. 'Cat. Sounds like he's got in the front bedroom and he's not allowed up there. Hang on a sec.'

She disappeared for a minute, closing the living room door behind her, and came back holding a large black cat who looked anything but contrite.

'This is Marlon,' she said. 'I'll just chuck him up the garden. If I don't watch him he leaves mice under my bed.'

She disappeared again and Kate felt a cold draught as the back door opened and closed. She raised her eyebrows at Hollis who was shaking his head in amusement. He knew that Kate didn't like cats. The sound of a tap running came from the kitchen and then Julie Wilkinson reappeared, drying her hands on a tea towel.

'Sorry about that. Where were we?' She dropped the tea towel on the table and sat back down.

'Did you ever hear of Dennis Lambert having a temper or being violent?' Hollis asked. 'Thorpe's a small place, people talk. Did he get into fights? Have a drink problem? Anything like that?'

Julie shrugged. 'Not that I remember. It wasn't the sort of thing that my parents would have talked about though – not in front of me. If you reopen the case, are you going to interview him again?'

'We can't,' Kate said. 'He's dead.'

Julie's eyes widened with shock. 'Wasn't expecting that. What happened?'

'He had cancer,' Hollis said. 'Caroline had come home to look after him.'

'Really?' Julie's tone was sceptical. 'I thought she'd moved away after her mum killed herself. She always said that she was going to move as far away as possible when she was old enough.'

Kate leaned forward again. 'You knew Caroline?'

'A bit. She was younger than me and Jeanette but I kept in touch with her after their Jeanette went missing. I bought Caroline her first legal drink when she was eighteen. I'm really surprised that she came back to look after her dad.'

'Why?' Kate asked.

'Because she hated him. Loathed him with a passion. I bumped into her in the Cross Keys one night, I think she was celebrating her A Level results. She was pretty pi – drunk. Kept going on about how she was going to finally get away from that bastard and how he could rot in hell for all she cared. She said that she was never coming back and I really believed her.'

'She hated her dad?' Kate said. 'So why would she come back and look after him? It doesn't make much sense to me.'

Julie sighed and shook her head. 'I really have no idea. From what she said about him I'd've thought that she'd have stayed away. I don't know why she felt like that but she was pretty wound up about him.'

'Do you think he was violent towards her after her sister went missing? Might that have been why she hated him?' Kate was thinking about the different reasons that Cooper had suggested for murder and she kept coming back to one in particular. Revenge.

'I honestly have no idea,' Julie said. 'I suppose it would make sense but I'm not a hundred per cent sure that he knocked their Jeanette about, either.'

Kate's phone rang just as they were concluding the interview. She looked at the screen. Barratt. She let it ring while they thanked Julie Wilkinson for her time, headed back to the car and then rang him back.

'Got anything?' Kate asked as soon as Barratt answered his phone.

'Maybe,' Barratt said. 'I've been talking to one of the neighbours opposite Lambert. A Peter Moody. He went to school with Dennis, had known him pretty much all his life.'

'And?' Kate prompted, trying not to be too irritated by Barratt's need to give as much background detail as possible.

'He says, when they were kids, that Dennis was cock of the school. Everybody was scared of him. He'd fight any lad who so much as looked at him wrong and he'd carry on fighting until his opponent was a bloody mess. Apparently he had a right reputation up until his marriage to Irene.'

Kate thanked him and hung up. It tied in with Jeanette's bruises and her fear of her father. What if his violent streak had been contained within the home after he married? It was possible that he'd lost his temper with Jeanette and gone too far. Is that what Caroline meant when she left the note? Was Jeanette somewhere where she could be found? Or her remains at least? She thought about the cross that had been marked in the book that she'd found on the shelf in Caroline's study. What if it marked more than just the house where she'd spent her childhood? What if it marked a grave?

'What now?' Hollis asked.

Kate sighed heavily, dreading what she had to do next. 'I'm going back to base to ask Raymond for the time and resources to dig up Dennis Lambert's back garden. If I were you I'd stay well away because you know how he gets about spending money. It won't be pretty.'

CHAPTER 30

The next morning's briefing was untypically subdued. Kate had spent half an hour in Raymond's office trying to persuade him to commit time and resources to searching Dennis Lambert's house and garden but he had been granite-hard in his opposition. He was unhappy that Caroline's disappearance had left so many loose ends and had implied that Kate was to blame. She was frustrated and disheartened when she met with her team at 8.30am but she didn't want to pass on this deflated feeling to them. She needn't have worried; it was their own lack of progress that seemed to have brought each of them down and made them tense and uncommunicative.

Kate called on O'Connor first. He gave her a rueful half-smile, clearly not wanting to admit defeat.

'I tried everybody I could find,' he began. 'There's only a handful of guys out there dealing in fake IDs. I did the rounds but nobody remembered a woman fitting Caroline Lambert's description. Only one of them remembered a woman at all. Most of their business is regulars wanting fake IDs to pass on to illegal immigrants and people who need to hide from *us*.'

Kate was uncomfortable with O'Connor's methods but she knew that he was exceptionally good at gaining the trust of some of the most useful small-time crooks and criminals in the area. She didn't want to know what he offered in return because his information often led to some high-profile arrests.

'You said there was one woman,' she prompted.

O'Connor grinned, obviously pleased to have the opportunity to show off his list of contacts.

'Ollie Skillen, who does a bit of running for Lee Weaver, said they'd had a woman round looking to buy a birth certificate and an NI number.'

Kate supressed a smile at O'Connor's casual name-dropping of one of Doncaster's most prolific offenders. Lee Weaver was well known to her team. She wanted to ask O'Connor what he meant by 'running' but couldn't face his smug smile as he explained.

'This woman turned up about three months ago. Skillen remembers it was a good few weeks before Christmas because he knew he'd get a cut if he organised the business and he planned to use it to buy his boy a dirt bike. It wasn't Caroline Lambert, though. The description was nothing like her – mid-to-late-thirties, dark hair, not very tall. She could have worn a wig but she couldn't have made herself shorter.'

'Sounds like Maddie Cox, though,' Barratt observed. Three faces turned to look at him as though he'd suddenly grown an extra head.

'It does,' he continued.

Kate had to agree with him, but it didn't make much sense. She looked over her shoulder at the rough timeline on the whiteboard. A photograph of Maddie smiled down at her with different coloured lines radiating out to key pieces of information. One line ended at an image of Caroline Lambert with a list of dates of their known encounters underneath. The first was November twenty-second.

'The date could just about fit,' she conceded. 'But why would she help Caroline? If they'd first met when Dennis was in hospital they wouldn't have had time to form any sort of relationship.'

'Maybe that's why Caroline gave her money,' Hollis suggested, his expression showing that he wasn't convinced by his own theory.

'I just can't see Maddie Cox knowing somebody like that,' Cooper added quietly. 'And, if Caroline convinced Maddie to help her, she must have had some serious leverage considering they'd just met. Brenda Powley allegedly made the call on November twenty-first. The timing doesn't fit. Didn't we think that the money from Caroline helped Maddie pay off her gambling debts?'

'So, it wasn't Maddie Cox?'

Four almost identical shrugs. They really were struggling with this one. O'Connor's moustache returned to its usual inverted horseshoe shape as his grin faded and Kate wondered if their luck was running out.

She was about to address the issue of Caroline Lambert's possible suicide when her phone rang. It was Morrison from East Yorkshire.

'We've done a search of the clifftop,' he announced after introducing himself. Kate seriously doubted that Morrison had been involved in the physical search and assumed that the 'we' referred to a team of uniformed officers on their hands and knees in the frosty grass.

'And?' Kate prompted as she sensed that he was waiting for some sort of response.

'I've emailed you some photographs of the product of the search. There's not much but there is one item that you might find interesting.'

'Which is?'

'Have a look at the images,' he said, hanging up.

Kate explained the call to the others as she logged on to the laptop connected to the projector and downloaded the images from Morrison's email. She flashed them up on the screen as a slideshow so that they could look at each in turn. At first glance they looked like the useless detritus that could be found on any stretch of grass or wasteland in the country. A squashed cigarette packet, a condom wrapper, a black sock.

'What's that?' Barratt asked when an odd-looking object appeared. Kate clicked off the slideshow and zoomed in on the photograph.

'It's a SIM tray from an iPhone,' Cooper said. 'You can tell by the shape. Looks like it's from a rose gold model judging by the edge.' She typed something on her keyboard. 'And Caroline

Lambert's possessions when she was arrested included a rose gold iPhone 7.

Kate tried to picture the scene. Somebody changing the SIM card in their phone, hands shaking with the cold, or fear; dropping the tray and being unable to find it. 'Why would anybody change their SIM card on a clifftop though? Unless they wanted to give the impression that the phone had gone out of service at that spot.'

'Wouldn't make any difference,' Cooper said. 'It's the IMEI not the SIM that's used to track phones. I'm sure a quick Google would show that information. Although, if I was going to destroy my phone I'd break the SIM as well, just in case it was found. It's really hard to get information from a broken SIM.'

Kate's thoughts were spinning. 'So, if this belonged to Caroline Lambert, and we're assuming that she didn't jump, she removed the SIM card, destroyed it and then threw the phone over the cliff? Why not just throw the phone into the sea?'

'Maybe she couldn't be sure that it would reach the sea? Or she might have been worried that something could still be recovered if it were found,' Hollis said. 'If she really wanted us to believe that she killed herself then she'd also have to consider that we'd try to track her phone – which we will. If it went out of service in the vicinity of Flamborough Head then she's right to think we'd probably look for it so she destroyed the SIM separately just to be sure.'

'You know what this means?' she asked, trying to inject some enthusiasm into her team.

'She might be alive,' Barratt said.

'It's the first concrete evidence that we've had that she might have planned this all along. Sam, get onto the phone companies and see if Caroline has registered another SIM with any of them in the last few months.'

'Long shot,' Cooper said. 'She might have bought one in a supermarket and topped it up there three or four years ago. She might be using a fake ID. She might have got somebody else to register the SIM.'

'I know,' Kate said. 'But have a look. She might have slipped up somehow. And, while you're at it see if you can chase up records for her phone. I want to know when and where she last used it. O'Connor – go back to your contact with a photo of Maddie Cox and try to jog his memory about the exact date. Barratt – hospital records. I want to know who admitted Dennis Lambert and when Maddie became involved. And have another word with Brenda Powley. Clarify the sequence of events leading up to Caroline going back to Thorpe. What did she say when she heard about her dad? Details please.'

The two men grabbed their coats, energised by the allocation of jobs, but Kate felt like they might be chasing more dead ends. Caroline Lambert was clever. She wouldn't have slipped up over something as simple as a phone and she really couldn't see Maddie Cox being involved in the fake ID. But there was another person who fitted the description that O'Connor had been given.

'What about me?' Hollis asked.

'You're coming with me. I need you to drive while I make a couple of phone calls. There's somebody else who might be the woman who met with O'Connor's contact. And, if I'm right, she's lied to our faces.'

CHAPTER 31

'Who's Rob?' Kate asked as soon as Julie Wilkinson opened the door. The woman looked from Kate to Hollis in bewilderment.

'I'm sorry?'

'When we called yesterday, your first response was "Is it Rob?". I'd like to know who Rob is,' Kate explained, struggling to keep the belligerence from her tone. If she was right, this woman knew far more than she'd let on and she'd withheld a lot of information the previous day.

'He's my ex,' she said. 'He rides a motorbike and I was scared that he'd had an accident. I spent years worrying that he was going to come off the bloody thing and the first I'd hear was a knock at the door from you lot.'

'That would be Robert Wilkinson? Drug dealer and general thug?'

The woman in front of Kate flushed and she couldn't tell if it was embarrassment or anger. She decided to press on regardless. If Julie wanted to get aggressive, Kate was ready. She slipped a hand into her pocket and checked that the handcuffs were still there.

'Known associate of Lee Weaver?' she continued. 'Not a very pleasant man by all accounts. Into all sorts, including fake IDs.'

The red flush disappeared almost instantly, leaving Julie pale and wild-eyed. She looked over Kate's shoulder to where Hollis was blocking the drive, leaving her nowhere to run. Eventually she sighed and slumped against the doorframe.

'You'd better come in,' she said, pushing the door further open, allowing Kate to pass. Julie followed Kate down the hallway, Hollis behind her in case she had any ideas about trying to run away, and the three of them settled in the living room. This time there was no offer of a drink.

'I don't have much to do with Rob anymore,' she said, looking Kate straight in the eye. 'We split up eighteen months ago because I got sick of him bringing his dodgy mates round. Some of them were running working lasses and I didn't want any part of that.'

Kate wondered exactly how much criminality this woman had turned a blind eye to until she'd had enough but she didn't want to antagonise Julie too much at first, not until she'd got the information that she wanted. Kate regarded the other woman thoughtfully, still a little unsure of her interview strategy. She'd used the shock of their reappearance and knowledge of Rob to throw Julie off guard so that they could gain access but that didn't really get them any further forward.

They weren't interested in Rob aside from his contacts but Kate didn't want Julie to work out the real reason for their visit until she'd backed her into a corner. She'd asked Hollis to stay quiet on this one and make notes, and he was following her instructions to the letter; leaning forward on one of the armchairs, notebook balanced on one of his improbably sharp knees as he tried not to allow his long limbs to spill too far into the room.

'So you knew some of Rob's associates?' Kate finally asked.

Julie nodded miserably.

'Including Lee Weaver?'

Another nod.

'Did he ever come here?'

'Twice,' Julie admitted. 'I didn't like him. Rob was fawning all over him like the bloody queen had just popped in for a cuppa but I didn't like the way he looked at me.'

'What way was that?' Kate asked.

Julie frowned at the memory. 'His eyes followed me round the room like I was prey. Like he wanted to eat me. He was really creepy. I didn't understand why the others were scared of him. He was a scrawny little runt.'

'And what about Ollie Skillen? Did you ever meet him?'

'Nope. Never heard of him.'

Kate watched Hollis scribbling frantically as he tried to record everything Julie said. 'So, if you couldn't stand Lee Weaver,' Kate said slowly, teasing Julie with what was coming next. 'Why did you go to see him in November of last year?'

Julie's eyes widened with surprise then narrowed as she appeared to consider her options. 'I didn't.'

'That's not what Ollie Skillen's saying.'

'And I've just said, I don't know Ollie Skillen. Who the hell is he to be telling tales about me?'

'He works for Lee. He deals with the small stuff that his boss can't be bothered with. One-off jobs like the odd fake ID for an individual. Lee doesn't trust him with anything bigger just yet.'

Kate was making it up as she went along but she could see that her words were having an effect. If she'd had any doubts about the identity of the woman who'd tried to buy a birth certificate in November, Julie's reaction had dispelled them all. Her eyes couldn't seem to stay focussed on one thing and her leg was jiggling wildly up and down as she started to realise the depth of the trouble she was in.

'I've got a detective on his way now, to interview Ollie again. This time he's taken a photo with him to confirm the identity of the woman that he remembers.' Kate didn't bother to tell Julie that the photograph was of a completely different woman.

'I'm expecting to hear back from him any time now.' Kate slid her phone out of her jacket pocket and placed it on the coffee table. Julie stared at it as though it were a ticking bomb and inched forward on her chair, her hands clasped between her knees. Kate sat back again, allowing the silence to do its work.

Eventually, Julie sighed and opened her hands wide as if conceding defeat. 'Okay. I did go to see Lee and I did meet Ollie Skillen although I didn't know his name.'

'When was this?' Kate asked, trying to keep the feeling of triumph out of her voice. Her hunch had been right and it looked like it was about to pay off. 'And please don't think about lying. As I said, I've got somebody with him right now.'

'It was the beginning of December. A few days after my birthday. Maybe the second or third.' Her responses had become stilted as if she was trying to give Kate the minimum amount of information possible.

'Why did you go to see him? Skillen says it was for a fake ID. A birth certificate.'

'That's right.'

'Which you know is illegal.'

Silence.

'I can't understand why you'd need a fake ID, Julie. Are you using it for some sort of fraud?'

Silence.

'If so, I'm going to arrest you here and now. We can get to the bottom of this when we get to Doncaster.'

'It wasn't for me,' Julie mumbled.

'Sorry, I didn't hear that,' Kate lied.

'I said it wasn't for me. It was for a friend.'

'Which friend?'

More silence.

'Julie. If you go "no comment" on me now, I'll make sure that this is as difficult for you as possible. I can put you in a line-up for Ollie Skillen to pick you out. I can charge you with obstruction if need be as well as obtaining a fake ID for the purposes of fraud...'

Julie jumped out of her seat. 'I just said it wasn't for me. I didn't use it for anything.'

She paced the room, picking at the skin around her fingernails. Kate knew that she was trying to work out what she could get away with and what the police already knew – which was very little other than conjecture and speculation. She needed to prompt Julie into a full confession.

'And I can't possibly believe that unless you tell me who *did* use the birth certificate. Who do you know who would have the money for something like that? Perhaps an old friend who lives in a big house in one of the poshest parts of Sheffield?'

Julie turned to Kate, fury scalding her face. 'If you already know, why this bloody silly charade?'

'I don't know,' Kate said calmly. 'That's why I'm here. Did you help Caroline Lambert obtain a fake identity?'

Julie slumped back into her seat. 'Tell me something first. Did she kill him? Did she kill her dad?'

'We're still trying to establish what happened to Dennis Lambert,' Kate said noncommittally. 'There may be a link with his daughter's treatment of him in his final weeks.'

'I bet there is,' Julie tried to smile, tears spilling from her narrowed eyes. 'I bet she killed that old fucker. He deserved it.' She wiped her nose on the back of her hand. 'I hope he rots in hell.'

The contrast with her sentiments of the previous day was striking. She'd claimed not to have met the man and seemed to have no firm opinion of his character when they'd spoken the previous day but her face contorted with hatred as she talked about him. Kate wasn't sure where to go next with the interview but she was certain that she was at a turning point. Julie Wilkinson knew much more than she'd let on so far.

'I thought you didn't know him,' Kate said. 'Why the venom?'

'I didn't know him. What I said yesterday was true. I never met him but I saw what he did to Jeanette nearly every day. I was trying to give you some clues but you're obviously too thick to get the message.'

Kate decided to let the insult pass.

'He was vicious. Any time Jeanette did anything wrong, he lashed out at her. I lost count of the number of times she couldn't get changed for games because she was embarrassed by the bruises on her legs and arms. I'm surprised that he didn't turn on Caroline when Jeanette wasn't there anymore. Or their mother.'

'How do you know he didn't hit Caroline?'

'She told me,' Julie said. 'She told me everything.'

'She's been in contact?'

'We never really lost touch. I got the odd card or letter most years. Since she moved to Sheffield we've met up a couple of times and written to each other every week.'

Kate was surprised. 'Written to each other? No email or phone calls? Not even a text?'

'Nope. Caroline was paranoid about anybody finding out that we still saw each other. So we wrote proper, old-fashioned letters. She asked me to destroy everything she ever sent, and swore that she'd done the same. The last letters I sent were when she was looking after Dennis. I couldn't believe that she'd got the guts to walk back into that house, never mind stay there with him.'

Kate looked over at Hollis and he'd obviously had the same thought that she had. He was sitting, open-mouthed, his pencil poised above a blank page of his notebook. Caroline had planned this for a long time. She'd made sure that her contact with Julie was untraceable. Kept it that way for years; until the time came when she needed help.

'You said she told you everything?' Kate prompted.

'Dennis Lambert used to hit Jeanette… a lot. I always thought that was why she eventually ran away. It devastated me that she was gone but even worse was that she never came back. I thought she'd gone to Manchester or somewhere and that she'd come back when Dennis couldn't hurt her anymore.'

Tears spilled down Julie's face but she continued her story, oblivious to the damp patch that was forming on her sweatshirt.

'Three years ago, Caroline wrote and said that she was moving back to the area and that she wanted to meet up with me. We arranged to meet at Meadowhall, at one of the cafes. I'd not seen her for over twenty years but as soon as she walked in I recognised her. She looks just like Jeanette. We had a coffee and she told me that she was back in South Yorkshire for a reason and it had something to do with her dad. She wouldn't tell me much more but we met quite regularly after that. One time I was in Sheffield for work and we went to the pub. Caroline got really pissed. I mean *really*, falling down, pissed. She started rambling on about Jeanette and how much she missed her and how she felt responsible for what had happened. How she was going to pay Dennis back for what he'd done. She said she could wait though. That she'd wait until he was helpless and then she'd make him pay.'

Kate heard Hollis clear his throat as if he was going to ask a question but Kate raised her hand, palm out, to stop him. She didn't want anything to interrupt the flow of Julie's story.

'I asked her what she meant but she wasn't making much sense. To be honest I was really worried about her so I rang a taxi and took her home. I told Rob that I was staying with a friend and spent the night on her settee. In the morning she was a bit sorry for herself but she didn't seem to remember what she'd said. Eventually I asked her what she'd meant when she said she felt responsible for what had happened to her sister and she looked shocked. I really don't think she meant to say anything. Not ever. But I wouldn't let it go. Jeanette was my best friend and I felt like I had a right to know. Her disappearance soured my teenage years and I wanted to know what had happened. So Caroline told me. Not everything. Not details, but enough.'

'What did she tell you?' Kate asked gently.

Julie sobbed. 'I can't say. I swore I wouldn't.'

'It was enough to convince you to help her though? You helped her to change her identity. You helped her to disappear. She's not dead, is she?'

Julie shook her head. 'No. But you'll not find her now. She's got a new name, a new bank account. She even looks different.'

Kate felt as though the air had been sucked out of the room as Julie's features froze. Everything felt brittle and sharp. 'You've seen her? You've seen her since we found her car?'

The noise upstairs when they'd been there the previous day. Was it really a cat? Had Caroline Lambert been hiding upstairs while they questioned Julie? 'She was here, wasn't she?' Kate asked. 'That was the noise upstairs.'

Hollis leapt to his feet, heading for the stairs.

'She's not here now,' Julie said. 'She went not long after you'd left. Said it wasn't safe for either of us. I have no idea where. And I don't know what she's calling herself. Have a look if you don't believe that she's gone.'

Hollis stamped up the stairs leaving Kate to consider what she'd just heard.

'You know I can arrest you for harbouring a fugitive?' she said. 'Or for the birth certificate? And you know that Dennis may not be the only person that Caroline has killed?'

Julie looked embarrassed. 'I know that something happened with a nurse from the hospital. She wouldn't tell me what. If she hurt somebody else it would have been an accident. It was only Dennis that she wanted to get rid of and I understood why. That's why I helped her. I'd do it all again, exactly the same. I'd do it for Jeanette.'

'So let's do something else for Jeanette,' Kate urged, trying to suppress her anger at Julie's disregard for Maddie Cox's life. 'Tell me what Caroline told you. Help us to find her. Let's put this to rest. I think she's dead. Is that right?'

A sob.

'She didn't run away, did she? She never left the house that night. Did Dennis kill her?'

Julie snuffled and wiped her eyes. Kate thought she was going to leave them hanging, to keep Caroline's secret but, eventually, she gave a barely perceptible nod.

'Julie, where is she? Where's Jeanette's body?'

'He buried her in the garden somewhere. He made Caroline help him and he told her that if she ever went to the police he'd make sure that she was arrested for helping him. She really believed that she'd go to jail.'

Kate grabbed her phone as she heard Hollis thumping back down the stairs. Raymond couldn't refuse her now.

CHAPTER 32

It was a dreary scene. The sky was leaden and overnight frost had coated the grass, giving the lawn a ghostly hue. The ice had cracked the soil on the remains of the flowerbeds making it look like something underneath was trying to get out. Kate leaned against the back wall of the house, hands tucked deep in the pockets of her down jacket, scarf wrapped tightly round her neck.

She'd spent much of the previous afternoon at Doncaster Central, interviewing Julie Wilkinson who had agreed to cooperate fully with the investigation. Kate still wasn't sure that there was much mileage in charging her with a crime – Raymond hadn't been convinced either. O'Connor's source wouldn't testify that she'd obtained an illegal birth certificate from him and she hadn't been intending to use it anyway. At worst, she'd conspired to help a fugitive; at best, she'd allowed herself to be used and the CPS wouldn't be interested in the latter at all.

'We're ready,' a voice called from the top of the garden. Two men huddled around an object which resembled an oversized lawnmower. They'd spent the past hour measuring the lawn and mapping out a plan to survey it with the ground-penetrating radar equipment and it was finally time to see what lay beneath Dennis Lambert's back garden.

Kate raised a hand and nodded, watching carefully as one of the men broke away with the equipment and pushed it along a near straight line following the back hedge. The other one walked over to her and sat on a camping stool, watching the progress of the GPR on a laptop. Kate peered over his shoulder, baffled by the lines and squiggles. It looked like it was going to be a long, cold day.

'So what are we seeing?' Kate asked.

The man turned and looked up at her. He didn't look much older than her son Ben and most of his lower face was covered by a trendy beard but there was a smile in his brown eyes. 'We're looking at a depth of two metres at the moment – most illegal burials are shallower than that because the soil tends to collapse in on the grave unless the sides are supported, and most people trying to get rid of a body don't want to draw attention to a massive hole in the ground. The transmitter sends electromagnetic energy into the earth and if it encounters an object the pattern changes.'

He pointed to the screen where the grey waves were fairly even apart from a tiny blip of black and white stripes.

'So, what's that?' Kate asked, pointing at the screen.

'Some sort of pipe. It's uniform in size and it's about this wide.' He held his hands about eight inches apart. 'Soil pipe probably. A burial will be more irregular and probably much wider. See that line there?' He pointed to another anomaly. 'That's a shift from one type of soil to another. It's mostly clay round here but some people add sand to veg beds to make it easier to turn over.'

Kate stared, fascinated, as the lines scrolled across the screen until a sudden shout from the GPR operator made her glance over to the end of the garden. He'd stopped and was staring at the small screen attached to his equipment.

'Can you see that, Alex?' he yelled to the technician. Kate looked back at the laptop. There was a large patch of black and white amongst the grey. She'd only had a quick explanation but she could see that something was there.

'Got it,' Alex said. 'Looks like it's about a half a metre down. Big enough to be a body?'

The other man shrugged. 'Could be. Only one way to find out.'

Kate took that as her cue. A Crime Scene van was waiting on the street, the SOCOs choosing to stay in the warm rather than spending the morning freezing their bits off watching the progress of the GPR search. She went to stand at the top of the path and gesticulated to the van driver. Less than a minute later two overall-clad figures appeared, one holding a crime scene case and the other wielding something that looked like a mattock.

'Ground's probably frozen,' he explained as he saw her puzzled look. 'Can't get through it with a trowel.' Kate studied the ground where the equipment had indicated something below the surface. It looked just like the rest of the garden around it; the frost was disturbed by the wheels of the GPR unit and its operator, leaving brighter green tracks in parallel lines. There was nothing to suggest that it had ever been dug up; ever been different from the surrounding lawn, but thirty years was a long time. If this was where Jeanette was buried, the ground could have resettled and repositioned itself until it was indistinguishable from that which surrounded it.

The first stroke of the mattock made Kate jump. She felt it in her feet as it bit into the frozen earth. The man wielding it was well built, his overalls straining at his shoulders as he swung again, breaking through the surface as easily as if he were dipping an oar into water.

Ten minutes passed with no sound except for the thump of the mattock, the click of a camera, and the increasingly heavy breathing of the overalled man wielding the heavy implement. He swung back for yet another stroke and then stopped.

'I'm through the frozen layer,' he said, gesturing to his colleague who passed him a trowel. He squatted on his haunches and scraped at the dark, damp soil.

'There's something there,' he said, putting down the tool and kneeling to get a closer look. His colleague joined him and they moved the earth more slowly with trowels, taking photographs as they cleared the earth. Kate felt like screaming at the sudden drop in the rate of progress; they might as well have been using teaspoons.

'Can you see anything yet?' she asked as one of them dug a brush out of the case he'd been carrying.

'Bone,' he said. 'Skull. There are some teeth still attached. Bits of wool as well. Could be a jumper or a carpet.'

Kate tried to picture the scene. Dennis Lambert wrapping his daughter's body in a bit of old carpet and dropping it in a hole in the garden. No wonder Caroline wanted her sister's body found. It was well past time for a proper burial. Kate leapt back as a purple-gloved hand held a jawbone out to her.

'*Canis familiaris*,' the SOCO said. 'Domestic dog. Looks like Fido's final resting place.'

He continued to sift around in the hole, pulling out more bits of browned bone but nothing recognisably human. The GPR techs lost interest and wandered off for a smoke while every last fragment was removed from the grave. Frustration had Kate almost wishing that she still smoked; a cigarette would be perfect for calming her nerves. She was worried that, if Jeanette's body were here, there would be nothing left to find after so long, and more worried that either Julie had lied to her or that Caroline had lied to Julie. Raymond wouldn't care which it was and she knew exactly who he'd blame if this turned out to be a waste of money and time.

With the dog exhumed, the GPR techs were free to continue their survey. The SOCO team retired to their van and Kate went back to her position against the back wall of the house from where she could see the screen of Alex's laptop.

Morning dragged into afternoon and the lines on the screen showed nothing except more sandy soil and the footings of some old fence posts. Finally, Kate conceded that there was nothing to find. Wherever Jeanette was, she wasn't buried in the garden.

Alex tapped away on the laptop keys and the screen cleared. 'I'll save the results,' he said, his disappointment clear in his movements which were lethargic despite the cold. 'Shame really. I thought we might find something. It's only my second time out with the police. I've just left university. I was supposed to go travelling but I wanted to earn a bit of money first. Oh well.'

He stood up, knocking over his camping stool. As he bent to retrieve it, something caught his eye. 'You know, we've not looked everywhere. How long's that greenhouse been there? Was it there when the girl went missing?'

Kate mentally reviewed the statements that she'd heard and read in the last few days. Brenda Powley had said something about the greenhouse. What was it? Dennis had put it up for his wife to grow flowers after Jeanette went missing. Was that it? Brenda had mentioned him doing work in the garden to help Irene cope, and Kate was almost certain that the greenhouse was part of the improvements that he'd made. It had to be worth a try.

'I think it was put up after Jeanette disappeared,' Kate said, walking across the grass towards the structure. She peered through the grimy glass, trying to ascertain what the floor was made of. If it was earth then it would be easy to dig. She couldn't quite make out what lay underneath the benches which ran along each side but the middle section was flagstones.

'Let's have a look,' she said and slid open the door. The light inside had a greenish cast from the algae which covered many of the glass panes but Kate could easily see the concrete beneath the benches. She squatted down. Each bench had six legs and each leg had obviously been embedded in the cement before it set.

'Looks pretty solid,' she said over her shoulder. 'Shit. I thought we might be able to dig here.'

Alex had followed her inside and was examining the feet of one of the benches. 'You know, we could get the machine in here. There's enough room under the benches to allow some movement.'

'Will it work through the concrete?'

'Easily,' Alex said. 'Utility services use it to locate pipes. We might not be able to go as deep, though. Let's clear some of the crap away and get set up.'

He bent down and moved plant pots and empty compost bags, throwing them through the door to land on the lawn.

Kate bent down to clear the other side, thinking that she could at least make herself useful by doing a bit of manual work. She removed the cylinder from an ancient push-along lawnmower and then found its handle lying further back. She reached in to grab one of the rubber grips but she couldn't move it. It was wedged between two legs of the bench and was too long to slide out. She'd need to work it further forward then slide it at an angle. She knelt down to get a better view. One of the cross pieces was stuck behind the leg of the bench. She leaned in and pushed it backwards, careful not to push too far and break the glass behind it. As it moved, she scraped a bright, grey slice into the filth and dust that covered the concrete. Something stood out darker against the pale smudge.

'You got a torch?' she asked Alex.

'No. Can you use your phone?'

Cursing her own stupidity, Kate took her phone out of her pocket and selected the torch function. She shone the beam under the bench, playing the light along the freshly revealed concrete surface. There were two initials there – obviously made when the surface was still wet – tiny and hard to make out but they were definitely letters, partially hidden by the thick wooden leg of the bench. She tried a different angle, then another, and suddenly they came into sharp focus.

J.L.

Jeanette Lambert.

Had she still been alive when the greenhouse was built? It seemed unlikely if Julie's story were true. Could Brenda Powley have been mistaken? Again, Kate was fairly certain that she'd said that the greenhouse had been a present from Dennis to Irene after their daughter disappeared. And then it hit her. Julie said that Caroline had been made to help Dennis bury the body. Was this her tiny act of remembrance for her sister? Had she crawled under here and scratched the letters just before the cement set, forever marking Jeanette's final resting place?

Kate stood up and brushed off her trousers. 'We need to start under here,' she told Alex. 'Jeanette Lambert's initials are hidden behind that leg of the bench. I have a feeling that her little sister might have done it to mark where the body is buried.'

Alex looked sceptical but called his colleague over and, within ten minutes, they were set up to examine whatever lay under the bench. Almost immediately Kate saw a change in the pattern on the screen. A blip of black and white ripples amongst the grey.

'What's that?' she asked, pointing at the laptop screen.

'Not a pipe, or a difference in soil or rock. It looks like there's some kind of void under the concrete.'

Kate dashed from the greenhouse and gestured again to the driver of the crime scene van. He must have sensed her excitement because seconds later she heard footsteps pounding up the path beside the house.

'What have you got?' Mattock Man asked.

'There's something buried under the bench. I think you might need a saw to get the bench out before you can dig. I've no idea how thick the concrete is though.'

'Less than three centimetres,' Alex chimed in, still glued to his laptop screen. 'Probably not much more than two in places. Should be easy to get through.'

Kate stood back as a saw was procured and the two men in overalls removed the bench, manoeuvring it carefully through the greenhouse door. They then swept and photographed the area beneath while Kate just wanted to grab the mattock and start swinging.

Finally the heavy work started and Kate and Alex had to stand outside, peering in through the dirty glass, trying to see what was going on.

'We've got something,' the SOCO with the camera said. 'Come in but mind where you step.'

Kate rushed back inside and stared down at the ugly fresh scar in the concrete. Beneath was dark soil and, mingled in with it was what looked like plastic or polythene. Kate squatted down and looked more closely. Mixed with the polythene were scraps of filthy fabric and, almost exactly where the initials had been was a brown smear of bone and a few strands of hair.

'Hello, Jeanette, sweetheart,' Kate whispered. 'It looks like we've finally found you.'

CHAPTER 33

Kate smiled at her reflection in the rear-view mirror as she checked her appearance for at least the tenth time since leaving Doncaster Central. Indicating right, she pulled into the hospital car park and let out a long breath. She wasn't sure exactly what the information was that Nick Tsappis wanted to share but he'd been insistent that they meet in person. He'd been going through Dennis Lambert's case notes and, when Kate questioned him about why she wasn't dealing with the original consultant, Tsappis was vague but charming. She didn't doubt that he'd found something significant but she was suspicious of his motives for wanting to tell her face to face.

She did one more quick check of her make-up, grinned at her reflection, and got out of the car. Hollis had wanted to accompany her but she'd put him off, explaining that she'd only be half an hour and, as Maddie Cox had been cremated two weeks earlier, anything that Tsappis said couldn't really do her or Ethan any good.

Despite having moved on to other cases, Kate's team were still frustrated and irritated by the feeling that Caroline Lambert had walked away without punishment. The previous day, Kate had voiced her opinion of assisted suicide being a grey area, based partly on watching her own mother fade away as the cancer ate her from the inside, and Hollis had practically yelled at her.

He was right. Kate knew he was right and even though she'd been talking in general and not about Dennis Lambert's death, she understood why he was so on edge. They all were. What Caroline had done wasn't merciful, it was murder, and they wanted her to face justice for Maddie Cox. Feelings about the murder of Dennis, however, were somewhat muddied by the discovery of the small body under the greenhouse. It had taken two weeks for DNA to confirm that it was Jeanette Lambert based on a comparison taken from the bones and from Dennis's body which was still lying in the morgue of the hospital that Kate was visiting. Sadly the remains were too degraded for Kailisa to be able to even suggest a cause of death but there was nothing to contradict Julie Wilkinson's account of what Caroline had told her.

The oncology receptionist looked Kate up and down before suggesting she take a seat as, 'Mr Tsappis may be some time.'

Kate couldn't resist a smug smile as his door opened before she'd had time to pick up a magazine; obviously he'd made time for *her*.

'Good to see you,' he said, ushering her to a comfortable chair in the corner of his office. He sat down opposite, allowing Kate the opportunity to study his face. In the direct sunlight, Kate could see that he wasn't what she'd have called conventionally handsome; his jawline was slightly asymmetrical and was covered by a sprinkling of dark stubble, his wrinkles put his age at about the same as her own but, where they made her look tired, they gave Tsappis a weathered look as though he'd spent a lot of time in the sun.

'I'm sorry I haven't called,' Kate began, suddenly embarrassed by their last encounter. Had she given him some hope that she might like to see him in a non-professional setting? She wasn't sure. She wasn't even sure that she didn't want to meet him outside work. It had been a long time. There hadn't been anyone since Garry and, even though she loved and blamed her job in equal measure, she was starting to wonder if she might be ready to open her life up to somebody else.

Tsappis said something, but she'd been too busy pondering her likelihood of going on a date with him that she'd missed it completely. She found herself apologising again and she could feel that she was blushing like a teenager with a crush.

'I said that I don't mind. I didn't expect to hear from you during a big case and I've been following developments in the newspaper. It must've been a shock, finding that girl's body.'

'It was,' Kate agreed. 'But it was a relief as well. At least we managed to close that part of the case.'

He nodded, keeping his eyes fixed on her own with an intensity that she found disconcerting.

Kate cleared her throat and tried to focus on why she was there. But she wasn't exactly sure. 'You wanted to see me? Something about Dennis Lambert's records?'

Disappointment flickered in his eyes. Had he been hoping that she'd been glad of the excuse to pay him a visit? He stood up and walked across to his desk, talking to her as he moved. 'I asked for Mr Lambert's records from Mr Read. I thought, as I'd already spoken with you, that it might be prudent for us to maintain the contact rather than you having to explain everything to Read.' His speech was unnecessarily formal and Kate was concerned that she'd unintentionally rejected him. But if his ego was *that* fragile, was he really worth the trouble?

'I finally have Dennis Lambert's notes,' he said as he grabbed a file from his desk and brought it back to the comfortable seating area. 'I'm sorry it's taken me a while but the wheels of the NHS move slowly around here. And I apologise on behalf of my colleague, Mr Read. Apparently he didn't receive my text message until he was at the airport on his way home.'

Kate sensed from his tone that he didn't fully believe his colleague's excuse.

'Anyway, I've managed to have a good look and there is one thing that strikes me as odd.' He passed her the folder and sat down with his legs crossed, chin resting on steepled fingers as she read. The notes were mainly medical jargon with lists of medication and tests that Lambert had undergone.

'I'm sorry,' she said, glancing up at him. 'You'll have to enlighten me.'

'Okay.' He smiled and the warmth returned to his expression. 'Dennis Lambert had all the tests and medications that I'd expect in such a case. There is nothing especially out of the ordinary there. The MRI scan shows that the disease was progressing at roughly the expected rate.'

'But?' Kate prompted.

'But, some of the medication was prescribed in much larger doses than I would have expected. The Diazepam for example. The dosage is correct but the number of pills prescribed is more than enough for a few months not a couple of weeks. The initial prescription was increased and repeated. Same with the Oramorph.'

'So why would a doctor give him more drugs than were strictly necessary? Aren't there rules against that sort of thing?'

Tsappis held her eyes for a few seconds. 'It wasn't a doctor. I've checked and double-checked with Read and with the pharmacy. The drugs were prescribed by a nurse practitioner and the second prescription was issued two weeks after he left her care. According to her supervisors, she was an exemplary colleague who was highly regarded by everybody who worked with her. Now, why would she do something so out of character, DI Fletcher?'

Kate already knew the answer; Tsappis had simply confirmed her suspicions. Maddie Cox was being blackmailed by Caroline Lambert. The money that Caroline had given her would have paid off her debts but had come with a much higher price and, ultimately, cost her her life. She would have lost her job if Caroline had told anybody what she'd done but, if she'd refused, how could she have given the money back without landing herself even deeper in debt? And Dennis was dying anyway. Having met his daughter, Kate was convinced that Caroline could be extremely persuasive and manipulative.

'I think Maddie Cox is probably the victim here,' she said. 'It looks like she was in an impossible position and being blackmailed.'

'Do you always do that?' Tsappis asked, smiling at her.

'What?'

'Look for the good in people? This woman would have lost her job if this had come to light. Who knows how much harm these drugs might have caused?'

'They did cause harm,' she said. 'They killed Dennis Lambert and Maddie Cox. But she's not the one I blame. At best she was weak and at worst she was stupid.'

Kate passed the folder back to Tsappis and he placed it on the table between them, making no move to hurry her out of his office.

'You know who killed her?' he asked.

'I think so, but I can't comment.'

He smiled as if he was pleased with her response. 'Very professional. I like that.'

Kate found herself smiling back at him. 'I'm not sure *I* do. You went very doctor-ish for a while when you were telling me about Dennis Lambert.'

His grin widened showing perfect white teeth which contrasted with his tanned skin. 'Sorry, force of habit. When you sat down, I forgot for a second why you were here. It felt like you'd popped in for a social visit. I didn't really want to be reminded that you're on duty.'

'Sometimes I feel like I'm always on duty,' Kate admitted. 'And this case seems to have taken over my life.'

'But you found the body of that girl. Surely that must give you some satisfaction?'

It had. But not enough. Kate knew that Caroline was still out there somewhere and, until they found her, there could be no justice for Maddie Cox. Kate wasn't sure whether Dennis Lambert deserved anything other than what he'd got, but the law stated that Caroline should be punished for that murder as well and it felt like she had got away with both crimes and was laughing at the police; laughing at Kate. There had been no sign of Caroline since Julie's admission that she'd let Caroline stay at her house for one night. They didn't know what name she was using; and Julie wouldn't give them a convincing description of what she looked like after altering her identity; she'd claimed that she couldn't remember – Caroline just looked *different*. Julie's phones were being monitored and her house was being watched but Kate knew that Caroline Lambert was too shrewd to be caught out so easily. They needed to draw her out, but how?

'The woman who killed Maddie Cox is still out there somewhere,' she said.

'I assume we're talking about Dennis Lambert's daughter?'

Kate didn't respond but she could see that Tsappis understood why she couldn't comment.

'And you have no idea where she is? What about her sister's funeral? Surely there'll be some sort of service for the girl? Won't she be tempted?'

Kate gave in. There was little point in pretending that she didn't know what he was talking about. Feeling a little unprofessional but unable to stop herself bouncing ideas off a sympathetic listener, she said, 'There won't be a service as such. When the coroner's finished the body will be cremated but there's no family left so it'll be a cheap, impersonal service. Caroline's much too clever to risk turning up.'

'And the father? Dennis?'

'Oh, he'll get a lovely send-off,' Kate said, watching as Tsappis reared back from her sarcastic tone. 'His "friend" Brenda has made the arrangements.'

'She doesn't believe that he killed the other daughter?'

'We can't prove it,' Kate said. 'Can't pin down a cause of death and everything else is hearsay and circumstantial.'

'But you believe it.'

'Absolutely,' Kate said.

As soon as the SOCOs had cleaned around the remains and lifted Jeanette's body from the shallow grave, Kate knew that what Julie had told her was true. She knew in her gut that Dennis Lambert had killed and buried his eldest daughter, and that he'd involved his youngest to make sure that she kept his secret. He'd probably told her that they'd both go to prison, or worse, if the police ever found out. It felt wrong that Jeanette received the bare minimum in terms of her funeral but her father was being sent into the afterlife like any well-respected, law-abiding member of society.

'It's the injustice of it that gets me,' she said. 'Same with Maddie Cox. I went to her cremation and watched her son, who's nearly a grown man, sobbing his heart out. Where's the justice for her? All she did was meet the wrong person at the wrong time and allow herself to get sucked into somebody else's crap.'

'You really care about this, don't you?' Tsappis said gently. 'It matters. These people aren't just cases, they're individuals with lives and hopes and dreams.'

Kate looked up at him gratefully. He got it. She hadn't been sure that she was getting her point across, but he'd heard her and understood. He was smiling at her but his expression was sad as if he wanted to shoulder some of her burden and, for a second, Kate wanted to let go; just unload everything and pick through the detritus with this strangely empathetic man. She wanted him to come to Dennis Lambert's funeral with her and hold her steady as she examined the face of every mourner. She wanted him to buy her wine at a quiet bar while the remains of Jeanette's body were being burnt to ashes with nobody in attendance.

And then it struck her. She *did* have a way to draw Caroline out. The funerals. An idea was forming and, if it worked, Caroline wouldn't be able to stay away. If she thought that everything she'd done had been for nothing, she'd have to come forward and make sure the truth was heard.

'You okay?' Nick asked. 'Your expression just changed completely. Something I said?'

'Not exactly. But you've helped. You've got me thinking and I might have an idea.'

'That's great,' he said, uncrossing his legs and leaning forward like a therapist who had just made a breakthrough with a tricky patient.

'I need to run it past my boss first but it might work.'

'And, if it does, you'll close the case and be free to socialise.'

Kate laughed. If only. 'I won't be free but I might be a bit less busy.'

'And you've still got my card?'

Kate blushed again as she remembered that it was sitting on top of the chest of drawers in her bedroom where she saw it every day. She stood up to leave, tripping over her own feet in her haste to get back to base and run her idea past Raymond. Tsappis reached out and grabbed her by the upper arm, steadying her and guiding her to the door.

She could still feel the pressure of his touch as she started her car.

CHAPTER 34

It had taken two days to implement her plan. Two days of negotiating with Raymond, finding a tame journalist at the *South Yorkshire Post* and placating Brenda Powley. The journalist had, surprisingly, been a friend of O'Connor's from school. She was astute and keen to help, and Kate had wondered if she had a thing for O'Connor, hard as that was to imagine. She'd charmed the editor into agreeing with their plan on condition that he could run a retraction after the event and Kate had agreed. The reporter, Emma, had written the story and emailed it to Kate for approval – it was exactly what Kate had requested and had been published the previous day. It was also the main story in the online edition of the newspaper.

Brenda Powley had not been quite as accommodating but eventually Barratt had won her round with a combination of gentle persuasion and willingness to eat all the cakes and biscuits she offered. Kate smiled to herself as she thought about how Barratt was always so attractive to women of a certain age who seemed to have the urge to mother him. She knew that Brenda wouldn't have responded so well if *she'd* asked and Raymond, with his brusqueness and loud voice, would have got nowhere. She'd already made a note in Barratt's record about his unique contribution to the investigation.

Kate scanned the office checking on her team. O'Connor was out somewhere on a mission for Raymond; Sam was at her desk, moving her mouse with one hand, the other buried in a bag of crisps; Barratt was on the phone; and Hollis was poring over a case file.

As the others had become more despondent and frustrated with the Caroline Lambert case, Sam Cooper had stepped up and was driving the investigation forward even though Kate knew that it was unlikely that they'd ever find the woman. Sam approached every task with a smile and an enthusiastic attitude and Kate was sure, on more than one occasion, that she'd even heard her humming as she typed. Kate had been proud to work with the team on this case and had written a note to herself to give them a boost or take them out for beer and pizza as a thank-you. They hadn't found their suspect but it wasn't for want of trying.

She turned her chair back to her computer and called up the website for the *Post,* hoping that reading the fabricated story one more time might give her a clue, a lead, anything.

REUNITED AFTER DEATH

Jeanette Lambert, reported missing over thirty years ago, is finally to be reunited with her family. The remains of the teenager were found in the garden of a house in Thorpe last month, finally concluding a case which had baffled police for decades.

In a tragic twist, Jeanette's father, Dennis, died in January, only a few weeks before his daughter's body was discovered. Neighbours describe how the disappearance of their daughter devastated the Lambert family with one saying that Irene, Jeanette's mother, 'died of a broken heart' after police were unable to find her daughter.

A joint cremation will take place at Doncaster Crematorium on Wednesday 8th March at 2pm when father and daughter will finally be at rest together.

Organisers of the service request that no flowers be sent, instead donations to Macmillan Cancer Support will be collected afterwards.

Kate scrolled back up to the top of the story and sighed. It was a long shot. Caroline wouldn't know who had organised the service but she'd expect Brenda to be there as well as other neighbours. Only Dennis Lambert's body had been released to the funeral home. Kate had no intention of Jeanette's remains being associated with those of her father but there would be a second, empty coffin at the crematorium for authenticity. She just wished that she could attend but she knew that, if Caroline spotted her, she'd know it was a trap.

'Guys,' Kate said, turning back to her team. 'I think we should call it a day. I'm not expecting anything else to turn up tonight, and I know you're working other cases which will take up your time tomorrow.' She watched as computers were logged off, bags and coats gathered and last swigs of tea and coffee drunk.

A few minutes later, Kate picked up her jacket and decided to take her own advice.

Frost was starting to form on the windscreen of her Mini as she unlocked the doors and threw her bag onto the back seat. She opened the boot and grabbed a can of de-icer, spraying the rear screen first and swiping at it with a plastic scraper. It cleared easily and she walked round to the front. A quick spray and that too was clear of ice. She threw the can and the scraper into the boot and slid into the driver's seat thinking about what she might have for dinner, which led to thoughts of Nick Tsappis and when she might make the call and perhaps invite him to a restaurant.

The roads had been gritted and she started the ten-minute journey home on autopilot, planning to raid her freezer for a ready meal and open a bottle of beer to keep it company. As she indicated to turn right onto her street a hand slipped round her throat from behind her seat and a voice hissed in her ear.

'Keep going. You're not going home tonight.'

'What the fu–?' Kate tried to turn her head but the hand around her throat tightened.

'Don't be stupid,' the voice said. 'I've got a knife and I'm willing to use it.'

Kate felt something cold tap her ear. A blade.

'Keep driving,' the voice continued. 'I'll tell you where to turn.'

Mind racing, Kate followed the instruction. She recognised the voice now. It had taken a few seconds to suppress her fear and start to think logically again. 'Caroline, I don't know what you're planning but I can tell you it won't work. I'm expected home and if I don't turn up…'

A laugh from the back of the car. 'Expected home? I don't think so. I've been watching you. I know you live alone. There's nobody expecting you. Keep driving.'

The last of the daylight faded as Kate followed Caroline's instructions, taking care not to hesitate for too long or to miss a turn. She knew most of the roads around Doncaster and had a good idea of where she was being taken, but not why. What could Caroline Lambert gain from killing her? She would probably just disappear again but what would be the point? Kate had done nothing to her, she hadn't even been able to track her down, so it wasn't like Caroline was in danger of imminent arrest.

Two more turns and Kate found herself driving down a darkened lane that she vaguely recognised. She passed the last streetlight and watched in the rear-view mirror as it disappeared into the gloom – a last beacon of hope. She was trapped in the dark, at the mercy of the woman holding a knife to her throat.

'Pull in here,' Caroline instructed.

Kate was able to make out a gravel parking area lit up by the twin beams of her headlights. She drove across it, the crunch of tyres unexpectedly loud in the silence, and pulled in.

'Now what? You're going to stab me and leave me here?' Kate tried to inject the words with a tone of bravado that she didn't feel, hoping to throw the other woman off balance. If Caroline didn't know that Kate was afraid, she might stand a chance of out-thinking her.

'Don't be stupid,' Caroline spat. 'I need you to listen to me and I need you to pay attention.'

'So why not call the police station? Why not send an email? Why the dramatics with the kidnap and the knife?'

The blade at her throat suddenly pricked her skin.

'Because I know what you've done. I know that you've planned that funeral to spite me. Or to trick me into turning up. What did you expect? That I'd march down the aisle like a jilted lover at a wedding determined to speak now rather than hold my peace? If you knew, you wouldn't have done it.'

'Knew what? Knew that your father killed Jeanette? Of course I know. Your friend Julie was only too keen to fill us in on the whole story.'

Silence from the back of the car. Had Kate's tone been too much? She was trying to taunt Caroline, to make her rethink whatever plan she'd hatched, but one false word and Kate could end up with a knife in her throat. Suddenly the pressure of the knife lessened and the rear door opened. Before Kate could even think about engaging the locks, Caroline was next to her, pulling open the driver's door, knife close to Kate's face as she leaned over and undid the seat belt.

'Get out,' Caroline said, her voice a whisper of suppressed anger.

'And what? Let you throw me in the canal like you did to Maddie Cox?'

The knife was back, under Kate's chin this time, forcing her to look up into eyes that were black with rage.

'I said get out of the fucking car! You want to know why I'm doing this, then listen to me.'

'I can listen to you in the car. It's freezing out there.'

Caroline grabbed a handful of Kate's hair and hauled her from her seat, dragging her from the car and throwing her down onto the gravel where she lay sprawled on her back, temporarily blinded by the Mini's headlights and stunned by the other woman's physical strength.

'I don't give a shit how cold it is. I want you away from the car, away from your phone and your radio or whatever it is you lot carry around with you. We're going to talk without interruption.'

She reached down and grabbed Kate's sleeve, pulling her to her feet. Keeping one hand wrapped tightly in the fabric, she stepped behind Kate, raised the knife to her neck, and said. 'Now, walk. There's a gap in the hedge. Go!'

Kate's eyes adjusted to the darkness as they walked beyond the range of the headlight beams towards the hedge. A half moon was rising in the clear sky, illuminating the canal bank as she was pushed towards the lights around the black-and-white lock furniture. Caroline manoeuvred her around until she was sitting on the edge of one of the lock gates with Caroline behind her, the knife still uncomfortably close to the tender flesh beneath her chin. All it would take was one hard shove and she'd be in the freezing cold water; Caroline wouldn't even need the knife.

'Right,' Caroline breathed close to her ear. 'Now listen and listen carefully. My sister cannot be buried with that man. I know that you know what he did but you don't know everything.' Kate felt the blade tremble against her flesh as Caroline took a deep breath and told her story.

1986

*I*t was the third time in the last few days that Jeanette had been home late. Her dad would go mad – again. He was always accusing her of being off with the lads but she just wanted to hang about with her friends. Julie had got a new radio cassette player and she'd taped the Top 40 so they could sit out in her garden and listen to their favourite songs. And then it had got really late and Jeanette had tried to run home but she'd broken the heel off her shoe and ended up limping slowly back up the street.

The house was already in darkness as she reached up and took the spare key from its hiding place in one of the hanging baskets that flanked the front door. She eased it into the lock and held her breath. There was no sound as the mechanism slid back and the door opened inwards. She closed it behind her and slid the bolt noiselessly. Now for the stairs. The second one up was loose on the right-hand side so she stepped carefully to the left and then tiptoed up the rest of the flight in silence. Her little sister's door was ajar and, in the moonlight seeping through the landing window, she could make out a small pale face watching her. Jeanette made a shushing gesture – putting her index finger to her mouth – and her sister smiled,

The last few steps were the most dangerous. Her parents' bedroom door was half open, the darkness beyond absolute. Three more steps and she'd reach the safety of her own room. She raised one foot, about to take a step when she spotted a movement. Thrown off balance she almost cried out in alarm. She didn't see the fist until it smashed into her face.

Behind her, Jeanette heard her sister's bedroom door close with a muffled click and then she was falling into nothingness.

'*Caroline, get out of bed and help me. Now!*'

Caroline pulled the blankets higher, covering her head, trying to blot out the sounds coming from outside her bedroom door.

'*I said now!*'

She didn't dare disobey. She'd seen the consequences of Jeanette's disobedience and there was no way that she wanted her father to turn the full force of his anger on her.

She crept out of bed and opened her door, just a crack at first, hoping that he would have managed without her but he was standing at the top of the stairs glaring at something below him.

'*There you are,*' *he said.* '*I need you to help me with your sister.*'

Caroline stepped out onto the landing and followed his gaze. Her sister, Jeanette, was lying in a crumpled heap at the foot of the stairs next to the front door. She wasn't moving.

'*Is she hurt?*' *Caroline whispered.*

'*She's had a bit of an accident,*' *her dad said.* '*I need to move her out of the way. Get the blanket off the top of your wardrobe. It's in the big suitcase that we took on holiday.*'

Mechanically, Caroline followed his instructions; she pulled her desk chair over to the wardrobe, climbed up and managed to get the case down without overbalancing. She flicked the latches on the case and the lid popped open revealing a threadbare blue blanket which she gathered in her arms and took to her father.

'*Now go back into your bedroom,*' *he ordered.*

'*Is she going to be all right?*' *Caroline asked.* '*Is she cold?*'

'*I said go back to bed!*' *her father yelled.*

Caroline scuttled back across the landing, closed her bedroom door, and buried herself beneath the covers until morning.

The next day, Jeanette was gone. Their dad explained that she'd run away after her accident but Caroline knew that he was lying. Jeanette couldn't have run away because Caroline had seen that one of her legs was broken. It had been twisted at a strange angle the night before, almost as if it had been taken off her body and put on backwards. Caroline's mum wasn't feeling well and had decided to stay in bed so

Caroline had to get her own breakfast while her dad fixed something in the bathroom. When he'd finished, he'd asked her if she remembered anything about the previous night. She remembered everything and told him so but he said she was wrong. He said that if anybody asked she had to tell them that Jeanette hadn't come home otherwise her sister would be in a lot of trouble. Caroline couldn't work out why this would be the case but her dad was a grown-up and he knew best.

The police arrived later that day. They asked her dad a lot of questions about when he'd last seen Jeanette and then they asked her and she told them her dad's lie. Her mum stayed in bed through it all.

There were a lot of visits from the police after that. Her dad kept telling them the same story and her mum kept saying that she'd not been very well and didn't know anything about where Jeanette might have gone. Caroline knew that her mum was poorly because she kept holding her tummy and her face was a funny colour as if she'd been sunbathing but just on one side.

Jeanette didn't come home.

After the visits from the police had finished, Caroline's dad decided that he would make the garden nice for her mum, to make her feel better. He dug new flowerbeds and then made a clear space in one corner for a greenhouse. Caroline wished that he'd finished working in the bathroom first because there was a bad smell that her dad said was the drains and that he'd fix it when he'd finished outside.

The greenhouse arrived on the back of a lorry. It was like a pile of empty window frames. Her dad put it together and it looked like the climbing frame in the park. When she said this to her dad though, he shouted at her and told her that she'd better not try climbing on it. He worked every day, putting in panes of glass and sealing them with putty that had a funny smell like Sunday dinners and bleach mixed together. Eventually all that was left to do was the floor which he was going to cover with concrete.

It was a hot night and Caroline woke up thirsty. There was a plastic beaker on the bathroom sink that she could use if she needed a drink after everybody had gone to bed but she lay awake trying not to think about water. She didn't want to go in the bathroom because the smell was really bad and she was worried that it might have soaked into the plastic of her cup and would make the water taste bad. Eventually she knew that she wouldn't get back to sleep without a drink so she got out of bed and opened her bedroom door. The light on the landing was on and there were noises coming from the bathroom. She slowly pushed open the door and saw her dad squatting on the floor. He'd taken the panel off the side of the bath and was dragging something out from behind it.

Caroline watched as he wrestled with a large package, finally pulling it free. She couldn't quite see what it was. There was something wrapped up in the plastic. Something brightly coloured. It wasn't until her father stood up, allowing the light to fall on the whole of the object that Caroline realised what she was looking at.

She screamed as she recognised the face of her sister pressed against the plastic.

Her father grabbed her and slapped her hard across the face, twice, but she couldn't stop sobbing. She kept trying to ask him what had happened but she couldn't get the words out between her sobs.

'Get back to bed and keep your trap shut!' her dad yelled at her but she couldn't, wouldn't, leave her sister. When she managed to gasp the words out her dad laughed like a villain in a film and told her that she might as well help him then.

He sent her down to the greenhouse in her pyjamas and told her to make sure that the hole he'd dug was deep enough. She followed his instructions as though she was in a dream even though she didn't know what he meant by 'deep enough' and she was standing in the greenhouse when he arrived carrying the bundle of her dead sister in his arms. She watched in silence as he placed Jeanette's body in the hole in the greenhouse floor and then covered her with soil.

'Right,' he said when the hole was filled in. 'You can help with the cement.'

He tipped up a bucketful of grey slop out on top of the soil and showed her how to level it with a length of wood, leaving her to complete the task while he went outside to mix more cement. It felt like hours before the floor was finally finished. He'd put in a wooden bench over where Jeanette was buried and cemented the feet into the floor and Caroline had to kneel down to smooth around the edges.

'Get that last bit done,' he told Caroline. 'Then get back to bed and never tell anybody what you've done. If you do, the police will lock me up and they'll lock you up for helping me. You'll never see your mum again.'

Caroline had to pass the wooden block across the cement three times before she managed to erase the tracks of her tears where they'd spilled over her sister's body. As one final small act of rebellion, or remembrance, she'd found a nail and written Jeanette's initials as small as she could in the corner of the greenhouse floor where her dad might never find them. Jeanette might not have a proper grave but at least Caroline had marked where she was buried.

CHAPTER 35

Kate could feel Caroline's breath against her neck as she told her story, her words becoming almost inaudible as she described how she'd tried to mark her sister's grave. The knife point had slipped and was resting against Kate's collarbone; she could feel it clearly through her coat, sense its coldness and purpose. She struggled against her rising panic – images from the previous summer, of a different knife and a different attacker, threatening to overwhelm her.

'I still don't understand why I'm here,' she said to Caroline, forcing herself to stay calm; hoping not to antagonise her captor too much until she could work out a way to get free from the loosening grip. 'I get that your dad was a complete bastard who killed your sister and screwed you up but what's the point of all this?'

She felt Caroline sigh against her.

'I'm so fucking tired. I had a plan but it's going wrong, coming unravelled. I wanted to be able to walk away, to start again but you won't let me do that, will you? You're going to hound me every day. I thought I might be able to get you to stop the funeral, if I could talk to you, explain everything, but I know that's not going to happen. If I let you go you'll just ring your work and somebody will come and get me. So now I'm in another mess and the only way out is to get rid of you. I don't want to. I don't want to hurt anybody else but I can't seem to stop what I've started. It's his fault. I can feel his poison in me, flowing through my veins. I wouldn't have been like this if it hadn't been for Dennis. I could have been happy; I could have had a life.

'I just needed *somebody* to know what he was like. What it was like for us after we buried Jeanette. My mum didn't know the details but I'm sure she guessed. She never used the greenhouse and she had no interest in the flowerbeds that he put in. And I was terrified for years. Terrified of *him*. Of his fists and his feet. Terrified that somebody would find out what we'd done and I'd be put in jail. He'd torment me with it, you know. He'd say that there was a police car on the street or that they were on the phone. He enjoyed making me afraid; enjoyed the power that he had over me. I was a complete mess until I did my GCSEs.'

'What changed then?' Kate asked, trying to keep the woman talking. If she stopped then Kate knew that she was as good as dead.

'I saw a way out. I knew that if I was clever enough I could go to university. My grades were excellent so I put in another two years' hard work and got my A Levels.'

As she listened, Kate saw something on the towpath. Lights. Probably a quarter of a mile away, bobbing up and down and definitely heading in the direction of the lock. Somebody was coming towards them. She made a play of trying to struggle free, shifting position on the wooden arm of the lock gate, angling herself so that Caroline wouldn't be able to see the lights if she wanted to keep hold of Kate's arm.

'Just. Sit. Still.' Caroline said, twisting round with her, away from the direction of the lights.

'What about your mum?' Kate asked, breathing heavily from her exertions; buying time.

'What about her?' Caroline asked.

'Did she really kill herself?'

Another heavy sigh. 'Yes. I know she did because I got her the sleeping tablets. I told the receptionist at the doctors that I'd lost her last prescription and they believed me and gave me another one. We wanted to make sure that she did it right. It was what she wanted and I helped her. I couldn't do it until I was eighteen – we knew that the chemist wouldn't give me the drugs if I was underage. She couldn't live with him any longer. He made her life a misery and nobody knew except me. Everybody on the estate thought he was a fantastic husband and father; that he looked after us both when Jeanette disappeared. He didn't – he terrorised us.'

Was her mother's death another murder? Kate couldn't quite work out the legality, her brain was too preoccupied with trying to keep Caroline's attention away from the lights, but Kate knew that Caroline could be held culpable for providing the drugs.

Where was the person with the light? Surely they should have reached the lock by now. She desperately wanted to turn round, to see who was approaching, and to yell for help, but the knife blade forced her to be still.

'So that's three people you've killed,' Kate said.

'I know. I don't need you to remind me. But I want you to know that Maddie was unavoidable. I think at first I was trying to frighten her into keeping quiet. But I could see that it wouldn't work so there was no other way. I was... oh, I don't really know what I was doing. I just needed time to get away. And I *am* sorry about her. But not Dennis. He got what was coming to him.'

'And I'm to be number four? Is that the plan? What's the point? If you kill me there'll be others coming after you. My colleagues know that you're alive. They'll find you eventually.'

'They already have,' said a voice from the darkness. 'Put the knife down, Caroline.'

Kate struggled again but Caroline tightened her grip and raised the knife until it was next to Kate's right eye.

'It's no good,' said another voice, this one from behind her. 'We've got you surrounded. You can't walk away from this. Let her go.'

Kate tensed, puzzled. She recognised Cooper's voice but the second, another woman, was a stranger. Kate could make out one dark figure near the lock but she couldn't see anybody else. Was Cooper a bloody ventriloquist? A sudden flash of light lit up Sam's face as she put her phone to her ear.

'I'm calling for backup, Caroline. Let Kate go. This is over.'

'I don't... I can't. I didn't want this. I just want it to be done with.' Her grip tightened and she wrapped her forearm around Kate's neck.

'Don't,' Kate said quietly. 'Just let go and it's over. Dennis is dead. We found Jeanette. Let it go, Caroline. There's nowhere left to run.'

After a few seconds of holding her breath, desperate for her words to have resonated somewhere in Caroline's warped psyche, Kate felt the woman behind her loosen her grip; the pressure from the blade was gone. She turned herself round quickly, grabbed Caroline's hand and twisted her wrist until she dropped the knife. She sagged against Kate, the fight gone. Gently, Kate eased her down onto the wooden lock gate, kicking the knife away from her feet as she sat down next to her.

'It *is* done, Caroline. We found Jeanette. Dennis is gone. It's over.'

Sam walked towards them, her head torch switched back on, spearing Caroline Lambert on the beam of light like a butterfly pinned to a board. The change in the woman shocked Kate as she saw her properly for the first time since Caroline had grabbed her in the car. The blonde hair was dyed dark brown and the understated make-up had been replaced by bold colours and red slashes of lipstick. Kate might not have recognised her if she'd passed her in the street.

'I'm sorry about Maddie,' Caroline said as though she was apologising for treading on Kate's toe or knocking her drink over. 'I just didn't know what else to do. She wanted us to go to the police and for me to admit that I'd been blackmailing her. Obviously I couldn't do that. It wasn't part of the plan. It was her or me, I suppose, and my need for survival turned out to be the strongest.'

Kate remembered the sodden body that they'd removed from the same spot a few short weeks earlier and the boy who'd sobbed at his mother's funeral. Suddenly the compassion that she'd felt for this pathetic figure dissipated like morning fog in a hot sun. She didn't deserve sympathy. She'd killed an innocent, vulnerable woman and whatever had happened to her in her past didn't excuse that.

Kate took a deep breath. 'Caroline Lambert, I'm arresting you on suspicion of murder. You don't have to say anything but...'

EPILOGUE

Cooper grinned as she passed Kate a white envelope.
'What's this?' Kate asked.
'Wedding invitation,' Sam said, blushing.
'You and Abbie?'

Cooper nodded.

'Congratulations. I'm glad you've worked things out,' Kate said, wondering what Nick's reaction would be if she asked him to be her date to a lesbian wedding. Only one way to find out, she decided. It would be a good test. They'd already been out twice; once for drinks and once for dinner. He was an interesting man and he wasn't pushy, allowing Kate to take her time to get to know him. The more she knew, the more she found that she liked him.

'We'd worked things out before that night,' Cooper was explaining. 'We're only going to live on the boat in the summer.'

'So no more walking along the canal bank on winter nights?'

Cooper laughed. They'd thoroughly debriefed about that evening, but Kate still couldn't quite believe that Sam and Abbie had managed to convince Caroline Lambert that they were there on purpose and that they'd known to find her on the canal bank. Abbie in particular had impressed Kate with her quick thinking and calmness under pressure. She'd suggested to Sam that Abbie might like to apply to join the police force but Sam had laughed and muttered something about the joys of separate lives.

They'd moved on to other cases, other deaths, but she knew that they'd grown together in the last few months. She was even feeling more charitable towards O'Connor. If he'd not found the link to Julie Wilkinson they might never have discovered Jeanette's body and Kate would always be thankful to him for that break in the case.

'Hey, you lot,' she said, clapping her hands to get their attention. Four heads turned in unison. 'It's half six. Any of you got anything that can't wait until tomorrow?'

Three head shakes and an unintelligible mutter from Hollis.

'Good,' she said. 'Grab your coats. It's beer and pizza time.'

'You paying?' O'Connor asked with a cheeky grin that made him look like an overgrown garden gnome.

'I am indeed,' Kate confirmed. 'But it's not like any of you deserve it.'

She slipped on her jacket and followed her team out of the office, smiling at the sight of Sam punching Barratt for some daft remark and Hollis pretending to pull her off.

THE END

ACKNOWLEDGEMENTS

As always, a huge thanks to the team at Bloodhound Books for continuing to have faith in my writing. I'd also like to thank the other members of the Bloodhound (Books) Gang for encouragement, advice, humour and support.

I'm grateful to Morgen Bailey, my editor, for her helpful suggestions, detailed feedback and for her patience with some of my worst habits.

I must thank my brother Graeme for sharing his knowledge and expertise on the subject of canals and narrowboats. I had no idea that a lock would be the best place to drown somebody.

The online blogging community deserves a massive thank-you. The book bloggers and reviewers work so hard to help authors to promote their books and it's greatly appreciated.

I also need to thank everybody who has bought and read *Closer to Home*, the first in the Kate Fletcher series. I hope you've enjoyed the second part of her story and, if you did, I hope you'll stick around for the third.

And finally, as always, thanks to Viv, first reader, critic and bringer of tea. Your support means everything to me.

Lightning Source UK Ltd.
Milton Keynes UK
UKHW010607010519
341862UK00002B/558/P